KILLI STRANGERS

RAM GOPAL

BlueRose Publishers
NewDelhi • London

First Published in October 2021

ISBN: 978-93-5472-204-2

BLUEROSE PUBLISHERS
www.bluerosepublishers.com
info@bluerosepublishers.com
+91 8882 898 898

Cover Design:
Shreya Kapoor

Typographic Design:
Namrata Saini

Distributed by: BlueRose, Amazon, Flipkart, Shopclues

ABOUT THE AUTHOR

Ram Gopal works in the field of information technology. He has an eye for global socio-political issues and is drawn by the events that don't seem to have an easy explanation. In his debut novel, Killing Strangers, Ram explores how the dichotomy and conflict in the complex world we live in and the psychological underpinnings influence human behaviour.

THE SHOOTING

April 10, 2020, 6:05 PM

Larry Watson was early for the job interview. Even though he'd lived in Atlanta for more than two decades, he'd never ventured into the Atlanta Tech Corridor, located in the city's Buckhead district. Instead of waiting in his car and playing with his phone, he got out and walked over to a nearby green area. He followed a path along the edge of a pond that appeared to be shaped like the number 8, and watched a row of ducklings paddling hard, to keep up with the mother duck. A stand of tall pines surrounded the pond, adding to the slice of nature within the tech corridor. The pond was near the south end of the corridor near the building where he would meet the man who potentially would be his boss.

At age fifty-five, Watson was determined to start a new career. Working in a security position in the tech corridor would give him a renewed purpose. Sitting at home watching television day after day and pondering his past was no longer an option. Not after twenty-five years as an FBI agent. Not after his wife had left him for a man who'd been his college room-mate, and who he considered his best friend.

Charles had been in love with Vivian in college, but they'd broken up when he'd enlisted and pursued a military career. He'd told Watson more than once that the biggest mistake in his life was breaking up with Vivian, and that Watson was a very lucky man. Vivian, for her part, told him that she'd always loved Charles and her heart was with him.

That was eight months ago, and a few weeks later, Watson's own heart failed him. Following his myocardial infarction, he resigned from the FBI, and took his pension. But he quickly realized, as he recovered, that he needed to get out, to do something, to meet people.

He pushed those thoughts out of his mind and prepared for what he expected would be one of the initial questions he would hear. Whenever someone found out about his career as an FBI agent, they always asked about exciting encounters on the job. The fact was that in his quarter century with the FBI, stationed in Atlanta, Larry Watson fired his .40 caliber Glock 22 only once while on duty, other than on the gun range, during mandatory practice sessions. That fact had disappointed his son, Ray, when he was a kid. Ray thought G-men and gun fights went hand-in-hand. Watson had made dozens of arrests of white-collar criminals that he and other agents had investigated. Only two of those suspects were armed, and both had quickly given up their weapons.

The one time he'd fired his weapon had ended badly. He was in pursuit of a gunman on the run across state lines and just before midnight Watson and his partner had found the stolen car the gunman was driving. It was stopped at a 7-11 in Marietta. The car appeared to be empty. Watson's partner went into the store while he stayed outside, his pistol in hand. Gunfire erupted inside the store and suddenly the passenger door of the stolen vehicle sprang open and a figure charged toward him. Watson fired, killing a 14-year-old black kid, who it turned out had been kidnapped. That incident affected him deeply. He received counseling and was put on a desk job for two years before he returned to field duty.

He looked up, as a burly man in his mid-forties with thinning hair and ruddy features motored up to him on a golf cart. "Larry Watson?" Before he could respond, the man thrust out his hand. "Higgins, George Higgins."

"You got me," said Larry and extended his arm.

"It wasn't hard. I did a little research after I got your on-line application. 'Six-two, 195 pounds, full head of hair, square jaw'. I saw your suit noticed the bulge from your shoulder holster. Completes the picture. Had to be you."

At the last moment before leaving home, Watson had decided to bring his Glock with him to the interview just to show Higgins he was ready to take on the new job.

"Hop in. Let's go for a ride. Are you familiar with the Corridor?"

"I know about it, of course. But I found out a lot more last night when I watched a YouTube video."

"Good. I can show you the patrol route, but first let's head inside and go over your application."

Higgins made a u-turn, headed down the path by the pond, then out to the road. "I have to say, George, that I'm a bit surprised that there's a private security force in place here."

Higgins shrugged. "Why's that?"

"Look where we are. Buckhead is the wealthiest neighborhood in Atlanta. Low crime. I can't imagine that street crime is much of a problem in the corridor. All these folks here are well paid, but I suppose white-collar crime might be another matter."

Higgins laughed. "That's true. But that's a job of your former colleagues in the FBI. We're mainly keeping an eye out for anybody or anything that's out of the ordinary. Work for a few days with keen observation and you quickly develop a sense of who belongs here and who is an outsider."

Higgins drove up to a three-storey building bearing the sign: 'Red Oak Event Space', and they disembarked. "We'll go in here first. This building and the one across the road are event-space buildings. Mostly the companies in the tech corridor use these facilities for their events. This is the bigger facility with an auditorium, conference spaces, and temporary office space for visitors. There's an event going on right now. We'll take a look, and then go over to the other building for the formal interview."

Higgins opened the door for him, and Watson stepped into a spacious lobby and noticed the large banner that said, WELCOME TO HAPP! 10th ANNIVERSARY CELEBRATIONS!

Several tables were covered with dishes of food and service people were busy setting up for a party. They walked past an open bar with two attendants preparing for the onslaught of party goers about to hit the counters. The lobby was empty expect for the service people.

"They're all in the auditorium," Higgins said. "Let's go take a look."

They stepped through double doors and entered unnoticed by the several hundred people in attendance. On stage, speaking to the crowd was a man who looked to be in his early thirties wearing a green sport jacket over a black t-shirt and jeans. Higgins leaned toward Watson. "That young man is the CEO. Most of these techies are under forty." Watson scanned the crowd and nodded in agreement. He turned his attention to the speaker who was concluding his speech.

"Folks, I again thank each and every one of you for your contribution. I am proud of the cultural diversity in our team. Our most significant opportunities are ahead of us, and I have no doubt that together we will continue to take Happ! to greater heights. I'm sure this will be an unforgettable day. Enjoy the evening!"

Everyone stood up, applauding, shouting, whistling. The CEO waved his arms, and everyone quieted down again. "Sorry. One more thing. Please sit down." He motioned with his hands. "Okay, all of you who joined Happ! in the first year, please stand up."

A dozen men and women, who didn't look any older than the CEO, stood up and waved to the crowd. "I am pleased to announce a cash bonus of ten thousand dollars for each of you." Thunderous applause ensued as they walked onto the stage to receive the 10th service anniversary plaques. Soon, CEO gave a double-thumbs up and shouted, "Let's party! We've got The Revivalists here for your entertainment."

A series of guitar chords greeted the audience as a wall-to-wall partition opened that nearly doubled the size of the auditorium and revealed another open bar and tables of food in front of a second stage where the band lit into their first song. Most of the Happ! employees quickly abandoned their seats and headed for food and fun. A few remained to shake hands and click pictures with the CEO and the other leaders.

"Guess they know how to party," Watson remarked.

"That they do," Higgins said. "But by ten o'clock it'll be wrapped up with just the mess left for the clean-up crew. Let's get out of here."

Watson took another glance around and frowned, wondered why he was feeling uneasy. Maybe because he was applying for a security job, he had turned on his FBI sensibilities; an awareness and a wariness. His wife had admonished him numerous times for the way he automatically stared at people's hands as they approached, as if they were armed and ready to attack.

The Happ! crowd was already scattered about the auditorium and the lobby. Phones were held high for selfies and videos. Lots of hugs, smiles, and handshakes. Must be a nice place to work, he thought, shrugging off the sensation. He and Higgins stepped out into the lobby where some of the crowd now moved along the tables of food and drinks.

They headed toward the door, but Higgins stopped. "Sometimes at these events, they invite you to partake. You thank them for the offer, but you don't, of course. No drinking, and you eat on your break."

"Certainly. Understood."

Higgins stared at him a few moments. "Look, Watson, when I saw your application, I thought you were way overqualified for this job. That you wouldn't be happy here. But then, I put things in perspective. Within six months, I'm taking a desk position and moving to headquarters in Houston. I'll be hiring people for positions like mine here, and the first one will be my own replacement. If things work out and you're ready for it, I think you might be the guy."

"I appreciate your confidence in me, Mr. Higgins. But let's see how I do first."

"Right. Let's go take care of the paperwork."

They walked outside, settled into the golf cart and drove over to the smaller building across the roadway.

# # #

In the auditorium and the lobby, the party mood took over completely. Some people were standing in circles enjoying the drinks and finger foods being served by the waiters. Others sat at the large circular tables that were placed in the auditorium and lobby.

As the first song ended, the crowd applauded the band, then returned to their conversations. A startling repetitive sound pierced the hum of the conversation, confusing people and the confusion increased as the sound grew louder. Pop, Pop, Pop...POP POP POP. Someone lifted both hands and signaled to the band members to stop as they were getting ready for the second song.

Those seated at the round table in the auditorium looked around, uncertain what to do.

"Did you hear that?"

"Yeah, pop, pop, pop."

"More like boom, boom, boom."

"Those aren't party balloons."

"I don't think so."

"That sound is freaking me out."

One of the men laughed. "So do we need to follow those asshole active shooter drill instructions?"

"I attended one of those drills," the woman next to him said. "Run if you can. Hide if can't run. Fight if you can't hide."

The man shook his head. "I never pay attention to that shit. It's like listening to the flight attendant tell you how to kiss your ass good-bye."

Screams and shouts echoed throughout the auditorium. Some people started running.

Messages started appearing on the social media. An Instagram user posted a video clip. It was shaky, taken from an iPhone, as the camera panned down a long, white hallway from a low angle. In the foreground was a body with blood pooling around the head. Another body was next to it. A man wearing a black camouflage outfit and carrying a huge backpack, was moving down the hallway. A ski mask covered his head. He held a rifle in one hand, the muzzle facing the ceiling. From the way he walked, it appeared the backpack was heavy with weapons and ammunition.

The exchanges continued on Happ!'s internal app and social messaging apps.

He shot someone right in front of me. Get the fuck out of the building.

Shut up! You're lying.

I swear to God. Get the fuck out. Now.

A dozen or more people ran into the lobby, dashed for the door and escaped. As more people ran towards the doors, a loud explosion erupted outside the doors. Someone pointed and shouted. "There's more shooters. Get back." Some hurried back into the auditorium. Others, including children, ducked beneath a long table draped with a tablecloth.

In the other building, Watson's eyes blinked rapidly at the muffled sound of gunfire from the other building. "Did you hear that?"

"What the fuck?" Higgins snapped. Both men bolted to their feet, drew their weapons, raced out of the door and over to the other building.

Chapter 1

One Year Before the Shooting

1.1 The Duck Pond

Dave Pruitt tossed corn to the ducks that had gathered along the edge of the 8-shaped pond located on one end of the Atlanta Tech Corridor. The mallards knew him because he came here every morning precisely at 8 a.m. and stayed for an hour. After he'd emptied half of his packet, he walked along the trail winding around the pine-shrouded pond. For Dave, the pond's shape wasn't an 8, but the symbol of Infinity. When the trail skirted the water's edge, he paused and watched reflections of the tall pines and noticed his own image on the surface.

Up until he was twelve, Dave didn't like looking directly at mirrors. He thought the person in the glass would say something bad to him. Now, at twenty-five, this mirror image caught his attention. His pointed nose and pronounced chin were exaggerated and he imagined his green eyes staring back studying him.

A pine cone splashed down shattering the reflection.

He continued along the walking trail until he arrived at his favorite bench where he sat to feed more ducks that recognized him. It was a daily routine that he never cut short. In fact, any change to the routine might trigger severe distress, a near meltdown. He started to read the latest edition of *American Gun Games* that had arrived in yesterday's mail. He'd already read the entire issue last night, and now started from the beginning again, quickly devouring an article about mistakes related to gun use, seen in movies.

Halfway through the second article, he caught his breath, looked up and stared across the pond at the Red Oak Event Space building. He let out a long sigh, then turned back to the article on 9mm hybrids.

He'd barely noticed his dad's black, six-door truck had pulled up to the pond. His father's three-man crew had arrived, and one of them stepped out and walked towards him.

"Hey, Dave! Your dad wants you to come to the office right away." When Dave remained engrossed in the article and didn't respond, he walked closer. "Dave, it's Harold. Are you just about ready to go?"

His head jerked up, a troubled look on his face. "What's the rush, Harold? You know I don't leave until 9 o'clock."

"It's something important about the design for a high-rise building. I don't know the details. Looks like they need to talk to you immediately."

Dave stood up, and took his time to feed the ducks that had regrouped in front of the bench. When the packet of corn was empty, he walked slowly towards the truck, counting the seconds. He was leaving three minutes and twenty seconds too soon, and he didn't like it one bit.

The crew members in the truck waved and smiled. He understood that it was a friendly gesture and returned the smile. It wasn't a spontaneous reaction, but a choice to return the smile. If the smile was from a total stranger in a random place, he would try to figure out why someone was smiling at him. Before getting into his ten-year-old sedan, he turned his baseball cap around so the visor faced forward. He started the car and the company truck followed him along the familiar eight-mile route.

Dave parked in front of the three-storey brick building in the Old Fourth Ward, a predominantly black neighborhood east of downtown. One wall of the building featured the company name, 'Pruitt & Sons – Plumbing Solutions', and was made out of huge brushed metal letters that were surrounded by a variety of decorative pipes and valves. The shop occupied the bottom two floors and Dave lived with his parents in the sprawling apartment on the building's top floor. The neighborhood was gradually gentrifying with new residents upgrading the older houses and increasing property values. But the building was just a few miles from a neighborhood known for drug trafficking and shootings, and so iron bars covered the storefront's bulletproof windows. There was a loaded Glock behind the counter.

Dave's dad, Robert Pruitt, inherited the company from his father, and it remained a flourishing family business, thanks to new homeowners who were gutting and renovating homes in the district, as well as frequent jobs from tech companies in Buckhead. Even though the company continued to take on residential work, P&S specialized in plumbing installations and repairs for commercial and industrial projects.

Dave climbed the stairs and entered the first-floor conference room that was dominated by a table and six chairs. The walls were covered with design sheets, checklists, and various brochures as well as framed plumbing licenses from the State of Georgia for the firm and individual employees. His dad and a couple of employees were looking over design sheets spread on the table.

"What took you so long, Dave? We've been waiting for you." Robert, at six-two was a couple of inches taller than Dave and at least twenty pounds heavier. His dark beard was threaded with silver and he wore glasses with black frames. Dave shrugged and dropped the magazine on the table. Robert shook his head, then turned to Steve, the firm's senior designer. "Go ahead and explain to him."

"Dave, we need you to focus here." Steve was a plump man with receding reddish-brown hair and a goatee. "The plumbing design we submitted for the new high-rise on Peach Street was rejected with the comment that the current design leads to a massive over-use of energy and water and doesn't meet the city's new green certification standards."

When Dave's attention seemed to stray, Robert interrupted. "I spoke to the sub-contractor who did the design. Those jerks say that they need us to redesign the plan to meet the new standards, and they want a new contract to do it! Their rough estimate increases the budget by nearly eighty thousand bucks. That means we could lose money on this contract, Dave, unless we can handle the re-design in-house. Do you think you can come up with a viable solution?"

Dave stared at the blueprint on the table and remained silent. He knew his father was upset, but he didn't like being rushed. Now Steve was carrying on in an animated fashion about all the technical comments they had received. Dave closed his eyes and rubbed his ears with his palms to block out Steve's grating voice.

"We've had great comments about your work on the last building. I know you can do this, Dave." Steve patted him on the shoulder and Dave jerked back, as if a hot iron had singed him. He looked at the door, ready to bolt.

Robert knew what was about to happen, and asked everyone except Dave to leave the room. "Look, son," he said softly, "This is a big-ticket item. A lot of money is at stake. I need you to look at it."

Dave stared in silence at the design sheets. After a minute, he raised his head and closed his eyes.

"What's wrong?" asked Robert.

Dave spoke slowly in a low, but firm voice. "Why did you send Harold and the guys to get me before nine o'clock? You know I don't like being interrupted."

"Sorry, Dave. Steve did that. He wanted to make sure that you didn't go anywhere else. But I didn't think they would get to you until nine."

Dave frowned. "Since they found me at 8:45, they must have left no later than 8:31 providing traffic was only one minute slower than when I drove there at 7:47. You should have told them to wait until 8:46."

"Well, it doesn't matter now. You're here and we have work to do."

"It matters to me."

"Okay, sorry. I tried calling you first, but you didn't answer."

"My phone is on vibrate. I don't like any of the sound themes. None of them."

"I know. You've told me." Robert pointed at the design. "So what do you think?"

Dave closed his eyes again. "I'm not sure."

"If you don't want to look at it right now, work on it in a little while, okay?"

"I don't like being interrupted at the pond. I even left my phone in the car so I wouldn't be bothered."

Controlling his frustration, Robert hesitated, then offered, "You get this right, Dave, and we can go to 'Bang for the Buck,' and bring our guns from the collection. Deal?"

Dave opened his eyes, glanced at his father. then said in a monotone, "Ok. That will be fun."

Robert tapped the top sheet. "Can you start right now? Do you want a can of LaCroix?"

"Dad, I never drink sparkling water until noon when I eat lunch. Mom knows that."

Robert shrugged, waited. He was used to such conversations.

"If you can get these moved upstairs, I will look at them in my room."

Robert nodded, relieved. "Good. No problem."

"Dad?" Dave made the briefest of eye contacts.

"Yeah?"

"We've gone to lots of indoor ranges lately. I'm going to one next week with a friend. Why don't we go to an outdoor shooting range, like Big Creek?"

"Who are you going with, next week?"

"Someone I worked with at my first job."

"I would've gone with you."

"Next time, Dad. We can go to the Big Creek together."

"Once the new design is approved, we'll go. I promise."

With that, Dave abandoned the conference room and crossed paths with Steve without looking at him. He paused in the hallway when he noticed that Steve didn't close the door, and listened.

"He'll do it," Robert said.

'How'd you talk him into it?"

"I told him I'd take him to Big Creek if he fixes this shit. I'd like you to come along when we go."

"Sure. But do you think it's a good idea? You've said that Mary wanted to discourage him from the firearms as much as possible."

"I've tried. But if I don't accompany him, he'll go alone or with someone else. It's the one thing he likes. I want to make him happy whenever I can."

"I'm not judging, Robert. But there was that one incident with the cops."

"I don't want to talk about that," Robert snapped.

"Okay, sure, I'll go with you. Let's see what he comes up with. But let's keep the sub-contractor warm as plan B."

"You know how much Mary and I've gone through with him. There's not a day we don't wish he was normal."

Dave covered his ears with his palms and walked away. He hated it when people talked about him as if he were dangerous or crazy. That's why he kept his gun collection secret. Not even his father knew all the weapons he owned. He climbed the stairs to the apartment and walked into the kitchen where his mother was putting dishes away in the cupboard. Mary was an attractive slender woman with short dark-hair, who stood a couple inches shorter than Dave. She'd done bookkeeping for the family business since before Robert's father died.

She turned to him and smiled. "Your dad was looking for you. Did you see him?"

"Yes, and I don't like that Dad invited Steve to go to an outdoor range with us."

"Steve's a nice man. He's an old friend of your father's from college."

"I know, but he doesn't even own a gun. He rents one at the range. That's sad."

She closed the cupboard and started wiping the counter with a sponge. "Well, not everyone is into guns like you, Dave."

"He doesn't like my interest in guns. I think he's afraid I'm going to shoot someone, someone like him."

Mary tried not to smile at the comment. "I know you would never shoot anyone, Davie. Not on purpose, and not on accident. You're very careful around guns."

"That's right. I know all the rules, and I follow them better than most gun owners."

She nodded. "But your father and I are concerned that your interest could lead to trouble if you get involved with the wrong people."

"I'm not going to sell my guns to anyone, if that's what you're thinking. If you have a collection, you add to it. You don't deplete it."

"Good. I thought Dad wanted you to fix a design plan."

"Yes, I have to do that first before we go to the outdoor range. It's complicated, but I think I can do it."

"I know you can."

He walked to his room, closed the door, then sat at his desk. He made sure all his pens, pencils and drafting tools were neatly aligned, that nothing on his desk was out of order. He was ready to work as soon as the design sheets arrived. His room was more than five hundred square feet with a low wall that separated his study from the bedroom.

He tapped his index finger rapidly on his desk, something he did when he was nervous or impatient. Today it was both. He was impatient to get to work on the project, and nervous about a notebook he'd found in his dad's closet. At that time, he was looking for a box of 9X23 Winchester Ammo that he'd bought last week. He'd left it on the kitchen table and forgotten about it. He'd asked about the ammunition yesterday while he was eating dinner with his dad.

"Oh, that. It's in my closet," Robert said.

"Why did you do that, Dad? That is my ammo. You don't even own a Winchester."

"Calm down, your mom handed it to me when I was in the bedroom. You know she doesn't like any gun-related stuff left on the kitchen table."

"Yeah, not even my magazines. She puts them on my bed. I hate that."

While his parents were watching TV in the living room, Dave walked into his parents' bedroom and into his dad's walk-in closet. He turned on the light and found several boxes of ammunition stacked neatly on a shelf, but none were his. Puzzled, he scanned the shelves, searching without success.

He was getting annoyed and began opening drawers and pawing through the contents. That was when he found a well worn red spiral notebook with one word on the cover, DAVE. His first thought was, *That's not my notebook.* Then he opened it and recognized his father's handwriting, and saw it was all about him going back to when he was a baby. He quickly closed it and was going to put it back, but changed his mind. After all, his name was on the cover, and he was curious to see what his father had written about him.

He'd secreted the notebook into his room, and tucked it in the lower desk drawer beneath his own notebooks that were mostly his drawings of guns with written descriptions under the best ones.

He took out the notebook now for the first time while he waited. There were no dates on the entries, just references to his age. He was about to start reading when he noticed a piece of stiff paper stuck between two of the pages.

It was a photo from Disney World when Dave was about five years old. He was on dad's shoulders, wearing a Mickey Mouse cap, and was smiling at his mother. He turned over the picture and saw a scrawled message—*Disney World, shortly after the diagnosis.*

What diagnosis? Then he realized for the first time that his parents didn't always know that he had Asperger's. They found out from a doctor, then went to Disney World. Why would they do that, he wondered. He stuck the photo between the same two pages, then turned back to the first entry. He seemed normal until he was four, his dad wrote.

Ten to fourteen months was the normal time frame for babies to begin saying words, and he said mama and dada at the beginning of his eleventh month. He uttered short sentences when he was two and full sentences when he was three. But by the time he was four, Robert and Mary started noticing certain peculiarities. They realized that Dave often avoided making eye contact, and he seemed easily distracted when they talked to him. They wondered if they weren't paying enough attention to him and they decided to spend more time individually with him.

Things went fairly well in preschool. Teachers commented that, although Dave was somewhat aloof, he followed the lessons and occasionally played with other kids. "Dave is very creative and enjoys both indoor and outdoor play. He is making good progress in small group activities. He is inquisitive in certain things and engages in the group activities with little adult prompts. Dave seems to like counting and arranging blocks in nice patterns."

He didn't remember any of that, but he guessed the notebook would include plenty of the terrible events in his young life. The next entry proved him right. It was labeled, *Tantrums,* and described how he would throw himself on the floor or the bed screaming at the top of his voice, and ignoring them completely. It happened outside the home too. They were in a mall once and Dave suddenly started throwing things off shelves, and when they caught him, he beat his head with his fists. It seemed like nothing would stop him until his energy was spent.

He had no memory of that incident. But the next one, oddly, he recalled one part of it, his fascination with a falling leaf. He and his parents were walking along a sidewalk. Dave was in the middle holding hands with his parents. He looked up and saw a bright orange maple leaf gently floating in the wind, moving in small circles.

He let go of his parents' hands and fell behind them where he reached his hands up, opening and closing his fingers as his gaze followed the leaf. The wind grew slightly stronger and the maple leaf suddenly changed course. Dave was fixated on the maple leaf and ran into traffic. Robert froze, and Mary lunged after Dave. The driver of a Honda Civic noticed Dave at the last instant, turned as hard as he could, and ran over the opposite sidewalk. Utter chaos followed. Three more cars came to screeching halts, but luckily no one was seriously hurt. One of the cars stopped a few inches away from Dave. When Mary reached Dave, he showed her the maple leaf he'd caught. He was smiling weirdly, and seemed utterly unaware of what just happened.

Back at home, Robert shouted, "What the hell were you thinking, Dave?" He said it over and over. Dave cried, and didn't seem to know what he'd done wrong. Mary told Robert to leave him alone. "It is time we take him to a doctor."

Dave couldn't read any more. He wanted take the notebook and use it for target practice somewhere out in countryside and shoot it until it was in tatters and unreadable. He heard a knock, and quickly jammed the notebook back in the drawer.

The door opened and his father came in with the design sheets. "All good?" Robert asked, trying to make conversation as he spread the sheets across Dave's desk.

"Fine." Dave avoided making eye contact and waited for his dad to leave.

Robert paused at the door as he retreated. "I know you will fix this problem like you've done before. I am so proud of you."

"I'll look at it," he answered in a monotone.

1.2 A Muslim American

Alim Mubarak was awakened from the sleep by the monotonous tone of his phone vibrating against his bedside table. He blinked and glanced at the time, saw it was 2 AM, and couldn't imagine why his longtime friend, Ajrami, was calling.

"Alim, I've been trying to call for half an hour."

He sensed panic in Ajrami's words. "Sorry. My phone was on silent. Is everything okay?"

"Please come to the mosque."

"At this hour? What's going on?"

"There's a fire."

"Did you call 911?"

"The firemen are already here."

Alim quickly dressed and rushed out of the house without waking up Rabia. May be it was just a minor fire; nothing serious. Perhaps someone had left a burner on in the kitchen and it had set off the fire alarm. As he drove he reviewed his day, and could never have imagined that it would end this way.

He had stopped at the mosque on his way home from the office to partake in the Friday sunset prayer. The mosque was not just a place of worship for Alim and other Muslims in Charlotte. It also served as a community center, offering classes in Islamic studies, Arabic and English as a second language, as well as an orientation program for immigrants unfamiliar with aspects of life in America.

Alim, who was born in Iraq, had lived in the United States for two decades now. He'd arrived at age twenty-two and was an active member of a local Muslim community. He'd launched an interfaith and outreach program in the mosque a few months earlier that he was particularly proud of. The mosque invited people of all faiths from the neighborhood to tour the mosque, watch a presentation on Islam, and participate in special events like a bazaar and health fair. Several times a year, the mosque offered free dinners on special occasions and each one featured cuisine from different Muslim countries.

Indian and Pakistani Muslims brought Haleem, made of meat marinated and tenderized by slow cooking for seven to eight hours and seasoned with spices, such as cardamom and cumin, and also wheat, cashew nuts, almonds, and other ingredients. It had a slushy texture and served with a garnishing of fried cashews, coriander and lime. A typical spread included mutton soup, salad and pita bread stuffed with vegetables and meats. Also pastries made with phyllo dough, fruit dessert and an icy noodle wonder, known as faloodah.

After Alim arrived at home following the sunset prayer, he and Rabia and their twelve-year-old son Zamir had gone out to dinner at their favorite Italian restaurant located in a shopping center a couple of miles from their suburban house. Alim was amused and proud of Zamir's American accent, his love for bagels and pancakes and his calm and confidence. There was nothing out of the ordinary about it since Zamir was born and raised in America. But it still seemed an impressive feat to Alim, who had encountered numerous confusing cultural roadblocks on his way to becoming an American citizen and gaining confidence that he was part of this country and culture. Back home from dinner, Alim worked on an idea for a sports and fitness program at the mosque, and went to bed a few minutes after midnight.

With growing anxiety, he gripped the steering wheel tightly, and accelerated ten miles an hour over the speed limit. He rarely sped, but this time was different, and traffic was light. He cut the usual twenty-minute drive by several minutes. He'd imaged a small fire confined to one room that would already be out, upon his arrival. But he was shocked when he saw the mosque engulfed in flames.

There was nothing he could do but watch as the copper-domed mosque vanished behind a wall of smoke and flames. By the time the firefighters doused the fire completely, the copper dome and marble slabs with religious quotations from the Qur'an were all that remained.

The small crowd that gathered in the darkness before dawn mostly comprised of local Muslims who arrived after receiving a phone call or a text. A portly police sergeant ran a yellow police tape between the street poles and ordered people to stand back. His partner, a tall, muscular African-American, pointed at someone in the crowd, who kept shouting that the cops didn't protect Muslims or respect their religion.

"Enough of that shit, test me again, see what happens."

Firemen emerged from of the blaze, their faces and yellow protective gear stained with soot. The shoulders of one of the firemen sagged. Two firemen supported an injured man between them, his head low, his arms around the firemen's shoulders. They dragged him forward, yelled for an ambulance. A new cadre of firemen arrived, their gear bright and shiny. They lined their hose, dragging it quickly to the blaze, then blasted the remains of the burning mosque.

Some in the crowd grew angry, others were stricken with grief or simply stunned by what they saw. Someone suddenly shouted in Arabic, "We will not take this silently. We will have our revenge. *Allahu Akbar. Allahu Akbar.* God is the greatest!"

Ajrami stepped in raising his hands, Don't do that. Don't take god's name and associate it with revenge and violence."

Few others joined the chorus, "We will have our revenge."

Alim stepped in front of the crowd and waved his arms to calm everyone down. "What the hell is wrong with you? This could be an accident. Let's not overreact till we have the facts."

"Who are you kidding?" a bearded man shouted in response. "Are you fucking blind to the hate around you?"

"Then why don't you pack your bags and go back to your native country?"

"I am an American citizen. I am not going anywhere."

"Then, why don't you behave like one?" fumed Alim.

While he'd admonished the man in an attempt to calm the crowd, Alim was fully aware of growing intolerance towards Muslims in America. More than a hundred mosques were targeted in the last couple of years. Muslims kids were getting bullied, and many of his friends and relatives told him that being a Muslim in America had become more and more complicated in recent years.

"What are we going to do now? Where will we gather for Friday prayers?" asked Ajrami. The 70-year old Palestine American was teary eyed, his voice shaky. He ran a hand through his thick gray hair and shook his head in despair. Alim reached out and hugged him. "We'll figure it out. Don't worry. Things are going to be all right."

Ajrami broke down completely. "They have desecrated our mosque completely. What sin or crime did we commit to deserve this?" He sobbed like a child.

"Our crime is being Muslim. Nothing else," someone shouted from the crowd.

Alim understood how his friends and fellow Muslims felt. He was naturally an empathetic person, but he knew that there were good people of many faiths around them, people who were going to be saddened by what happened here tonight.

He repeated what he'd said a few minutes earlier. "This could be an accident. Let us wait for details."

"No, it's not," Ajrami said. "We've gotten threatening phone calls and hate mail from people telling us to close the mosque or else, and finally, the bastards did it."

"Did we complain?"

"Yes, and I'm sure you heard that someone threw a rock through a back window a couple of weeks ago. We reported it, but the cops don't give a shit."

"That could not be true," Alim responded.

"Stop living in denial," an angry replied from behind him. "There were pickets in front of the mosque two days after the window was broken—people who think all Muslims are terrorists—and now this."

"All right, all right," said the stout officer. He took off his cap and waved it as if to shoo the crowd. "Nothing more to see here. Move along. Go home."

"Let's get back to our families," said Alim. "We can't do anything more now. The cops will investigate."

"What good will it do?" Ajrami said, shaking his head.

The next morning, Alim called his boss at Happ!, an Atlanta-based software company that had an office in Charlotte. He told him that he would like to take a week of personal leave, and explained what happened.

His boss, Alex, was sympathetic, but asked Alim to cut the leave to two days. "You know how important your project is to the company. We're already behind schedule, and there's zero tolerance for missed deadlines on this one."

1.3 - The Young CEO

Maverick Investments was located in an obscure corner of Buckhead, a few miles from downtown Atlanta. The firm operated from an historic antebellum house, the kind built during the reconstruction. But in the twenty-first century, the majestic structure was located in the shadow of an overpass on an otherwise abandoned block. Because of the location, the house was zoned for office use. The outer parlor with its large bay windows on either side of a picture window looked out onto the back side of commercial buildings and the overpass. As usual, all the shades were drawn blocking out the view.

The inside parlor had been converted into an office , where Mark McCarthy was surrounded by a tablet, laptop, and a desktop. At twenty-seven, he had a solid physique and deep voice. He had dark hair, broad forehead and high cheek bones. His eyes and looks were deep and thoughtful. Women often did double takes, especially when he walked by in one of his thousand-dollar suits.

Four flat screen televisions were all on at once, each tuned to a different business channel. One channel was covering the story of an American e-commerce giant's decision to shut its China online store and how homegrown e-commerce rivals were giving the global giant a hard time. Another channel covered the impact of the crackdown of the U.S. on Iranian oil. The market analyst was predicting a big drop on the supply side that would boost the commodity price as the White House announced that it was ending a six-month waiver from U.S. sanctions for importing Iranian oil.

A social media giant setting aside $1 billion for payments related to privacy infringements was covered by another channel.

The news that caught Mark's attention was about S-UnLimited. The energy company was forecasting a first quarter loss of $60 million, but the company was predicting that it will return to profit by the fourth quarter. Startup companies always lost money, a thought that he found especially reassuring today.

Stacey Cranston, his fiancée and interim secretary, walked into the office. He appreciated her help and at least for now the one-year-old company didn't need a full-time secretary. From his aesthetic point of view, it was also nice to have an attractive, shapely blond moving about the office. At least, that's how he had thought about her presence when she first started working for him.

"You've got a meeting with Deck to review finances. Should I call him in?"

"Sure."

Deck Dressler was the lone finance employee of the firm. He worked mostly from his home office, and dropped in for these monthly reviews of the company's financial status.

After Mark's father's death from brain cancer, Mark gave up his job with an insurance firm and decided to go on his own. He wanted to fulfill his dad's prophecy that one day he would achieve spectacular success and make him proud.

The process of starting an investment firm took a few months, but it was pretty much doable. He did some research, talked to his acquaintances in investment banking and hired a lawyer to provide legal advice and guide him throughout the process of filing the paperwork and paying the necessary fees. He cleared the mandatory written exams to get the required licenses and became an investment advisor in the state. He chose the company name and completed the registration requirements with state and the federal governments. The firm was in business.

The company's tag line was "Reap Rewards with Minimal Risks." Its expensive brochure said that it offered an approach to generate excellent returns without undue risks. Mark hired a team of portfolio managers who invested customer funds in various financial instruments and discussed changes on a weekly basis. Whenever required, Mark as CEO would arbitrate and make final decisions.

Deck walked into the room, greeted Mark, then connected his laptop to one of the monitors. He was more than a decade older than Mark, had thinning hair, a round face, and the beginning of a paunch. He proceeded to give a summary of the affairs, quickly covering the basics and provided a one sentence summary. " The monthly expenses are higher than monthly earnings by 90,000 dollars."

"That's fine," Mark responded. "Burning cash till the cash flow turns positive is an expected routine for any new firm."

"Can I say something?" asked Deck.

"Shoot."

"I've dealt with many small firms and I think the expenses are on the higher side for a company of this size and revenue."

Mark started tapping the table with his fingers. "I'll be getting some additional funding. We can easily sustain this burn rate for at least another year. So, I don't want you guys to worry."

"That's great!" pitched in Stacey.

She was probably wondering about her pay check," Mark thought, smiling at her.

"Yeah, I'm also getting new customers, which means we earn more while keeping the cost at current levels."

Deck nodded. "But, I think we can tighten on upfront costs. I think…"

Mark jerked his head around. "That is enough! Just tell me the expenses required for the next two quarters. I have a ton of things to do and don't have fucking time to waste."

Deck turned silent, but Mark wasn't in a mood to let it go. "Do you get it?" he asked, raising his voice.

"Sure."

"So, the upcoming expenses?"

Deck mumbled some numbers, and Mark waved a hand. "Don't worry about it. We're covered."

Deck picked up his computer and headed to the door. He flexed his burly shoulders and looked as if he was about to put his fist through the wall. When he was gone, Stacey asked if she could do anything else to help the situation.

"I could look for less expensive office space. The lease is coming up for renewal in two months, and I can find something before that."

"Have you been paying attention to the news, Stacey?

"What news?"

"A renewable energy start-up reported $60 million loss for the quarter."

"So?"

"They indicated that they would return to profit by the fourth quarter."

"Your point?"

"My point, Stacey, is that is how business works. Especially a start-up firm, like mine. I'll continue to burn cash to attain growth and turn around the cash flow. That is how it's done."

"That looks like a big company, Mark. How can you compare your small investment firm with it?"

"That's just an example. All startups like mine lose money before they start generating profits."

" Just tell me if I should look out for new space."

"No, we're good."

"Cool." She headed back to her desk.

"Hey, thanks for helping me with all this. I can hire a secretary anytime. Just let me know when you're bored."

She stopped in the doorway. "No worries. I like doing this."

"Thanks!"

"One more thing, Mark." She hesitated. "It is about Deck. I think you were a bit rude to him."

"I didn't hear him complain."

"No, but I wanted to mention it to you, since I referred him to you."

"And I thank you for that, Stacey. His voice was tinged with his annoyance. But I don't want him to challenge my judgment."

"It's not only about what you say. It's also about how you say it. You are the CEO. The big boss. Can you please be nicer to him?" Stacey smiled.

Mark mellowed down. "Anything for you, Honey, but tell Deck not to challenge me when I'm speaking. Okay?"

"Sure, I'll tell him." She reached out and squeezed his arm before stretching out both her hands to make finger gun gestures and asked "Shooting range, this weekend?"

Mark smiled, "Yup, I can blow off some steam."

THE SHOOTING

6:28 PM

Watson and Higgins entered the Red Oak Event Space, darted across the lobby toward the hallway, and pressed their backs against the wall of an alcove. They peered down the hall and spotted two bodies lying motionless in pools of blood. Higgins called 911 and briefly described the scene. Watson, meanwhile, texted his former FBI partner, Esteban Barrios, and told him where he was and who he was with. Barrios, still an active agent, wrote back that he would link with the cops.

Higgins glanced over at him. "Let's make a move. Ready?"

He nodded. They stepped out into the hallway, then moved around the bodies. Two more victims appeared. Neither were moving. From the damage to the bodies that he could see, Watson guessed that the killer was carrying an AR-15, probably with 30-round magazines for maximum kill. He noticed a pack of cigarettes on the floor next to one of the bodies. The shooter must've gotten interrupted in his plan by smokers. If he hadn't gotten into the auditorium yet, they needed to take him down quickly to limit the death toll.

A man in a sport coat came around the corner, walking oddly, his hands up. "Don't shoot!" A man wearing a ski mask held a rifle to the back of the man's head.

Watson crouched low and aimed at the gunman, but the hostage blocked his way. The shooter was staring at Higgins and didn't see Watson. For a moment, he had an open shot, but then the killer shoved the hostage forward, blocking his aim. Higgins and the gunman both fired. Higgins' shot struck the hostage in the shoulder, the man collapsed on top of Watson, and Higgins fell next to him. The killer shot Higgins again, this time in the back.

By the time Watson freed himself from the hostage, the killer had moved on. He crawled over to Higgins, who whispered, "Go get him," as light faded out of his eyes.

Watson's breath came in gasps as the fight or flight mechanism kicked in. His body tensed, adrenaline took over. He had no time to take stock about what had just happened, what an incredibly dangerous situation he was in. The only thing that came to his mind was his doctor's comment that he should continue to take it easy for a while.

He took one more look at Higgins—dead less than an hour after he met him—then turned to the wounded man who was sitting up against the wall. Watson stripped off his tie, slid it underneath the man's arm and tied it tightly around his shoulder to slow the loss of blood. He helped the man up, wrapping an arm around his rib cage. He looked down at Higgins' pistol, wishing he'd picked it up, but now he had to get the injured man to the entrance where he was sure help would be waiting nearby.

He could tell the man, who was in his early twenties, was in shock and might pass out at any moment. "Hey, what's your name?"

"Jerry."

"I'm Larry. You're going to make it. But we've got to get you out of here." They started down the hallway. Jerry gulped air and struggled to walk. The difference between being shot by a .22 in the shoulder and Higgin's .40 Smith & Wesson M&P from close quarters was enormous. Watson knew he might lose his arm.

"Jerry, did you see which way the shooter went?"

"Yeah, this way." He'd no sooner spoken when they heard the report of several loud pops coming from the direction of the lobby.

"Shit." Watson held his Glock next to his ear, the barrel pointed at the ceiling, while he moved forward holding the gasping man upright.

He needed to text Barrios to give him an update. He was confident his old partner was in contact with the locals, and if they were following immediate deployment protocol, the standard now for active shooter control, they would hold off on entering to give him time to deal with the situation. They would think that he and Higgins, the security chief, were their best bet.

They edged closer to the lobby. When it came into view, Watson saw bodies, but no shooter.

Either he'd fled out the door, or went into the auditorium to continue with what was probably his original plan of attack. The answer came as he heard gunfire from within the auditorium. Unless someone with a gun had taken down the shooter, the rampage was just beginning. By now, police would be arriving by the dozens—on-duty and off-duty ones called into service—and organizing outside the building. As they crossed the lobby to the entrance, edging around a couple of bodies, screams and more gunfire erupted in the auditorium.

It was raining outside, and the glass doors looked like an abstract painting featuring flashing red lights. He jammed his pistol back into its holster, and was about to help Jerry outside when the door to the auditorium burst open, and a crowd of people piled out and rushed for the door. Watson stepped aside, allowing them to flee. The last one to make it was a big guy with hair tied in a man-bun. He stopped and looked at Watson and Jerry. "Do you need help?"

"Yeah, can you take him and get him medical help right away?"

"Sure." He wrapped a long arm around Jerry as Watson stepped aside. "Hey, what about you, aren't you coming?"

Watson didn't hesitate. "I'm staying inside. I'm armed, ex-FBI. They should know about me. Tell the cops Watson is alive and working the scene."

"I will. Good luck."

As the two men made their way out, Watson saw the line of police and emergency vehicles, blinking lights, and rifle-bearing cops in tactical gear. For a moment, he considered fleeing, letting someone else better armed and protected to take over. But instead he turned and headed for the auditorium.

# # #

Videos appeared on Twitter. In one, several men were trying to open one of the doors to the auditorium, but found it locked. Nearby, people were hugging and sobbing, others were on their knees praying. Some had ducked under tables.

In another, several children were being ushered under tables in the lobby. A six-year-old girl with orange hair grabbed the collar of a three-year-old boy and jerked him back. The little boy was giggling, clapping his hands, tapping his feet and squirmed to be free from the girl's grip. Popping sounds erupted, growing louder and louder. The girl managed to hold onto the kid and they vanished under a table just as the video began to jerk about wildly, then ended.

# # #

USN reporter Blake Radcliffe stood on the far side of the pond where police had moved all representatives of the press. He held a microphone in one hand and an umbrella in the other as he stared across the pond toward the event space building.

Radcliffe positioned himself so that the camera would show the backdrop of police and emergency vehicles. He nodded to the cameraman, and a moment latera red light on the camera came on.

"Tactical response teams are still arriving on the scene here in the Atlanta Tech Corridor where an active shooter is believed to be holding hundreds of people hostage. Authorities received the first reports of a shooter in the Red Oak Event Space building a little over twenty minutes ago. Of course, police forces around the country are prepared for these events, and so the quick response, though impressive, is not surprising. I was in the tech corridor on another story when the report came in, and by the time I got here police were already setting up a perimeter and condoning off the press."

The camera panned the line of police cars and emergency vehicles and the clusters of officers standing behind them watching the building.

"We've been told that employees from an Atlanta tech company, called Happ!, which is located here in the corridor, were in the event space auditorium celebrating their tenth anniversary when shots were heard. Because these folks are so connected with social media, the reports were on the internet at the same time they were coming into the police. Okay, it looks like we have some activity near the entrance now."

Radcliffe paused and looked toward the building, which was barely visible through the rain and darkness. "I can see a stream of people with their arms raised starting to the leave the building. Let's hope it's over and the social media rumors about multiple deaths are wrong."

More distant pops of gunfire were heard. "Maybe it's not over yet," Radcliffe added. "It looks like about fifty people have emerged, but now I don't see any more escaping. They're coming in this direction. It looks like they're being taken to another building across the street. Let's see if I can get any comments as they pass by the police line."

Radcliffe moved closer to the yellow ribbon and held out the mike toward passing Happ! employees, their hair and faces glistening with rain in the light from the camera. Their hands were clasped behind their heads and they were accompanied by several officers dressed in tactical gear. "Hello, can you tell me what's going on?"

Several passed by in silence, their heads down before a young blond woman turned to look at him. "It's awful. I saw dead people, people I worked with." She started crying, shaking her head, and hurried on.

Radcliffe followed her along the line. "Where was the shooter when you left?"

"I don't know. People were afraid to leave because there was a loud blast in the lobby, like an explosion. We don't know how many shooters there are. But some of us ran for it."

She moved on and Radcliffe turned back to the camera. "Fortunately, some are escaping, but we don't know what's going on inside." He turned as a man who was basketball-player tall strode along the police line, his shirt covered with blood. "Sir, are you injured?"

The man whose hair was knotted at the crown of his head, slowed down. "No, I was helping someone who was shot."

"Can you tell us anything about what's going on inside?"

"There's an ex-FBI agent in there, and he's armed." The man moved on.

Radcliffe looked down a moment, then stared into the camera. "I've covered far too many active shooter stories in my time at USN. Over the years, the police tactics in dealing with these terrible events have changed. At one time, when police arrived at a school or other building where a shooter was active, they would create a perimeter and wait until a three or four-person tactical team arrived. It was a tactic borrowed from the military, infantry patrol tactics, and was considered radical at the time."

He paused a moment and looked earnestly at the camera. "That approach usually involved waiting on the outside far too long. Tactics have evolved over the years so now the first officers to respond no longer wait for SWAT teams to arrive and suit up. It's now recommended that whoever arrives first go immediately into the building. Statistics show that the sooner officers enter the building in question, the sooner the incident ends. Often times, shooters will take their own lives."

Radcliffe paused and looked over his shoulder. "Does that mean there are officers inside? We don't know for certain. But we just heard from one of those who escaped tell us that there's an armed FBI agent—or ex-agent—inside."

Radcliffe looked down at his phone for a few seconds. "As I said, there are many rumors being spread around on the internet about what is going on inside the Red Oak facility. Some people who have escaped say that there are at least two shooters, maybe even three. There are reports of a Middle Eastern man who might be involved. But again, we want to emphasize that these are unverified rumors."

Radcliffe moved his umbrella to the side as the rain let up."Happ! employees have been sending out photos and videos relentlessly since the incident began. Hopefully, these images can help authorities not only see what's going on, but to identify the shooter or shooters, and locate them. We already know that Instagram pictures show bodies in a hallway and the lobby, as well as pools of blood and bloody footprint trails."

Chapter 2

2.1 Aspie the AssBerger

Dave sat on his favorite park bench at the duck pond and stared out at the Red Oak Event Space building. As usual, the building looked empty and quiet. The only people he'd ever seen enter the building were maintenance types, who were cleaning or changing lights and whatever maintenance people did. If there was any activity here, it would probably be during the evening or on weekends when conferences were held.

Only once in the three months that he'd been visiting the duck pond did he encounter anyone on his bench. A woman smartly dressed for an office job sat right here and stared at her phone. He'd stood next to the bench on her left, waiting for her to move on. After thirty seconds, she looked up, slowly turned her head, and studied him. "Can I help you with something?"

"Just the bench. I'm waiting for the bench."

She pointed to her right. "There's another bench, unoccupied. Go sit there."

He shook his head. "No, this is my bench until 9 o'clock."

"What? Oh, never mind. Fucking crazies. I'm out of here." With that, she got up and walked off, shaking her head.

He'd frowned, confused by her reaction. After all, she was the intruder, not him. He never knew how people were going to react to him. Except for Laura. She understood him, but she was gone, and he pushed her out of his mind.

He reached under his arm and pulled out the red notebook entitled, DAVE. He hadn't opened it since his father had brought the design sheets for the plumbing of the high-rise building to his room. The original design was devised by a sub-contractor with a single agenda of keeping costs low and meeting bare minimum energy efficiency requirements. There was absolutely no intent to create a solution that would control energy costs and water usage once the building was operational.

He'd finished the re-design two days ago. In spite of additional costs, the company would still make a lot of money. It had taken him six days and his dad and Steve had gotten more and more worried with each passing day. One morning, after his visit to the duck pond, he'd walked through the shop and overheard Steve say, "For all we know, Robert, he's up there drawing pictures of ducks on a pond."

"Please don't say that. I'm confident he'll get it done and get it right," Robert replied. "Let's give him a couple more days, then we move to plan B with the sub-contractor."

Early yesterday morning, he'd dropped a neatly drafted note detailing changes to be made to the current design. Dave's solution was to divide the entire building into multiple pressure zones and replace the very large booster pump with pressure reducing valves and a central water heating system with a booster pump package and a water heater for each pressure zone. He included the precise calculations on how the new design would reduce the energy usage by one third compared to the old design and how over the lifetime of the building the new model would yield magnificent dividends.

Armed with the thorough information Dave put together, Robert and Steve were able to negotiate new terms yesterday with the builder, who was mightily impressed with the solution and promised more business for Robert.

He opened the notebook and found where he'd left off reading. The next entry was about a visit to the family doctor after the incident with the falling maple leaf. Robert and Mary explained all the peculiarities they had observed in Dave over the past year, and how they'd tried to be flexible to his idiosyncrasies. The doctor listened closely, then recommended they make an appointment with Dr. Wilma Sutton, a neurologist and autism specialist.

When they arrived at the building where Sutton's office was located, they stepped into an elevator and Robert asked Dave to push five. Dave pressed the buttons with the numbers 1 to 5 on the control board and called out loudly, "One, two, three, four, five." That was an example of how Dave took everything literally, Robert wrote.

Dave felt as if he were reading about someone else's life, since so far he remembered almost nothing of what he'd read. He closed his eyes and said the doctor's name a couple of times to himself. Suddenly, an image appeared in his mind's eye, a memory from long ago. It was a room that looked like a preschool classroom with a child-sized table and chairs, puzzles and other small toys, and shelves that held books and little dolls. Dave remembered being fascinated by the toy cars during his visits here. As he read his father's summary of the visit, he imagined that he was there again.

# # #

When Dr. Sutton arrived, she leaned down close to Dave's face and asked how her buddy was doing. Dave didn't answer. "I see you like that little car," she smiled, then turned to Robert and Mary. "How's that medication working that your pediatrician prescribed?"

"He's been a tad better, I think," said Robert.

"Has the stimming let-up?"

"The what?"

"I'm sorry, that's the official term for the hand-flapping you described. It's something some children do to self-regulate and get organized and overcome anxiety. The medication should help not only with some of the impulsive behaviors, but that too."

"I think there has been some improvement," Mary said. "I haven't noticed him doing that so much."

"Okay, good. Well, as you know, you're here today for a brief screening to see if we can get closer to Dave and understand what's going on."

"What does this involve?" Robert asked.

"Today, we're just going to observe Dave being Dave in his six-year-old world." She looked at Dave who had turned one of the cars over and was still spinning the tires.

"Dave, what is that you're holding?" she asked, smiling.

No response, he wasn't listening. Dr. Sutton pulled out the small chair next to him and sat on it. She rested her chin in her hand and got closer.

"Dave, can you please show me the car?"

He turned the car over and placed it on the table, but didn't offer it to her.

"What color is the car, Dave?" she asked.

"Blue," he said.

She held up her hand and said, "Give me five." Dave complied with the requested hand gesture. Thanks to his mother, he already knew what that expression meant.

"How many cars are there, Dave?" she asked, pointing to the table on which some toy cars of various colors were arranged neatly.

 A few seconds later Dave said, "Fifteen."

"Count again Dave. You might be missing some," said Dr. Sutton.

Dave didn't bother to re-count. Instead, he said, "Three blue cars, seven yellow cars, and five red cars. That is fifteen cars."

"I see twenty cars, Dave. Four rows with five cars in each row" said Dr. Sutton softly.

Dave slowly walked to the table, picked up five toys from different rows and placed them on the floor and squatted next to them. He looked in the direction of his mother rather than Dr. Sutton. "These five are not cars. Two vans and three trucks."

For a moment Dr. Sutton was taken aback. "You are right Dave, and you can take home any of the cars that you like." She quickly correctly herself with a smile, "Including the vans and the trucks."

After another high five, she scribbled something in the file and smiled. She looked up at the anxious parents and said, "There is great hope for Dave. I see signs that are very, very good. What I'm going to do is have my assistant come in and work with Dave for a while. She'll engage him in puzzles and drawing exercises. Hopefully, it'll be fun for Dave. It's part of the assessment. Meanwhile, we can go to my office next door and go over any concerns you have."

Moments later another young woman arrived, and Dave seemed to be exceptionally compliant. His interest expanded to several other toys on the other tables. He didn't even seem bothered when his parents left him alone in the room with the assistant.

There was an overstuffed sofa in Dr. Sutton's office, and on the other side was a large desk. "Take a seat on the couch and relax," she said as she settled herself into her desk chair. "Let's talk a little about home life and what you're experiencing with Dave."

# # #

Dave paused and looked up from the notebook as a uniformed officer stopped in front of him. Instead of looking at her face, Dave stared at her holstered weapon. He couldn't see much of the gun, but he knew it was a full-sized Glock 22 Generation 4. The Atlanta Police Department bought twenty-three hundred of them in 2013, replacing the Smith & Wesson M&P .40 caliber. He didn't know what the police department did with the old S&Ws, and wondered what happened to them.

"Are you already done feeding the ducks, Dave," asked the middle-aged officer, who wore her hair shorter than his.

He looked at her name tag, reaffirming that it said, Sheila Smathers, someone he knew. "Yes, the ducks were fed very fast today. I was in a hurry."

Smathers smiled. "You don't look like you're in a hurry."

He tapped the notebook. "I'm reading about my past. My father wrote journal entries about me."

"Oh, and now he's letting you read them."

"No, I found it in his closet and I'm reading it."

She was about to respond when her partner, a younger black officer, joined them. "What's up, Sheila?"

"I think he swiped his father's notebook. But since it's about him, he deserves to read it."

"I don't know what you're talking about and I don't even want to know. Let's just move on. Have a good day, Dave."

Dave watched the two cops walk away. He didn't know why Officer Will didn't know what she was talking about. She told him exactly what he was doing. The pair patrolled the tech corridor weekdays and had approached him soon after he'd started coming here. He remembered that they laughed at him when he asked if they were married. Why was that funny? Sometimes it was best not to ask questions, or try to explain anything.

He turned his attention back to the notebook, and continued reading about his time as a six-year-old at Dr. Sutton's office. Again, he tried to imagine the conversations and the scenes in his mind's eye.

# # #

"Besides our own observations and feelings about Dave's behavior, we've also received some comment from his teachers," Robert said.

"Oh? Tell me more about that," Dr. Sutton said.

"They tell us Dave is very bright in some aspects. He knows his math in his head, doesn't even need to write things down. It just doesn't make sense." Robert shook his head. "In the same breath, they tell me that overall he's immature and the other kids don't like him, and they bully him. I don't understand any of this."

"He has a wonderful home life," Mary said. "He's loved, and he's offered all kinds of opportunities to go places and do things. He never wants to go. You could leave him in his room alone all day long, and he wouldn't want for anything."

"He can be a beast, too," Robert interjected, "especially if he's interrupted from some TV show or game he likes. And getting him to sleep is a fight every night. I don't understand."

"Hmm, what does he like? Dr. Sutton asked. "To do, to play with, I mean."

"Oh Jeez, Dave is obsessed with some Turtle movie. He knows all the characters names. We have a video that he watches over and over and over. He knows the words as if he wrote the script. He sits two inches from the TV screen, wide-eyed. I mean he's a happy kid. Well, at least, when he's doing what he wants."

"Does he like to play outside with neighborhood kids?"

Mary shook her head. "No. Even when we take him to the park, he sits on a swing alone while all the other kids are meeting up and chasing each other. I've tried to get him into cub scouts, but he just doesn't seem to connect well with other kids."

# # #

Dave paused as he reached the end of the entry. He dropped his head back and stared at the pine boughs high overhead. Most of his life he'd wanted his parents to leave him alone so he could do the things that interested him, not going on a boring trip somewhere that was supposed to be fun, but never was, not for him.

The next entry was about the third visit to Dr. Sutton's office. His father had put a label on this one, *Worst Fears Confirmed*. Did he really want to read this stuff?

What did he care what some doctor had said about him two decades ago? But he had the notebook and he was determined to read it.

# # #

"There is some good news and some bad news. Let me give you the bad news first," said Dr. Sutton. "Dave is a wonderful kid, but you have to accept that he is not completely normal."

She paused, looked from one parent to the other, then continued. "From all the tests we've done, he is surely on the Autism Spectrum. To be on a spectrum means to be on a level of functioning from severely disordered to high-functioning and anywhere in between. Our diagnosis shows that Dave is on the high-functioning side, which is a big deal. We call it Asperger Syndrome or just Asperger's."

Robert and Mary looked devastated, and didn't respond.

"I know this is hard to accept, but let me break it down for you." Dr. Sutton pulled up an image on her computer screen and pointed to the red rectangle.

"As you can see broadly there are three categories. When someone's falls under severe autism category, which is level three, their behavior severely impacts their life and they need a substantial and constant support including full-time aides and intensive therapy in some cases."

She moved her finger to point to the yellow rectangle. "When someone fall under level two, they too need substantial support and their lack of social and communication skills and odd behaviors are obvious to the casual observer, even when support is in place. They may require speech therapy or social skills training. It is a relief that Dave is not in these two categories."

"I don't know if any of this is a relief to us," Robert said.

"What does that mean for Dave's life ?" Mary asked.

Dr. Sutton point to the blue rectangle. "When I say Dave is on the highly functional side, he has mild symptoms and with the right support, won't significantly interfere with his education, work, and to some extent relationships."

"But will he be able to lead an independent life as an adult?" Mary persisted.

"Yes, that's the good part. His communication skills are much more advanced than others on the spectrum, and that means he will have a good chance at living on his own."

"He doesn't speak a lot or share what's happening at school, but he can usually tell us what he wants," Robert said, and Mary nodded in agreement.

"Good. However, there are couple of things you need to understand so that you know what to expect and how to react. First, the lack of social emotional reciprocity. People with Asperger's don't possess theory-of-mind abilities, which mean they aren't able to recognize and understand the thoughts, beliefs, desires and intentions of other people in order to make sense of their behavior."

"Could you explain that a little more?" Mary asked.

"Sure. As Dave grows up, he will have difficulty in social situations. He will see issues as black and white and won't recognize the shades of grey. In other words, he won't be able to read between the lines. He will say things without considering the emotional impact on others."

"In other words, people will think he's an asshole," Robert said, grimly.

"Until they get to know him and understand he's not acting that way on purpose.

She continued after a pause, "The other thing is, Dave will have narrow areas of focus. He will have restricted, repetitive, and stereotyped patterns of behavior. He will have a preoccupation with specific patterns of interest. He will adhere to specific routines and have repetitive mannerisms."

"He'll be an oddball."

"Don't call him names, Robert," Mary said.

"High functioning autistic individuals have made great achievements through their narrow focus of interest. There are many real-life examples of inventors, engineers, designers, sculptors and artists, musicians with exceptional talent who struggle daily with their autism. They are typically overwhelmed by social settings involving more than one or two people. The fast pace of life with all the sounds and movements are a confusing blur to them. They are high achievers who understand very little of what is outside of their focus."

# # #

Dave read Dr. Sutton's explanation of his life over again, and then again. It was his life, but he'd never seen it explained so clearly. He glanced at his watch and shot to his feet. It was 8:59, time to leave. He started to walk, then broke into a trot when a runner passed him on the path. He didn't like to run and couldn't keep up to the man, who he recognized as a regular who ran six times around the duck pond between eight and nine every morning. A very thin woman who was as old as his mother made three laps every morning, then ran off somewhere else. He would rather count their laps than run with them.

"Right on time, Dave."

He looked up as he was unlocking his car to see a man who wore a black windbreaker. "How do you know my name?"

"The officers told me. They said you were a good guy."

"I feed the ducks."

"I know. I guard the buildings in the corridor. My name is Higgins. He held out his hand. Dave stared at it a moment, then reluctantly held out his own. The man firmly shook his hand, then turned and walked away. Dave saw that the back of his windbreaker said LEVEL 1-A SECURITY.

Dave was still interested in reading the notebook, but he didn't want to do it at home where he might be interrupted. After he'd turned in the completed project, his dad was so pleased that he told him to take a couple of days off before they went to the outdoor shooting range.

He knew exactly where he would go now, the one place where he had privacy and would be surrounded by all that was dear to him. He drove to the entrance to Interstate 20 and headed west until he exited on State Road 29 and continued south for several minutes until he turned off on Campbellton Road. Several miles later, he found the dirt road that was a quarter mile past an old red barn. He followed the winding road for two and a half miles until he came to a wood-framed house with a front porch. The entire property was fenced and he used a code to enter through the gate. He drove slowly along the double-track past the house and to a storage shed. It measured eleven by twenty-one feet, had polyethylene walls re-enforced with steel, a metal roof with two sky lights.

He keyed the padlock and opened the door. He stepped inside and flipped on the light switch. The interior wall to the left displayed eleven of his guns, everything from 9mm pocket pistols to tactical weapons. They were the guns his parents didn't know about. On the opposite wall were shelves filled with his collection of gun magazines that dated back three decades. The shed was furnished with a small table with a single chair, a cot, and a port-a-potty. He loved this place. If he had running water, he could live here.

He dropped the notebook on the table and ran his fingertips over several guns. He stopped in front of the A-15, his newest purchase made at a gun show. He should take it apart and clean it, he thought. But right now he wanted to read more about himself. He was fascinated by his father's chronicle, but he didn't know what to think about it. It was the first time he ever thought about himself through another person's eyes. It was strange and somewhat frightening because he knew things got worse as he grew older.

He sat down and opened the notebook to the last page that he'd read. His father summarized what happened in the months after the diagnosis. It took them several months to come to terms with the new reality. As recommended by Dr. Sutton, they had follow-up sessions with her assistant Dr. Brenda Hayes. On the first appointment, she explained the difference between a meltdown and a tantrum.

"For you to be able to relate to what Dave goes through during meltdowns, imagine you are in a room full of people, each speaking a different language you never heard and understand. They have circled you and are yelling at you. Some seem confrontational, some are laughing, and some are pleading. You see everything, you hear everything, but you don't understand a thing, you are overwhelmed."

"That's a meltdown?" Mary asked.

"Yes, Dave experiences that sense of being overwhelmed in a situation that probably appears completely normal to you. During such situations Dave's behavior might give you an impression that he is throwing a tantrum, but it is not a tantrum."

"A meltdown," Robert said. Mary's eyes were full of tears. Robert held her hand to comfort her.

"Before the meltdown they generally exhibit signs of anxiety," Dr. Hayes continued. "They can start pacing, seek reassurance asking the same question again and again, and there might be physical signs, such as rocking or becoming very still." She also explained how to watch for a pattern of the specific things that causes Dave to have a sensory overload, how to minimize the triggers and anticipate the meltdown."

In the final session, she also explained how to react during a meltdown. "Please understand that you cannot stop a meltdown when it is happening. So, don't judge Dave if he doesn't respond to what you are saying. Give him the time and space that he needs. If there are people around you, ask them to move along, not stare, turn off the loud music, the bright lights or whatever you think is the trigger. Dave is wonderful boy and with your understanding and support, he will do well."

As they stood up to leave, Mary said: "I got that Dave doesn't easily understand the emotions of others, but does he experience emotions like everyone else?"

"That's a very good question. While Dave may not readily understand the emotions of others and nonverbal cues, he has feelings like anyone else— happiness, sadness empathy, compassion, and so forth. But he has difficulty expressing those feelings to others so it might appear that he lacks emotions."

Robert wrote that he and Mary started understanding and making note of Dave's hypersensitiveness to specific sounds, tastes and lights as well as his difficulty with give and take in conversations. Dr. Hayes made it clear to them that there was no cure for Asperger's, but suggested they try different therapies because each child is different and there is no one-size-fits-all approach.

Dave went through school scoring high marks, but he struggled in the outdoor activities and ironically his inability to discern intent sometimes protected him from insults. Robert related a story to that affect that was told to him by a teacher.

Dave was in fifth grade, when the teacher took the class on a field trip, and all the kids were on the playground to discover tadpoles and frogs around a retention pond at the corner of the field. One of the boys called out to the rest announcing the great find, a bunch of White's tree frogs that change color depending on their location. The girls were squeamish and looked from a distance, but the boys gathered closely, fascinated with picking them up and observing them.

Dave wasn't with the boys or even watching alongside the girls. Instead, he was sitting on a tire swing, twisting around, then letting go to enjoy the spinning and dizziness effect. Dave was in his own world, the teacher explained to Robert.

One of the boys pointed and called out to the class to look at Dave the Dope on the tire swing. The class laughed and pointed and yelled out names to him. "Whatsamatta? You scared of little froggies?" The boys laughed, and even some of the girls chimed in. Dave didn't understand and didn't seem to care. He didn't know why the group was pointing at him and laughing, but he went along with the fun. He inappropriately waved back at them and pretended to laugh along with them, which further amused the boys and one of them shouted, "What a freak you are, Dave."

Unknown to the teacher at the time, a couple of the boys hatched a plan to bring a few baby frogs back into the classroom the next day to scare Dave. They placed several frogs into Dave's meticulously organized pencil storage case knowing he'd open it during the math lesson. The teacher wrote the equation on the chalkboard, and Dave went to work on it. He already had his pencil out, left on his desk from before gym class, and was writing down the problem. Much to the boys' chagrin, he didn't need to get into his pencil case where the frogs were.

The teacher asked the class to spend the next few minutes solving the equation quietly alone. One of the boys announced he didn't have a pencil and asked if he could borrow one of Dave's. The teacher looked at Dave and asked if he would share a pencil. As Dave opened his pencil case, several tiny frogs jumped on Dave's arm. He started flapping and waving his arms, knocking the pencil case and its contents to the floor.

The classroom roared with laughter. The teacher, who didn't know about Dave's Asperger's or see the frogs, asked him if he was trying to be funny. Dave didn't know how to explain himself or understand the trick played on him. He wasn't mad or angry, just confused. After that incident, the teacher and Dave's classmates came to know that he was diagnosed with Asperger's, and one of the kids made up the nickname 'Ass Berger,' and most called him 'Aspie.'

Dave's parents kept detailed notes of Dave's development history, his strengths and weakness, situations and environments that triggered a meltdown.

Various therapies over the years helped Dave develop self-expression to some extent, better understand social cues, and control his outbursts.

At school, the special education director helped in evaluation of Dave's academic strengths and weaknesses and created an individualized education program that provided accommodations such as longer duration for tests and a quiet lunchroom setting to minimize sensory overload.

Dave took a break from reading the journal. He had no memory of the frog incident. He must've blocked it out. So many things had happened that he didn't remember.

He placed his hands over his ears as he'd done when he was young and struggling with a meltdown. After a minute, he slowly lowered his hands, aware again that he was in a safe place, his place, and no one could bully him, no one could touch him. He wanted to drive home now and return the notebook to his father. But he struggled with forming a response to the journal. If he were reading it in his room right now, he might take it downstairs, throw it down and scream. But he had time to think it over and come up with a better reaction.

He decided to keep reading.

Dave's journey through high school was challenging, his father wrote.

It was a different school and he was repeatedly bullied in his first months. High school administrators assured Robert and Mary that there would be no more bullying.

Dave completed freshman and sophomore years without further trouble. But bullying incidents resumed in his junior year and took an ugly turn. Those were the most frightful weeks in Dave's life, and he'd refused to go back to school for several weeks.

To help him recover, Robert took Dave duck hunting. That led to his intense interest in guns, an interest that became a passion, and now it had become a full-blown obsession. Dave remembered his high school years much better than his younger years. But he didn't want to think about that incident in eleventh grade that led him to temporarily drop out of high school. He skipped over that journal entry, and continued reading.

After he returned to school, he focused on his studies in a way that only people with Asperger's could do. He aced all his math courses, scored high enough on his SATs, and went on to major in civil engineering at Georgia Tech, all the while working for his dad at the plumbing business to pay for tuition.

The journal, to his surprise, continued to describe Dave's life after college. He remembered these experiences well, and filled in details as he read his father's summary.

While he was in his final year of engineering, one of his professors referred Dave for an internship at Green Works, Inc, a construction company in Atlanta. Armed with the professor's recommendation, Dave met Harold Wallace, the company's chief engineer, for a short interview.

Introductions and exchanging pleasantries didn't come naturally to Dave. But Wallace made him feel at ease and Dave became comfortable when the conversation turned technical and about projects he'd completed at the university. Wallace was impressed, and offered Dave an internship. After six months, he was hired for a full-time position. Things went well until Wallace left Green Works for another company.

The new boss, Brian Peterson, didn't seek out Dave during his first week, and Dave made no effort to approach him. The following week Dave walked into the break room to refill his coffee cup when he came upon a few of his colleagues talking to the new boss. Dave overheard the end of the conversation before they realized he was there.

"He's some brainiac that Wallace hired last year. Do you know he was excused from coming to the team meetings if didn't feel like attending them? Special privileges? Maybe he's certifiably loony. He's a loner and he's one French fry short of a Happy Meal." Peterson laughed along with everyone.

Dave stood there, frozen as they realized he was in the room. He knew the comments were specifically about him. In the ensuing uncomfortable moments, everyone except the new boss got up and left.

Peterson approached him at the coffee machine. "So, you're Dave."

"Yes, sir."

"I've been here a week and this is the first time I've talked to you. Just wondering what the problem is here. Wondering why the guys talk about you."

"Problem? None that I'm aware of."

Peterson took a step back and sized Dave up, then smiled wickedly. "Are you the Rambling Wreck guy?"

"Excuse me? I do not ramble."

Peterson laughed, "I take it you don't follow football?"

"Sir? No. No time for football."

"Georgia Tech?"

"Yes, yes... oh! You're referring to the school's fight song." He knocked his palm against the top of his head. "Sorry. I guess my mind is on my project and the deadline."

"Fine. Keep your mind on the job. Nice to finally meet you."

"Yes. Bye." He turned to leave.

"I've got my eye on you!" Peterson called out, stopping Dave in mid-step. "Remember that. One more thing, I need you to join all the team meetings. I can't exempt you from the meetings nor can I have separate meetings with you." Peterson walked past him, and left the break room.

Dave had no clue what the hell just happened. All he knew was that he needed his inhaler when he returned to desk so he could prevent the asthma symptoms that seemed to arise alongside a panic attack. He tried to remain calm, but it was too much for him to handle.

New boss, remarks from his colleagues, remarks from Peterson. It was all too much to handle.

By lunchtime, he couldn't focus any more, and decided to work on the project at home. He placed his phone on do not disturb and left a note with the front desk that he could be reached at home. He didn't leave the office early very often, but at times like this, it made sense to him.

Later that night, he shared the break room exchange with his mother. He told her it upset him, but he didn't know why. "Maybe the people in the office are against me."

"They just don't get you, that's all. But I do! What happened to Mr. Wallace? He liked you a whole bunch and it seemed you liked him. This Peterson guy sounds different."

"He's not like Wallace at all."

"I hope he doesn't hold it against you, you know, that you took your work home this afternoon. There are laws about making accommodations when you have a condition. But why don't you try making the team meetings."

"Mom, you know about my social anxiety. Meetings causes panic attacks, then I can't focus on my work."

Dave feared going to the office the next morning. Maybe he was in trouble for leaving early. His mind jumped from one negative possibility to another until all he could do was collapse into his bed. The next day he mustered courage and drove to the office, but as soon as he reached the parking lot he turned around and went home.

That was the end of his job, and he had similar issues on his next job. That's when his father decided to bring Dave into his business again. Robert understood that it was challenging to get Dave to focus from nine to five like other regular employees. But when he did focus, he provided great results.

He used Dave on tasks that were challenging, but didn't have tight deadlines. Dave cracked some of the toughest design problems, saving him thousands of dollars. Robert was mindful of Dave's routines, like feeding the ducks every morning in the tech corridor's pond, his peculiar eating preferences, and how he brushed his teeth precisely at nine o'clock every night, then rinsing loudly three times. Any change to the routines would cause a meltdown and Dave would lose control. At those times, Robert grew concerned about Dave's fascination with guns.

But he wrote that Dave had never mishandled guns. "He is aware of his diagnosis and has always been very meticulous about sticking to the safety norms while handling firearms. Nevertheless, I'm worried."

That's where the journal ended. Dave closed his eyes and fought off an urge to scream as loud as he could. Reading about his own life leading up to the present was disturbing, and he needed to calm down. He decided not leave the shed until the feeling of confusion and disorientation went away. Dave knew that if he was a normal person, he would return the journal to his father and tell him he was sorry for all trouble he'd caused. But he knew he couldn't bring himself to do that. He found it odd that he'd even considered it. He would sneak it into the closet where he'd found it.

Just before leaving the shed, he picked his latest purchase off the wall, a Colt 6920, a formidable tactical weapon. He would take the AR-15 with him and show it to his father when they went to the outdoor range. But he wouldn't tell him that he'd opened a new credit card to pay for it.

2.2 From the Ashes

Throughout the weekend, Alim and other members of his community were engaged in talks about rebuilding the mosque. By Sunday evening, he was utterly exhausted. He needed a drink so that he could just sit and unwind. While he'd seen numerous media reports about rising anti-Muslim feelings, he never thought he would experience it first-hand. But that was a growing possibility. Most likely the fire wasn't an accident.

He drove to a hotel bar, ordered a bourbon cocktail, and took a seat at a corner table. He let his thoughts drift to the past. He'd travelled to America from his birthplace, Baghdad, with a student visa. After getting his PhD in computer science at the University of North Carolina, he'd moved from Chapel Hill to Charlotte, North Carolina, one of the new technology hubs in the South. The city had strong job growth, affordable housing for software engineers, and was popular with millennials.

Although he was in a foreign country, he generally felt welcomed. He was intelligent, educated and had a good job, distinguishing him from refugees who had nothing. At the same time, he initially had a difficult time adjusting to the permissiveness of American culture. He was confused when he heard that the South was conservative and that many people here wished religion and the Bible would play a greater role in government. But Americans had no idea what it was like to live in a country where conservative religious values and government were closely entwined. He was sure that women from the South would be appalled by religious strictures among the most conservative sects where women not always by choice wore ankle-length burqas, head scarfs and veils, where men might physically abuse their wives and escape any punishment. Besides that, in eighties less than one in four Iraqi women graduated from high school, and even fewer held jobs outside of their home.

It wasn't long before he adjusted to American culture as he pursued his career in computer engineering, and was considered capable and successful. He built a comfortable life for himself and his family, and embraced Southern hospitality and manners, not to mention basketball. Alim became especially enamored with barbeques, as long as they didn't involve hogs, anathema to him as a Muslim. Indeed, he enjoyed most, if not all things, American. But eating pork was one of the last taboos he refused to break.

Alim was Muslim, devout but moderate in his religious involvement. He drank caffeine when he needed a jolt for work, not that it was forbidden, and he would have a beer sometimes with friends, or at a corporate picnic. He knew most Muslims considered alcohol haram, or forbidden. But he didn't agree with that interpretation of the religion. Still, he atoned by stepping up his involvement at his local mosque — at least he'd taken part in their community outreach and social events.

After the tragic events of September 11, 2001, Alim put an American flag sticker on his car and made sure to have the real thing waving in front of his house. Whenever he felt eyes sizing him up, or heard muttering under his breath, he indulged in kindness, with extra helpings of politeness. Nonetheless, he was incensed when, even before the sand had settled on American tanks in Afghanistan, Alim's adopted country had decided to invade his homeland. But to whom could he complain? How could he say anything when he saw the bloodlust in the eyes of his co-workers? And he didn't want to incite fellow Muslims at the mosque. Instead, he worked to be the example to which Southern Republicans could point as one of the good ones.

Alim also made sure to get his green card, and he applied for citizenship as soon as he could. To this day, he was genuinely happy to tell anyone who might ask the story of how he got a perfect score on the exam. For twenty-plus years now, he has sent a third of his salary back home to his mother and sisters and prayed every day for the political situation in Iraq to stabilize enough to allow him to bring his family members to his new country.

He was distracted from his musings by the conversation from the next table over. Several people had arrived a few minutes ago and now they were getting boisterous. A man exploded with expletives. "He's a fucking son of a bitch. I wish the bastard would get hit by a bus."

"Ouch. Who're you talking about?"

"My boss, Dick Miller."

Everyone at the table looked to be in their thirties, Alim thought. They were all dressed casually. The guy who was complaining had short red hair and a moustache.

"That's his real name?" someone giggled.

"No. It is Rick Miller. He says he likes to be addressed as Mr. Miller. Mr. My Ass. We call him Dick when he's not around."

"That's kind of mean," one of the two women at the table said. But she was smiling when she said it.

"Not for him; it isn't. He treats all the guys like shit. The SOB only wants to talk to women employees and likes to throw everybody else under the bus based on hearsay.

Someone lightened the mood by saying, "It's not you speaking, Carl. It's the single malt bottled up for twelve years."

"No, no," pitched in another guy, loudly. "I understand where he's coming from. I used to have a terrible boss named Chuck and we all called him 'Upchuck' behind his back."

Everyone at the table laughed at that. But Carl wasn't done. "If Mr. Dick got hit by a bus, I'd stay and watch him suffer," he said, then waved off the instant reactions of disapproval.

"That was nasty!"

"I can say that because that's how he makes me and others feel. Miserable. We agree on something, then he asks me to e-mail him a note about it and cc it his boss. Then Mr. Dick will respond by writing that he has a better idea. He does it just to make him look better. He derives sadistic fun if has to fire someone."

This time one of the women pitched in, "My boss is a pig. She is obnoxious and shouts at everyone in the meetings and calls. She is talented and hardworking but so uncivilized. No professional etiquette and class at all."

"Yeah, tell me about class," one of the other guys said. "My boss has an accent that's really hard to follow. He's from Turkey, I think. His accent is horrible, much worse than the people from India on the customer service lines."

Someone noticed Alim at the opposite table and hushed the others. Heads turned to look at him and everyone started looking at their phones.

Alim finished his drink and left amidst the silence. That night, he continued to follow TV news reports on the mosque fire. Arson was suspected, a fire official told a reporter. The video clip showed the community praying in the open with the ruins of the mosque in the background. The anchor talked about firefighters losing the battle to save the mosque after fighting the flames for three hours. Then she went on to say that dozens of residents came together to offer their support to the Muslim community. She noted that an online site had been set up to raise funds to rebuild the mosque and it was receiving phenomenal response from all around the world.

That made him feel better, but he still couldn't help thinking about the continuing turmoil going on about Muslims, Islam as a religion and sharia law, or Islamic law. Some of the videos he'd seen on YouTube left him feeling disturbed. One of them showed a reporter on the streets of Little Palestine, a neighborhood in the Chicago suburb of Bridgeview where Middle Eastern bakeries, grocery stores, and specialty fashion shops are abundant along with business signs in Arabic. The reporter asked everyone he stopped how they liked living in America. The uniform response was that they appreciated and loved the country , and it was easy to be a Muslim since freedom of expression and freedom of religion was the American way

The reporter then pressed on. "Do you feel more comfortable living under American law or sharia law?"

"Hmm. Sharia law. I am a Muslim, so I prefer sharia law."

"If I asked your friends, would they say they feel the same way?"

"Yes, May be most of them. For a simple reason." The man tapped his temple with his finger. "American law is made by people. Sharia law is made by Allah, and it should be the law for the whole world, not just America. *Inshallah* God willing one day it will be."

One guy intervened, "As a Muslim, I may practice aspects of sharia law in my personal life. As a citizen of America, I respect America for its constitution. I appreciate the American way of life, and America should protect the right of Muslims to practice sharia law in aspects that are not at loggerheads with the American constitution. If there is a conflict, the U.S. constitution should prevail."

The reporter continued: "How do you feel about the controversy on balancing freedom of expression with respect for other faiths? There are people who prefer no limits on freedom of expression, like depicting religious figures in the way they want."

"That really pisses me off. That makes me very angry. Yes, there is a lot of freedom, but my freedom cannot be used to insult other faiths."

The reporter pressed on. "Do you understand the motivation of people who use violence to attack and even kill people to protect the honor of their faith?"

"Yes. When you face hatred, frustration, and suspicion every day, you become mad at what people say about your values and your faith, and you start to hate yourself." He began to get choked up and his voice started to tremble. "Your heart cannot take so much hatred. You can't stop yourself. You don't care. You can commit suicide, or you can go and kill someone."

"So, would you like to live in America, or in a Muslim country?"

"Though I have freedoms here, I may prefer to live in a Muslim country."

The reporter left it at that. Alim shook his head. The reporter should have asked, "Then why are you still here?"

Yet, Alim saw another side of the Muslim community which made him feel better. Two Muslim women had been elected to the U.S. Congress and both were very progressive. They took a strong pro-LGBTQ. stance. A recent poll had shown that acceptance for gay marriage was stronger among American Muslims than among white Christian evangelicals

It was indeed a big deal because so many Muslim scholars said that being homosexual was a sin. Under sharia law in nearly a dozen Islamic countries, those engaging in same-gender sex could be sentenced to death. Many Islamic scholars did not differ on the opinion that being gay was a sin. They differed in the mode of punishment, not on the end result, but how it ought to be delivered: by stoning, by sword, by fire, or being thrown from a high wall. A prominent US Muslim scholar had written, "Homosexuality is an immoral and criminal act. By birth no one is a homosexual. Just like no one is born a gambler, a rapist or an atheist. Due to lack of guidance they pick up evil habits and turn into monsters."

Amidst such a backdrop, Muslim youth across the globe were raising their voice and fighting such interpretations. A small number of Islamic scholars, mainly in the West, had started reexamining Islamic teaching on same-gender sex and concluded that blanket condemnation is a misrepresentation.

Alim personally believed that fear and hatred of Muslims made it essential for the American Muslim community to show that it could really assimilate with American culture. He thought the fulcrum was shifting. He'd read that until the middle of the twentieth century, the Protestant majority saw Catholics with the kind of suspicion many Muslims now felt. The writer said that American Catholicism evolved, and in the process, it changed Catholicism all over the world in a significant way. It was unfair to think that a similar transformation couldn't happen with Muslims.

Alim had no doubt that transformation would happen for sure. The only question was how. Would it be through proactive interventions from within the community or due to pressure from outside? Or both?

While Alim overcame many challenges that he faced in his childhood and teenage years, he was very nervous how his son, Zamir, would be able to handle the new challenges he faced. Despite Alim's busy schedule, he always took time to talk to his son. He would initiate conversations and wait patiently for Zamir to answer him with more than one or two words. He eventually would steer the conversation to what Zamir thought about high school, grades and friends. He made an earnest effort to stay connected with Zamir at a deep level beyond everyday mundane matters.

Just a day before the mosque fire, Zamir had asked him to drive him to a friend's house, a kid he knew from the mosque. During the drive, Zamir started to talk about things happening at the school.

"Dad?"

"What's up, Zamir?"

"I want to tell you something?"

"Sure."

"They nicknamed me ZBL at school."

"ZBL?"

"Zamir Bin Laden."

"What? Who?" Alim's voice rose, despite his best efforts to control his feelings.

"Steve and his buddies."

"What else did they say?"

"They asked me if I was a terrorist, and if I will become one when I grow up and shoot them."

"They didn't! Were they joking?"

"Kind of making fun of me, I guess."

"Yeah, a nasty joke at your expense."

"I just thought you should know."

"Zamir. We need to report this to the school."

"No Dad. No Please"

"What did you tell them?"

"I didn't say anything, but Rick and others told Steve to stop it and shut it."

"Zamir, it's important that you tell anyone who tries to bully you that it's wrong and makes you feel uncomfortable and that you'll report it, if it happens again."

"Okay, but I have one question, dad. It's not like I haven't been called names before. It's been happening, sometimes less and sometimes more. But it's not just me who gets bullied. There are others too."

"Okay, what's your question, Zamir?"

"Other kids are bullied about their color, food, accent, but only Muslim kids are bullied that we are all bad people who will attack and kill others. Why, dad?"

The question floored Alim. He gave a lengthy explanation about terrorism and how some Muslims misinterpret the Qur'an, and how that reflects on all Muslims. After a couple of minutes, Zamir stopped him and said, "Okay, dad. I get it." Alim stopped as he knew his son is too young to understand what he wants to communicate.

# # #

One week after the fire, Alim stood behind the yellow tape on the outskirts of the mosque property. A bulldozer plowed into one of the remaining walls of the destroyed mosque. Another bulldozer piled the rubble in a growing mountain of crumpled concrete, broken wood and tiles, drywall and rebar, while a third bulldozer loaded the refuse into a waiting dump truck.

The demolition devastated Alim. Although he still advised everyone not to jump to conclusions on the cause of the fire, he recognized there was a strong likelihood that it was a hate crime.

The conversation he'd had with Zamir concerned him, and now in the aftermath of the fire, it frightened him. He feared for the safety of his family. He wondered if everything was somehow interconnected–hostile workplaces and schools, unbridled individualism in some cultures, brainwashing from childhood in other cultures, polarized neighborhoods, rising intolerance and the burning down of places of worship. He wished he understood the big picture so that he could make sense of what was happening around him.

His phone vibrated. It was an email from his boss at Happ! about the upcoming review with the management team in Atlanta. That night he rolled from side to side, then onto his belly and it took more than 30 minutes before he slipped into sleep.

Loud bangs on the front door brought him alert. He threw his legs over the side of the bed and rushed toward the front of the house. Someone was trying to break in and they were kicking the door and shouting angry curses. His wife Rabia and Zamir came up behind him.

"Call 911," Alim shouted.

"I already did," Rabia said, as she peered through the blinds. "I can see a car."

Suddenly the door burst open. Three masked men rushed in. Two of them leapt on Alim and Rabia landing punches and pushing them onto the floor. The third one grabbed Zamir and dragged him to the car. The other two joined him and the car peeled away.

"Zamir!" screamed Alim and Rabia.

Alim woke up with a start. His heart was racing. He looked at Rabia. She was asleep. He rushed to Zamir's room. He too was sleeping. Alim hurried to the bathroom and threw up. He hung his head over the sink, gasping for breath. After a couple of minutes, he climbed back into bed. As he tried to sleep again, he assured himself that Rabia and Zamir didn't face any danger. He took Rabia's hand and placed his cheek on her palm. He vowed that if anyone hurts his wife or son, he would make them pay.

2.3 Mark Takes Aim

Mark closed his laptop after confirming what he had already known. The money he got after his father's death was depleting rapidly, and would only sustain his firm for six more months. A couple of minutes later, he stepped out the front door of the historic house that served as his office. The bright sunlight momentarily blinded him after hours in the office. He desperately needed a turnaround to make Maverick profitable, but he had no idea if it was going to happen anytime soon.

Frustrated by the slow pace of the company's growth and his inability to attract new investors with large pocketbooks, he'd decided to get out of the office and go to the shooting range. Top Gun was just a few miles away, but considering the usual traffic, he knew it would take him about twenty minutes.

He settled behind the wheel of his Beemer and was about to start the engine when he snapped his fingers. Just getting out of the office allowed his mind to relax and see another perspective, another possibility. He'd been occupied with his hunt for clients and he realized that he'd overlooked one obvious possibility. He snatched up his phone and looked up the number of one of his college roommates. He remembered that Brian Connelly worked in a venture capital firm. Brian was one of the guys who Mark thought of as a close acquaintance. They kept in touch and met occasionally. But Mark had been busy and they hadn't talked for months now.

"Hey, Brian. It's Mark McCarthy."

"Of course it is. What's up, buddy?"

"The last time we talked I told you about my new investment company, and I just wanted to get back to you about it. As you know, I'm the seed investor and looking forward to the next step, getting some venture capital to kick in. I thought your company might be interested. Can I tell you..."

"Mark, sorry, I quit that job. I'm not there any longer."

"Wow. When did that happen?"

"Just a month ago. I was hired by a tech company called Happ!—H-A-P-P exclamation point—as their finance manager."

"Hey, congratulations. Where are you located?"

"In the Atlanta Tech Corridor."

"Oh, right here in Buckhead. Nice. We'll have to do lunch soon."

"Let me see if I can connect you with some of my contacts."

"That would be great. I'll buy lunch."

"By the way, Happ! is a great stock with good potential. You can recommend it to your portfolio managers to invest with a long-term view. Take a look at our investor presentation on the Happ! website."

"Sure."

So much for that lead, he thought. He felt even more stressed after the call. He closed his eyes to calm himself, and after a few seconds the image of a rifle came to mind. He even sensed the smell of well-oiled steel and the feel of the weapon in his hands. It was time for the shooting range.

# # #

Stacey had initiated Mark into the world of guns and shooting. Both her older brothers were excellent shooters she said and had taken her to the range, starting when she was fifteen. When she turned eighteen, she was finally able to go to the range unaccompanied or with someone else eighteen or older. Mark had felt overwhelmed when he visited the indoor shooting range for the first time to take lessons. He rented a Glock 43, a single-stack 9-millimeter handgun, which Stacey had recommended. He also rented ammunition and a target, as well as goggles and earplugs, which were required. At Stacey's recommendation, he hired an instructor for a basic lesson. Stacey assured him no one would think any less of him for getting an instructor. In fact, quite the opposite, she said. Most shooters want everyone on the range to know all the rules.

He and Stacy took adjacent lanes on the fifty-yard range, and Mark's instructor, a grizzled older fellow named Boon, guided Mark. He began by pointing downrange toward the target and telling Mark that his gun should always be pointed in that direction. Then he told him to button his shirt tight to his neck. He explained that all semi-auto pistols and rifles release hot brass cases after every shot and you don't want it getting inside your shirt.

Following Boon's instructions, Mark took aim, slowly exhaled and pulled the trigger. He could see the bright muzzle flash. His body jolted from the recoil. The muffled sound was still surprisingly loud, and the acrid smell of burnt gun powder hit his nostrils. The explosion of sensations and head-rush that followed was startling and even fearful.

Mark felt that standing his ground and pulling the trigger was a way of overcoming primitive fears of coming under attack. It was all about character, he thought. By the time he completed the training lessons he started really liking it. It soon became a stress-busting exercise for him. He had more than enough reasons to feel stressed, including the financial position of the firm, his mother's deteriorating health, and most of all the pressure to become extremely successful so no one could push him around or denigrate him. Initially, he visited the shooting range with Stacey, but he soon started going on his own. He still didn't know much about guns, but trips to the shooting range were just what he needed.

However, today his concerns followed him to the range. He was deeply troubled by the dearth of new investors and feared the company was failing. On top of that, his relationship with Stacey was sliding into an abyss. He regretted that he allowed her to move in with him. She was too snoopy and was pressuring him about marriage.

How had things gotten this way with Stacey, he wondered. He clearly recalled the day they'd met when he'd shown up at her office to inquire about office space. The cowbell hanging on the door clanged as he entered the small realty firm at 212 Main Street. She was stooped over a coffee pot, filling a mug. She snapped her blonde head, startled, and her big blue eyes locked his eyes for a moment.

"Oh, it must be 9 o'clock and you must be Mister Mark!" she said, regaining her poise.

She took a few steps towards him and extended her hand for a shake. It was small and soft, and he was aware that he probably squeezed a bit too hard before she politely pulled back. Her perfume wafted toward him, then dissipated, and the addictive scent of vanilla and musk left him wanting more.

She held up her mug and offered him a choice of coffee or sweet tea, both of which he declined with a smile. She flirtatiously curled her index finger motioning him to follow her to the back of the office. Mark felt a tingling in his groin as she beckoned, and he imagined a boudoir instead of an office awaiting them.

It was a tiny office. No window. A little blue bag with a Tiffany logo rested on her desk, and it told him she was a woman who liked fine things. The walls were decorated with framed artist-signed prints of some of Georgia's most notable landmarks. Considering her Southern drawl, her stylish attire, and her well-appointed office, she probably came from money, he gathered. She would look good on his arm at business events, he thought, a real class act.

Mark didn't remember much else about that first meeting or even the details about the lease he signed. But it was crystal clear in his memory that he wanted to rip off those clingy black pants, push her over the desk right then and there, and make love. That little office fantasy gave him private pleasure that night and others in the weeks that followed before they became a couple.

She showed him several office spaces suitable for a small firm and he zeroed-in on the most posh and expensive one. During the process he invited her for lunch and dinner meetings and they enjoyed each other's company. Mark didn't say much, but Stacey wouldn't stop talking.

She was a tease, a natural flirt with Southern charm, and she seemed to toy with him. She was flirtatious and he was hesitant. When he gathered courage and made a move, she resisted his advances. When he was direct in his come-ons, she'd pull the "good girl" routine, and she had a way of flipping her hair off her shoulder as if she was brushing him off. He hated that, but it turned him on at the same time. Maybe this lady needed a little incentive.

Then, one day, things changed. Perhaps it was the stroll they took after meeting for business at a local restaurant. As they walked past several boutiques' cute little shops, she finally warmed up to him. Mark kidded that if she'd go out with him, he'd buy her the freshwater pearl necklace she admired in the window of a jewelry shop and take her with him to a business meeting in the Caymans. Stacey's eyes lit up. She pulled his arm so he leaned into her, and she whispered in his ear, "That's a deal, hon."

Stacey wore the pearl necklace out of the store and put the velvet box in her purse. From that moment on, she was his, at least in his mind. Godiva chocolates, Victoria's Secret lingerie, and other little surprises paid off well for him. A promise of an overseas business trip with a planned shopping excursion bought him months of giddy pillow talk and lots of affection.

It was in one of those moments Mark completely exaggerated about the deep financial reserves he had, and how he intended to be independently wealthy before he hit thirty. He saw that Stacey was mightily impressed. He had a fancy office and a posh apartment, and he was a CEO at twenty-seven. He was burning cash and claimed he had deep pockets and seemed to know the moves to make it big.

She kissed Mark and asked, "Tell me more about it."

"About what?"

"About becoming a multi-millionaire. How far are you from it?"

"Depends on how many millions you're talking about." Mark adroitly changed the subject. "Hey, you know, I'm lucky to have met you, and I think you're going bring me more luck."

"You think so?" said Lacy lifting her eyelids, slightly tilting her head and with a smile on her lips. Her large blue eyes looked even larger.

"Yes. Look I don't have lot of friends and don't easily trust just anyone, but I think I can trust you. I need you on my side on my journey to the big league."

He waited as Stacey stared at him. She finally replied, "I need to think about it, if you're asking what I think you are."

He didn't mean that he wanted to marry her, if that was what she was thinking. They'd only known each other a few weeks. "That's fine. You know there's a lot of stress when you are building a company, and I lose my temper sometimes."

"I can understand."

A week later, Stacey made a comment that Mark didn't understand at first. "You have a big apartment. Don't you get bored?"

"It's okay." Mark wasn't paying close attention. The apartment was their love nest and occasionally Stacey stayed overnight. They both liked ordering meals and eating in as they watched television, rather than going out for dinner. Once in a while, they prepared dinner together.

"I'm okay, too," Stacey said with a shrug. Mark still didn't get it.

The next morning the alarm buzzed at 6 AM and Stacey got ready to leave. She would go to her place to get ready for work, then meet Mark at the office.

"I hate this," she said as she slipped into her jeans.

"What?"

"Leaving in a rush like this. I wish I could cook us breakfast and go directly to work from here."

"That's fine with me." Mark didn't like cooking.

Stacey's eyes narrowed. "I mean not just today. You know what I mean, right?"

He belatedly realized she was proposing that she move in with him. He didn't immediately reply. Overnight visits were one thing; living together was another matter.

For the next few days he noticed that Stacey was becoming more formal and strictly professional. He was afraid that too much familiarity and constant companionship would limit his freedom, but he didn't want to lose her. So against his better judgement he asked Stacey to move in with him.

The real estate market fluctuated so much that Mark knew that Stacey appreciated the regular paycheck as well as the free rent at his place. But it wasn't long before she started suggesting they make plans for a wedding. He wasn't too keen on the idea, but he humored her and he said they could start making plans for the event for some time in the future. It quickly became apparent that "future" meant two different things to them, according to each's envisioned timeline. Stacey pushed for a firm date, but Mark remained non-committal. That's when the personal conflicts started, but at least, for now, their work relationship was functional.

# # #

An accident slowed traffic, but he finally arrived at the shooting range twenty-seven minutes after leaving the office. He usually rented a semi-auto pistol, but today he wanted the full auto experience, even though it was going to cost $300. He handed his credit card to the woman behind the counter and was given a choice of several rifles. He picked the Colt Commando, not because he knew anything about it; he just liked the name and the ultra-short barrel, and he was impressed when he was told that Navy Seals used it. He found out that the steep rental price included a range officer who would stand right next to him and give him pointers.

Once at the range with his goggles on and his ears covered with a sound-blocking headset, he raised the rifle to his shoulder ready to destroy the target. The range officer, a tall black man named Joe , who had spent twenty years in the Army, had assured him there wasn't much to it, and had shown him how to adjust his stance to better prepare for the impact. He suggested firing off a few bursts to get used to the feel of the gun.

He squeezed the trigger for several seconds then released it. He took a deep breath, exhaled and fired again for several more seconds, feeling the recoil throughout his upper body. He looked over at Joe. "Wow, very impressive."

"I think you got it Mark. Now you can just blast away if you want and imagine you're wiping out a force of invading space aliens."

"Got it."

He fired away, emptying the magazine. He reloaded, took a couple more tips from Joe, who then said he would leave Mark on his own for the rest of his time. That was fine with him. He raised his gun, then opened fire again. He completely forgot about his problems. He was in another world, eliminating everything and everyone that was in his way, that was keeping him from achieving all that he wanted.

"Cease fire !"

The call came not from Joe, but from the range safety officer. Mark released the magazine and stepped back from the firing line as the officer walked down the line making visual inspections as he went. After he passed by, Mark looked at the adjacent lane and noticed a guy close to his age wearing a Georgia Tech t-shirt. He called out to him. "Hi, how is it going?" But the man was looking at his phone, and didn't respond beyond throwing a quick glance at him. Before he could say anything more, he heard the officer call out, "The range is going hot." A few moments later, he heard the command, "Commence firing."

Once he was outside of the range, he saw the same man in the parking lot. The way he walked, the way he carried himself suggested to Mark that there was something unusual about him. He was somebody who Mark would remember, if they ever crossed paths again.

Chapter 3

Nine Months before the Shooting

3.1 Face Off

At forty-three, Alim Mubarak had twenty years of experience in computer engineering, and earned hefty fees as a consultant. Most of his former bosses had posted very positive comments about him on LinkedIn. Even though Alim's job increasingly kept him at the office late into the evenings while he worked on a new software project, he continued to be involved with the mosque project. To that end, he'd joined the committee working on rebuilding the community's sacred place of worship. In one of their many conference calls, they named their group "Committee al-Nur," or "Committee of Light," a fusion of the language of their new world with the mother tongue many of them had learned in their home countries. Sometimes, they met in the basement of the United Methodist Church.

When Alim first walked up to its doors, he stopped short to read the words on the banner across the threshold of the church. "Open Doors. Open Hearts. Open Minds." Walking down the long hallway, past colorful signs outside the church's day care, Alim recalled a sermon he had heard an imam give at a mosque in Ohio. He'd told his congregation that when a woman comes to a mosque in America, the community ignores her and makes her feel unwelcome. However, if she walks into a bar, she is given a hearty greeting from the patrons. Alim chuckled remembering the sermon. He'd laughed politely when he'd heard it that day, and it was still humorous remembering it now.

He made a mental note to be sure to try to convince the mosque leaders to make room for a day care in the new mosque they were designing. He was so tired of mothers being scolded for their children's chatter and innocent play. The mosque had been a men's club, like so many mosques. They had to change that.

Opening the door to the meeting room, Alim was thrilled to see old friends of the family: Haleema, a pediatrician from Hyderabad, India; Christina, a convert from Minnesota; and Malik, a student from Nigeria. He was not so happy to see Amjad, an engineering student from Houston. He was a young zealot who drove to the Washington, D.C., and New York suburbs for weekend seminars run by an online network, Al Mihrab Institute, started by young American Muslims from Texas. Its leaders designed slick graphics for its courses, but Alim knew what they were teaching: an Americanized version of the Salafi interpretation of Islam that was regressive and confrontational about ideas of assimilating and integrating in America.

Sure enough, before the meeting could even begin, Amjad started railing for revenge. "The destruction of our mosque—that was an act of aggression against us, as Muslim! We must get revenge. The Qur'an makes it our divine mandate to strike back against aggressors who threaten our way of life by destroying our sacred place of worship."

Alim tried to interrupt, but Amjad spoke over him. "I know who did this. We all know. It's the Guardians of the South. You know them. They've been picketing in front of our mosque for over a year now. Do you know where they take their motorcycles and trucks after they're done? To Mickey's Fishbowl. We have to strike back. Like a snake. Otherwise, next time, they will *kill* someone!"

Alim couldn't take it anymore. "Enough! That's enough!" he thundered. "There will be no hateful talk of violence in a place of worship! We are here representing our mosque."

"This is no place of worship," Amjad responded. "Their Jesus is no God. Their cross is a false symbol. Christians have lost their way, chasing a false god. They are *mushrikun* now!"

This was getting worse by the minute, Alim thought. Now Amjad was accusing these Christians, who had stepped forward to give them a space to meet, of *shirk*, a crime worse than murder in the conservative interpretations of Islam. Their crime was giving the Jesus equal status with God.

"What do you think? They first burn down the mosque and then allow us to meet in a church to discuss on the rebuilding plans, and you see generosity in that?" Amjad said as if reading Alim's thoughts. "They all hate us Muslims. They all hate us."

Alim was enraged and speared Amjad with a fierce gaze. "Are you kidding me? It is people with a mentality like yours who say that every Muslim is the same as 9/11 attackers. A terrorist! There are 1.8 billion Muslims in the world and most of them are living in perfect harmony with people of other faiths and vice versa."

Malik backed him up. "I know it is insane when anyone says every Muslim is a terrorist, and I confront them, But we cannot shy away from identifying and eliminating bad things in our own community."

Alim knew that Malik had grown up with Christian families in his neighborhood. He'd told Alim that he loved singing Christmas carols with them. He just lip-synched over the part about "the Father, the Son, and the Holy Ghost." It was no skin off his back. His Christian neighbors believed in a higher spirit, just as his family did. That's all that mattered to him. That was the Islam that his parents had taught him, and the Islam that Alim embraced.

With two men challenging him, Amjad grew flustered. He could care less what Haleema and Christina thought, but these two Muslim brothers? "You two, you might as well wear skirts for the Christians," he said in disgust, then added: "*Astaghfirullah!*" Literally, it meant, "I seek forgiveness from Allah." It was the new go-to phrase for the indoctrinated Salafi Muslim.

Alim saw Christina's eyes roll at the comment. Like a lot of converts, she had gone ultra-orthodox in her first two years as a Muslim, covering each strand in a tight hijab, marrying a student who needed a "green card," divorcing him the next year when he finally admitted he had a wife and daughter back home. She would quickly utter, "*Astaghfirullah*," if she accidentally cursed. "*Astaghfirulla*" this or "*Astaghfirullah*" that, especially if she heard a sister say that she had second thoughts about Islam.

Amjad had seen the eyes roll too, and sneered at her. Alim guessed that Amjad was thinking. *How dare she? A white convert disrespect me? These Muslims were* munafiq, *hypocrites.* "I don't belong here," he said. "I'm not going to waste my time with you people anymore."

With that, Amjad pushed his chair back and stormed out. No one followed him. Instead, they all breathed a sigh of relief. With that interloper gone, they spoke late into the night about their vision for rebuilding the mosque, and dreamt of Turkish tile and Home Depot chandeliers, and the latest designs in bathroom and kitchen fixtures.

# # #

On the drive home, Alim couldn't help but think about Amjad's certainty that the Guardians of the South were behind this attack. Maybe he was right. Maybe we needed revenge to stop future bloodshed. That's how they did it back home. It was called the strongman approach. You had to show your adversary that you were the stronger person. You had to out-shame your adversary. Did Muslims need to assert their power in America with violence in order to protect themselves?

As he nosed his car into the garage, he tucked that question away with his shoes, stepping into the kitchen in his socks. Alim smiled, as Rabia turned to greet him from behind the kitchen sink and felt bad. He knew that his work on the mosque project at night meant his wife had to attend all the duty at home to keep up the house. He never wanted her to be a traditional wife, and didn't mind helping out in the kitchen, cleaning the bathrooms or doing the laundry. But he had no time for any of it now, and he so appreciated how she held the household together with grace and patience... even when she grew frustrated.

Their marriage wasn't like so many of the other marriages of men at the mosque. They were partners not only in the home, but in community service. They had met at the University of Baghdad thirty years earlier in the summer of 1989 when they were both students. He was majoring in computer science and Rabia was studying in the Oriental Studies department, where professors taught literature from the Turkish, Persian, and Hebrew languages.

# # #

Alim liked her the moment he saw her, across the hallway. She had a beauty and gentleness, a natural ease to her personality that he found enchanting. She was someone who was comfortable with herself, open and interested in others. He'd stepped up to her. Iraq was very modern in its relations between women and men.

Not as forward as the West, but not as conservative as some countries, where men often couldn't even see a woman's face.

"Salam," he said, casually.

She didn't avert her eyes. She looked straight at him. "Salam."

"I'm Alim," he said, extending his hand to her.

She took his hand and said, "I'm Rabia."

He let her name roll softly off his tongue. "Raa-bia," he said, adding with a smile, "Rabia of Baghdad?"

She smiled and told him that her grandmother had named her for Rabia of Basra, a Muslim saint and Sufi mystic who had lived in the Iraqi city of Basra in the ninth century.

"Ah, I've heard of her. I think I saw a movie about her once." He knew that the Sufi interpretation of Islam went beyond the dogma and ritual of religion and emphasized spiritual experience.

"Yes, in fact there have been several movies made about her life in the Turkish cinema. She's quite popular among the Turks, I guess."

Later, Alim looked up Rabia of Basra. It was said that she was captured as a slave and that when her owners started trying to force her to be their sex slave, she would escape her suffering by traveling out of her body. Her last owner was so intimated by her spirituality that appeared as a glow around her body when she prayed that he set her free. Rabia of Basra became a symbol of spiritual transcendence for both Sunnis and Shia

Muslims. While it's sometimes misunderstood as a sect of Islam, it's actually a broader style of worship, a mystical practice that guides followers to turn inward.

"My grandmother was a Sufi scholar at the University of Baghdad," Rabia said.

Beautiful, he thought. She came from a very educated family. He took a risk. That weekend, he was going with his sister to Mazar Ghous an Islamic religious complex dedicated to Abdul Qadir Gilani, the founder of the Qadiriyya Sufi order. The complex consists of the mosque, mausoleum, and the library known as Qadiriyya Library, which houses rare old works related to Islamic Studies.

"Would you like to join us?"

She thought carefully. "Maybe. Can I bring my sister?"

"Sure." They made plans to meet after lunch on Sunday. He walked away, wondering if she would show up.

# # #

"Hurry up!" he exclaimed.

"I'm coming! I'm coming!" Safiya, Alim's sister adjusted her knapsack, and they jumped off the city bus. She was eighteen and full of romantic ideas. She would play along, just in case this really was the woman of Alim's dreams, as he kept telling her.

The shrine rested at the heart of Baghdad, and it was a beacon for Sufis. As they approached the shrine, Alim could see the magnificent medieval building with its blue-and-white dome, surrounded by a sprawling complex where visitors stayed overnight and got meals. A sweet scent wafted over him. The caretakers sprinkled perfume all around the complex to activate the senses of visitors. The square surrounding the complex is named Kilani square.

Alim peered into the crowd for a glimpse of Rabia. How would he ever see her among the thousands of pilgrims in the complex? He scoured the many faces before him. And then he spotted her and waved. He motioned to Safiya and they made their way closer to her. She looked even more stunning than he remembered her.

He smiled, and she smiled back, and introduced her sister, Sarah, who was just about Safiya's age. Safiya and Sarah exchanged knowing looks about the budding romance of their siblings, then locked arms. "Have fun!" Safiya said, and the girls skipped into the crowd. "Meet you back here in one hour!"

Alim shook his head, happily. His sister. Such a romantic.

One hour. They didn't have much time. Together, the two slowly walked to the shrine holding the grave. Rabia didn't normally cover her hair, but she slipped a perfumed *chaadar*, or wide scarf, over her head, and then, inside, she draped it over the grave. It was a symbolic offering, seeking protection. Secretly, in her heart, protection for Alim and her. She liked him. She liked his confidence, his good looks, his smile.

A hush fell over the crowd and it parted to make room for the widows of the Iran-Iraq war. It had begun in 1980 when Alim and Rabia were children and it was still raging, with tens of thousands dying every year. Rabia and Alim slipped out quietly.

For months they met like this, at the most, holding hands briefly, pretending to be a married couple. Meeting in the day time was as forward as they would get. Alim wanted to marry Rabia, he knew, not just date her.

His Rabia was like a transcendent being. She thought big thoughts. She dreamt big dreams. America. Discovery. A spiritual relationship with Islam. She felt like a mirror to his world view. Not that he ever thought of himself as a spiritual being.

One afternoon, Alim recited one of his favorite poems by Rabia al Basri, *O my Lord*, to his new-found love:

O my Lord,

if I worship you

from fear of hell burn me in hell.

If I worship you

from hope of Paradise, bar me from its gates.

But if I worship you

for yourself alone, grant me then the beauty of your Face.

In love, Alim could only think of his Rabia of Baghdad when he thought of the beauty of the face of the divine. Six months after they went to the shrine for a special blessing, Alim asked Rabia's father for his blessing to marry her. His parents had already given him their blessing. She came from a good family.

"Yes," her father said.

With that blessing, Alim felt his life was complete. He would never feel troubled again. His life was perfect. Or so he thought.

# # #

For the first year of their marriage, Alim and Rabia lived with his parents. It wasn't always easy for a bride to live under the same roof as her mother-in-law, but his mother left in the morning, like they did, for her work as a school principal. Alim would drive Rabia to campus on his scooter, their hair blowing sweetly in the wind. There were no helmet laws in Baghdad and there were no laws that required women wear hijab.

It was a simple life, but they were content. Mostly. There was still the dream to go to America. How would they realize that dream? Every day they exchanged ideas. Should they try to get tourist visas? No, then they would have to return. Get a job there after they graduated? That seemed impossible. Why would any U.S. company hire graduates from Baghdad?

Only one option seemed possible: going as students. Alim would be finishing his bachelor's degree, and he could apply for a PhD program. So could Rabia.

Whoever got the opportunity, the other would also seek enrollment. They went to both of their families for their blessing. The opportunity would be a good one for the family. Yes, their families said, try to go to America.

So, each night, they started their queries.

"Rutgers University?" Rabia asked.

"Where is it?" Alim asked.

"New Brunswick, New Jersey. Near New York City."

"Yes!" Alim exclaimed. The Empire State Building. The Statue of Liberty. Manhattan. He wanted to see it all.

"Kansas State University?"

"Kansas?" Alim asked.

"Manhattan...Kansas!" his wife said, smiling.

"Manhattan, Kansas?" Alim answered, hesitantly. And then he thought: why not? "Yes!"

And so they continued night after night, application after application, until one day the most unexpected letter arrived: an acceptance letter for Rabia from the University of North Carolina at Chapel Hill in the emerging Arabic language program. Soon after he dispatched his application to the engineering department, Alim received a green light too.

They slept on the rooftop that night, staring at the stars as if their futures too were distant lights, sparkling, awaiting their arrival.

"...if I worship you for yourself alone," Alim whispered into Rabia's ear, as she slept beside him, *"grant me then the beauty of your Face."*

"Shhhh!" she scolded him, smiling.

# # #

So many years later, in Charlotte, Alim and Rabia talked long into the night as if they were still newlyweds. They belonged to the mosque, but they subscribed to an interpretation of Islam that was rooted in the history of their Iraq, but, alas, abandoned centuries ago. The Mutazilites were philosophers, scholars, and thinkers who had lived in the tenth century. They were rationalists. They believed in critical thinking, a concept called *ijtihad* in Arabic and Islamic history. Women scholars were among the leading thinkers of the day.

Alim and Rabia didn't share their belief in the Mutazilites with even their friends in Charlotte. They talked with each other how they wanted to raise their child in America... With critical thinking. With rationalism. With unconditional love.

But their world view led to clashes. Most American mosques recruited white converts as their PR officials, and the Charlotte mosque was no exception. Aisha, a convert, had assumed that role and one day she met with Rabia to show a new group of women refugees from Syria around the mosque. When the women arrived an hour late, with children in tow, Rabia smiled. She knew how long it took to get children ready.

Aisha took the lead. She directed the women first to the women's bathroom to show off the faucets they used for *wudu*, or the cleansing ritual before prayer. It wouldn't have been her first stop, Rabia thought, but oh well. They moved to the balcony where many of the women prayed. Some like Rabia prayed in the main hall, but it was a constant tug-of-war, depending on whatever ideologue was appearing at the mosque. Some demanded a curtain across the main hall to separate the women.

"Women cause *fitna*," the last young radical, Mohammed, had said. It was a loaded word that meant chaos. Alim didn't abide by it. He protected the right of the women to at least pray behind the men, without a partition between them. He confronted others, "Are we so weak minded that we get distracted by mere presence of women while praying?". The argument never settled.

In the balcony, the children ran freely. There weren't many people in the mosque, so no problem, for now. Aisha started her integration training. "There is Monday night women's swimming at the local YMCA. They cover the windows so men cannot look inside," Aisha said and continued, "Remember, when you meet the kafir," Aisha continued, using the Arabic word for non-Muslims, "just say *Hi, Good Morning or ask How are you?*,". Rabia turned to Aisha and asked her, in a hushed tone: "Why is that?"

Aisha pulled out a pocket prayer guide. It said explicitly: The Muslims are in higher in status and should not humiliate themselves by saying Salam (peace),to non-Muslims first as it would tantamount to honoring them. But if we are greeted first with Salam, then we should return the greeting in similar or better terms. If there is a need to greet a non-Muslim, kaafir, first there is no sin in that but it should be something other than the greeting of salaam (peace), such as How are you. In that case the greeting is for a reason, not to honor them.

Rabia reacted with horror. "How dare you? Do you have no humanity? Do you understand that this book is taking things out of context? "

That night, she told Alim about the confrontation. He listened intently and drew her closer, kissing her gently on the forehead. "I love you, my Rabia of Charlotte."

When Aisha's husband, Farouk, called to tell him that his wife had been hurt by Rabia's rebuke, Alim told him, "She must live then by the golden rule. Treat others as you wish to be treated!"

Farouk sighed. "I agree."

A few weeks after the destruction of the mosque, Alim and others had taken plans for a new mosque to a public meeting at city hall. Everyone thought it went well, but that wasn't the case a month later. Normally, very few people showed up at the planning commission meetings, but on that day there were more than a hundred in attendance. Alim recognized a few familiar faces from the neighborhood, but most of the people were strangers to him.

Everyone was asked to sign in with their names and addresses. When it was Alim's turn to sign in, he noticed that many of those in attendance were from different parts of the city and a few came from towns outside of Charlotte. It quickly became clear that most came to protest the rebuilding of the mosque. They asked the commissioners to delay the approval.

Things turned ugly when Alim made his presentation that included the minor changes that were requested by the planning staff at the last meeting. Someone stood up and shouted, "Nobody wants your cult in this place."

Someone else called out from his seat. "They're going to practice the Sharia law, and we don't need that in our community."

The protest leader approached the guest podium after Alim sat down, and said, "We want this thing delayed at the very least. I will do everything in my power to stop this."

The man turned to Alim. "We don't want this because everyone of you is a potential terrorist."

The ones who'd come to protest all stood up and clapped. The chairwoman pounded her gavel, and when everyone settled down, Alim raised a hand. "Come to the podium, Mr. Mubarak, and have your say," directed the middle-aged woman with short dark hair and the gavel still in her hand.

"Thank you, Madam Chairwoman. Islam is a religion of peace. In fact, we greet each other and also non-Muslims by saying, *Salam.* That means peace."

As-salam alaikum, a supporter called out from the back of the room.

"Did you hear that?" One of the protesters called out. That's one terrorist calling out to another."

Alim shook his head. *As-salam alaikum* means peace be upon you."

A blonde woman marched up to the podium and Alim hoped she was a supporter from the neighborhood. He stepped aside. She looked at him and said, "I don't care what you say or what you think. You can say whatever you want, but every Muslim is a terrorist."

The clapping and foot-stomping became louder, and the chairman pounded her gavel again. The woman still wasn't done. "With everything I have in my power I will stop you. This is not an outpost for ISIS."

A white man in his thirties stood up and Alim expected more of the same. "They have every right to worship in the way they want, and it doesn't bother me. Most of them, by the way, happen to be Americans just like you and me."

Several people booed and someone called out. "I don't want Sharia law in Georgia. They train their children to do terrible things to Americans."

The man shook his head. "Practicing Sharia law. That's like saying you follow the Ten Commandments. So what."

The blonde woman intervened, "So What? So What? Unbelievable! Do you know what they are taught? If they are in majority they must do everything to convert everyone to their cult even if it means to use violence and kill a few as an example. When they are in minority and majority is not united, like we are now, they ask for more concessions, more mosques, implementing Sharia law like they are doing now. Only when majority is united and strong they align." She turned to Alim and challenged him, "Can you deny that?". She shot her arm forward pointing her forefinger towards Alim and repeated, "Can you deny that? Putting your hand on your heart?"

Alim took to the podium again as the blond woman retreated, nodding her head as she went. "Yes I deny that. We never taught anything like that in our mosque. We continuously advocate that Muslim majority countries and communities need to embrace pluralism and diversity. I agree that more needs to be done to in some countries. But I am talking about America here. We have been living in this community for decades. We raised our families here. We are American citizens and our kids go to schools here. Have we ever shown any traces of violence? Why would we jeopardize the society that we live in?"

One of the planning commission members, an older man with gray hair, responded. "You have everything in order for rebuilding your place of worship. However, considering the sentiments of the community that you see here, I think it would be a good idea to go on record condemning the violent acts that have taken place in the name of your religion. I haven't heard that. Not in a prominent way."

"We have been doing that, and of course I condemn violence in the name of Islam," Alim replied. "We have shared websites that give link after link about how we condemn the violence. I don't know what else we can do to reach out to the community."

The protest leader stepped in again. "I don't believe you. Can you name one fucking country with majority Muslims but run as a secular state? Wherever you guys are in majority they are not secular nations. I know that for a fact."

Alim again shook his head. " You ask for one and I can name ten. Indonesia, Turkey, Albania, Bosnia. Please look up for facts."

"I know what to look up for.", the man dismissed Alim's explanation.

A few minutes later, the meeting ended after the planning commissioner decided to table the issue for four weeks at which time a final decision would be made based on the recommendations of the commission's attorneys.

3.2 Second Man on the Moon

Mark hated doing housework, but his once-a-week housekeeper wasn't enough for Stacey, who was obsessed with cleanliness and complained that he wasn't doing his share. So here he was on a Saturday morning sweeping the kitchen floor and afterwards he would unload the dishwasher, then make the bed and clean the bathrooms. Stacy had left half an hour ago to take her mother shopping, then to lunch. Before leaving, she'd asked if he would clean up the place while she was gone, and told him that she was tired of being the one who did all the daily chores. As she was going out the door, she said: "Don't forget the little hairs from shaving in the bathroom sink. That really annoys me. Good-bye, hon."

He should've never allowed her to move in with him. He realized now that he'd only known her superficially. Now he was getting a complete view and, as a result, their relationship was faltering. So many aspects of her personality that had seemed cute were now irritating. From the moment she moved into his apartment, she started taking control of everything.

But what irritated Mark most was that she was snoopy. She asked too many questions about his past, his business, and his finances. That made him feel edgy and on guard. It constantly played on his mind that he'd lied to her about his financial status. When he objected to her continual inquiries, she said, "Shh. No secrets between us now. Don't create rules and boundaries between us. Ask anything about me. I will tell you everything. I don't want trust issues between us."

"Okay, how many men have you slept with?"

"None of your business," she snapped, then laughed and touched her fingers to her lips. That was cute, but also annoying.

"See, you've got your secrets."

"*That's* different. You're not supposed to ask that kind of question, at least, not to me. But you can ask me anything else."

Mark shrugged and shook his head. He was never a great communicator and negotiator and knew only one way to react. He felt a lot of internal conflict and stress, but the only way he expressed it was by either turning silent or blowing up. Sometimes she took his angry retorts in stride and other times she would fight back. At one point, when he was in a calm mood, he told her, "I'm not the type of guy who likes to talk about everything going on in my life, or about things from the past. I don't know how I can be clearer."

Stacey replied that she understood that he was more reserved than she was. But it wasn't long before she started questioning him about why he wasn't more forthcoming with information, what he was doing at work, or what he was thinking about. Eventually, her persistence would trigger a fight and they would shout at each other. Then they would stop talking altogether, until one of them made an effort to make up.

Mark was fixated on his financial mess, and resented Stacey for not recognizing his need to make it big. His whole life hinged on becoming a spectacular success and making his dad's prophecy come true. His earliest remembrance of his father was not his face, but his words, "My son is special. He will make us proud."

# # #

As he cleaned the apartment, Mark's thoughts drifted to the past. He recalled the day he came home from sixth grade and proudly showed his father his report card. He had one A+, four A's and one B-. His dad immediately pointed to the B- and asked what the problem was. He made eleven-year-old Mark feel that he'd done poorly. His father expressed no appreciation for the A's he'd received. He behaved curtly with Mark for a few days. Mark worked harder and by the next report card he received all A's. That time his dad showered him with praise and bought him presents.

The following weekend, he took Mark to Stone Mountain, a mix of nature park and theme park, named after the mountain with an enormous grey rock at the top. The restaurant offered hotdogs, burgers, grilled ribs, and salads, but what Mark loved most was the dessert made of a brownie with toasted marshmallows on the top. When he commented about how yummy it was, Dad immediately got him a second one.

After eating, they took the Swiss cable car ride that gave them a beautiful view of the Atlanta skyline. Mark was impressed by the massive carving of four soldiers riding horses that was cut right out of the mountainside. "That is the Confederate Memorial Carving—General

Robert E. Lee, General Stonewall Jackson and Jefferson Davis, the Confederate President of the Confederate States. Great leaders of the South's campaign," his dad told him.

After the cable car ride, they sat down at a spot with a nice view; his dad cruised into his favorite topic about life and how it ought to be lived. "You know who the first man to walk on the moon, don't you, Mark?"

"Neil Armstrong."

"Good. Who was the second man to walk on the moon?"

Mark frowned, trying to recall the name. "I don't remember. But I know it was Apollo 11 that took them to the moon."

"That's right. It took Apollo 11 four days to reach the moon. There were three people in that mission. One astronaut remained in orbit around the moon to do experiments and take pictures. Neil Armstrong and another astronaut took the lunar module Eagle and landed on the moon. They both walked on the moon for hours. Mark, why do you think you only remember Neil Armstrong?"

"Because he was the first person to walk on the moon."

"Bingo, Mark! No one remembers who came second. That is what happens in life, Mark. The purpose of life is to achieve. Not just achieve, but be the first."

Mark's father was very fond of heroes. The field didn't matter: politics, sports, film. He admired the best. Today, he was particularly animated about the topic.

"What is the history of humanity if not the history of a few individuals who changed the course of history? We are just like any other species. We are born, we grow, and we die. The world remembers only special people who shape the future and alter the destiny of humanity...the winners, the ones who come in first. There are no exceptions."

Mark gazed up toward the Confederate trio carved on the mountainside. They came in second, he thought. They lost the war. Yet his father admired them as if they were winners. He kept quiet about that inconsistency as his father continued with his lecture and jabbed his index finger toward Mark. "You know what? When you truly believe that you are destined to become a great person and work towards it, it becomes a reality. Trust me."

"Really dad? Am I special and will I do great things? I am not even the topper of my class."

"'It is never too late to become what you might have been.' That's a direct quote from the famous writer George Eliot. She overcame the obstacles of her time—the Victorian era—when women weren't allowed to achieve in the same way as men."

"George Eliot was a woman?"

"Her name was Mary Ann Evans. George Eliot was her pen name, and that's how she managed to achieve her highest goals. You are special, Mark. Even though you're not the number one student in your class, you can improve and succeed in a very big way. You will make us proud one day." He patted Mark on his back.

Why is he not always this nice? Mark wondered. His dad had terrible mood swings. He would be super generous when Mark did well in school and super critical if he didn't stand out. Mark's mom had different ideas about life. For her, it was all about love, warmth, relationships and taking part in a journey. For her, every achievement was an occasion to celebrate, and to say life was inconsequential without great success was ridiculous. She expressed her thoughts to him, but was not as aggressive as his father.

Initially, she tried to intervene forcefully, which led to a big fight. Her husband was crystal clear. He did not want Mark receiving confusing signals under any circumstance. When he was in a good mood, he would beg her to pitch in and support him in his conversations with Mark. When he was in a foul mood, he would become very aggressive and demand that she support him fully when he spoke harshly to Mark. Though she did not like it, she obliged him.

It became a routine for Mark. Lavish praise when he achieved, and shabby treatment when he failed to meet his father's criteria for success. It was a binary measurement for his dad. Anything less than the best was failure. "No one remembers the second man who stepped onto the moon just nineteen minutes after Neil Armstrong."

Mark didn't have any close friends at school. To most, he appeared shy, withdrawn, and even secretive. He interacted with others minimally on a need-only basis. Throughout his school career, Mark became close to only a couple of kids who lived in his neighborhood and who sometimes went to his house to study with him. Overall, Mark got better grades than the other kids, and their presence was somehow comforting to him. They actually looked up to him because he was so determined to score the highest scores on tests.

Mark came to believe that his dad, mom, and the world at large would show affection to him, and love him, only if he achieved his highest goals. He felt a strange bitterness that he must continuously achieve to be recognized, admired and loved. That feeling was continually cemented by his father's behavior.

In seventh grade, Mark won a silver medal in an inter-school quiz competition and came home happy. Again, his dad was disappointed that he missed gold.

"What happened, Mark?"

"There was a tie, and Kevin hit the buzzer first. I knew the answer too."

"Don't you think you should have taken a risk and pressed the buzzer first? After all, it was the decider."

"But I had to listen to the question fully before I hit the buzzer."

"Kevin didn't win because he is smarter, but because he was brave and clever. He took the risk. Remember, no reward comes without some risk." His dad raised his voice. "I'm getting sick and tired of telling you that no one remembers the person who comes second. You should have gone for it, Mark. All or nothing, buddy."

Mark nodded, but his father wasn't done with him yet. Throughout the week he tormented Mark for not taking the risk and for being second.

A few days later, Mark went to the backyard, dug a small hole and buried his silver medal. His mom asked him why he looked stressed, but Mark didn't answer. After he slipped into bed, he began fantasizing.

It was the inter-school baseball final playoff game, and Mark was the last batter. The other school was ahead by two runs, and everyone sat on the edge of their seats. The pitcher fired a fast ball, but Mark was ready. He hit it, sending the ball deep into left field. All the eyes followed the ball as it cleared the fence for a homer. Mark circled the bases, stylishly and leisurely. Thanks to him, his school clinched the title. His schoolmates rushed onto the field and carried him on their shoulders shouting, "Mark! Mark! Mark!" The girls jostled each other to shake his hand. The fantasy calmed his brain, and he slipped into sleep.

It gradually became a habit. To fantasize and feel good. Later that week, he talked to his mother about the inter-school quiz competition, where he had won the silver medal. "Mom, you know, Kevin cheated."

"What are you talking about?"

"The quiz. Kevin hit the buzzer even before he heard the question. He knew the tie breaker question."

"Really? Who told you that? Dad and I will come to the school today and ask about it."

"No, mom. I don't want to tell anyone but you."

"Tell your dad about this."

He shook his head.

"Why not?"

"Kevin will feel bad, and I don't want that. Promise me, mom, you won't tell dad. He will make a big fuss."

"How did you find out he cheated? Tell me that much."

"I can't tell you. Do you hate me for not getting the gold?"

She knelt on one knee and hugged him. "Listen. Gold or silver. Medal or no medal. We always love you, Mark. Always."

Mark hugged her back. He wasn't so sure that his father would love him, if he failed. He put his arms around his mom's neck and whispered in her ear. "Mom I will make you and dad proud. One day I will."

# # #

Mark headed into the bathroom to continue his chores. Even though he despised doing any maintenance work himself, he didn't want Stacey to come home and start badgering him for ignoring her request, and then that would expand to some other issue about him that perturbed her. He'd held off on hiring the housekeeper for a second visit each week, because the apartment wasn't really dirty, in his estimation. But now he was having second thoughts about it. With two people in the house, there was more of a mess, and he was also noticing that Stacey had brought more of her stuff into the apartment from her storage unit.

120

As he continued cleaning, his thoughts turned back to his childhood again.

He realized now that by the time he was a freshman in high school, conditional love throughout childhood turned him into someone with a fundamental lack of trust in people. In high school, when anyone tried getting close to him, he backed off. He was suspicious of people's affections (i.e., "What do they want from me?"). He continued to engage in fantasies that fulfilled his desire for excellence and recognition. His high school courses were challenging, and his self-esteem fell as he realized he wasn't in the top 10 percent of students. He got along with the few kids whom he called friends, but the relationships were superficial. He already knew he'd never see these kids again after they graduated and moved on to college.

For fun, he would create fake on-line IDs to log into message boards and forums and felt powerful when he posted pompous messages. He became abusive at times and enjoyed disrupting friendly chatter on blogs with caustic comments, and turning all the attention to himself and his contrary comments.

After graduating, he was accepted into a business school where the competition was intense and he was a mediocre student. As a result, he was overlooked for the most lucrative corporate jobs in investment banking, financial management, and consulting, which paid more than a quarter of a million dollars a year, plus bonuses. He settled for a relatively low paid job in the healthcare industry. He was unhappy with his prospects and just went through the motions. He hit new lows when he saw on an alumni site that a few of his business schoolmates were driving luxury sport cars. He hated his regular sedan.

He couldn't help but make backhanded compliments when folks more successful than him posted or shared about the great things happening in their lives. When a fellow business school mate shared news with the group that she was selected by a blue-chip firm after clearing six rounds of interviews, Mark replied, "WOW! Lucky you. I didn't expect you to cross the finish line! Congratulations though!"

When someone in the group invited everyone to a party after receiving an unexpected big-fat bonus he replied, "Nice! Now hanging out with you will be fun!" He had no real friends and even his close acquaintances were limited to four or five folks with whom he was in touch.

One day, his mom called him with the news that his father had a massive heart attack and was in ICU. His dad's madness that life's singular purpose was achievement had mellowed down, but he'd never made an effort to reconcile with Mark. After a second attack that night, he passed away. More than grief, Mark felt relieved that he no longer needed to speak with his dad.

After the funeral, Mark did a Google search and found out the name of the second man who walked on the moon.

# # #

Mark's dad left a substantial life insurance plan, and he made both his wife and son equal beneficiaries. Mark saw a chance for instant recognition in his social group by floating his own company. He was no longer going to repent that he was not hired by a large investment firm. He was going to start his own investment firm. He was going to be the CEO. He was going to be the hero of his own story. With the money he got from his dad's insurance he started Maverick Investments. The company was now fifteen months old and under water. The capital was eroding fast, and his stress levels were increasing.

He'd received a few recommendations from Brian, his former college roommate, and that led to several presentations. But none of the companies were impressed enough to buy into Maverick's offerings. He tried to think of other contacts from the past who might help him, but he'd never invested the time and effort needed to nurture such professional relationships. As a result, he had nowhere else to turn.

Then came two calls that suddenly changed everything.

The first one was from Barry Spitzer, a certified public accountant, who owned a thirty-person accounting firm. Six months ago, Spitzer had parked a modest amount of his clientele's assets with Maverick to invest in short term instruments , like money market accounts that have high liquidity. Though the value of individual transactions was low, the volume was high, and the arrangement was profitable for Mark. Spitzer's accounts slowed the drain of Mark's remaining assets.

One of Mark's portfolio managers, Nate Rothman, had introduced Spitzer to Mark, and he handled Spitzer's transactions. Then one day, Spitzer called Mark.

"Hello Mr. Spitzer. How can I help you?"

"Well, in ways where both of us can outcome with big numbers in our pockets." Spitzer chuckled.

"Sounds good." Mark had no idea what Spitzer had in mind.

"Talk to Nate. He'll explain the details."

Mark promptly called the portfolio manager and they agreed to meet at St. Regis that evening for drinks. The bar was almost empty when Mark arrived at 5:35 and found Nate seated at a booth with a drink.

Mark caught the eye of a waitress as he sat down and ordered a screwdriver. They shook hands, greeting each other. They were both dressed in suits, but Nate's tie was loosened, and his fleshy cheeks looked flushed. He was overweight and had an unkempt appearance, with longish hair. Stacey liked Nate, but had told Mark that Nate needed to drink less and join a gym. Sitting across from him, Mark felt as if he were fit, in comparison.

"Good to see you again, Mark. So are you and Stacey still doing your thing together? Is that working out?"

"Yeah, pretty good, pretty good. You know how it goes. It's not always heaven."

Nate laughed. "Yeah, it's never quite like the first time, right? But, hey, you're a lucky guy, she's a keeper, for sure."

Mark's drink arrived and they touched glasses. After a couple more minutes of small talk, Nate asked, "So, Mark, your company now over a year old by a few months, right?"

"It is, yes."

"You've got quite a posh office."

"Thanks."

"I hope you don't mind if I ask you something about the business."

"No, go head. You got me my new newest and biggest clients. I greatly appreciate that." He also wanted to know what else was going on with Spitzer and Nate, and he had the feeling that he was going to find out.

"Then I'll be straight forward with you. In the past, I've worked with many small investment consulting companies like yours, and I know how hard it is to get started. So, I'm curious, have you broken even yet?"

Mark was surprised by the question and couldn't help wondering if Deck had been talking to him about the company's finances.

When Mark didn't reply immediately, Nate continued. "You know, Mark. I have connections with some high net worth individuals and smaller venture capital firms that are looking for opportunities to invest. That's the reason I am asking."

After Nate's mention of venture capital, Mark was certain that Nate knew he was in a financial mess. Any new prospects would be great, but he didn't want to appear as if he were desperate.

"You know how it goes, Nate. The firm is doing fine. But what funding are you talking about?"

"Didn't Spitzer mention it? It's about giving your company a big injection of income."

"You've got my attention."

Nate smiled, then leaned forward. "You know high reward comes with high risk. Right?"

"What are you talking about?"

"Look Mark. I want you to take your time on this and think carefully. You can make a choice and I will respect that."

"Okay, get to the point."

"Look Mark, there are many firms who would jump on this opportunity, but I like you and want to help you. You are young and hungry, and the best part is you think big."

"That is true. Making it big is what drives me."

Mark heard laughter, looked around, and saw that several more people were now seated at the bar.

"Look, Spitzer has been using your firm like a parking lot. He's happy with what he has seen in the last six months. Now he wants to take you to the next level, if you're willing. He is talking about massive investments."

"I like what I'm hearing."

Nate signaled the waitress to bring re-fills, then turned back to Mark. "He is ready to pay more than the standard commission—a lot more—and in cash."

Now Mark was getting suspicious. "Okay, what's the catch, Nate?"

"Yeah, there is a catch, and that is what I need you to think carefully about before you respond. I'm okay with whatever your answer is. But if it's no, we will never discuss this topic again. Is that understood?"

"Of course. So what's it about?"

"Look, so far Spitzer has parked funds from legitimate businesses with you, but his connections go beyond the ethical world."

"I get that. So what is it?"

Their drinks arrived and Nate handed the waitress a credit card.

After the waitress moved away, Nate leaned forward again. "Spitzer has clients who make a lot of money illegally. Drugs, Girls, clubs who cares? They're always looking for ways to launder it. If you're game, I can arrange a face-to-face with Spitzer."

"I'm a bit stunned right now, Nate, but I guess I should've figured it came from illegal stuff."

"Shh. Keep your voice down, man."

Mark looked around and saw more people arriving.

"Look, I brought it up, because I know you're looking for something big to happen. But if you say no, I understand and we'll go on with business as usual. But..."

Mark leaned in closer. "What?"

"If your answer is yes, things will quickly be set in motion, and you can't go back on your word. Not without consequences."

Mark nodded. "I get that."

Nate signed for the drinks, then tilted his head back as he gulped down the remainder of his drink. "So take your time and call me if you want in. If I don't hear from you, I'll know your answer. Nate slid out of the booth, but motioned Mark to stay seated. "Relax, think about it, and finish your drink. I've gotta go."

"What if I have questions?"

Nate placed his hands on the table. "It's all or nothing, Mark. Once you're in, you'll get all the answers you need."

"Wait. I can't decide if I don't have any details. Tell me at least one thing."

"Shoot."

"What kind of volumes are we talking about here?"

Nate glanced over his shoulder, then bent over the table as if he were going to wipe it clean. He spoke rapidly in a low tone. "Seven-digit volumes per month and five-digit commission to your firm, and the same amount in cash to you. I'm not going to answer anything else. I'm out of here."

"Thanks, Nate. Hey, if you're into this thing, why have you been working for me?"

Nate stood upright and ran a hand through his already mussed hair. "Gotta look legit." He patted Mark on the shoulder, turned and left.

Mark stayed to finish his drink and ordered another as he tried to make sense of all that Nate had laid on him. The meeting had left him shaken. It happened so fast. Mark had always thought of Nate and Spitzer as highly professional and smart guys. But this evening he saw another side of Nate, a shady side, and he was feeling wary.

While he'd always wanted to become a huge success and was willing to cut corners, if necessary, he'd never considered getting involved into something illegal. He had an urge to pick up the phone and blast Nate for thinking that he would do something so reckless and dangerous to make it big. Then he reminded himself that it was Nate who brought in Spitzer who remained his biggest customer. He would just not call Nate, and that would be it. Nate would understand that he was not interested in any fucking shady deals with him and Spitzer.

# # #

Two days passed and Mark was determined not to call Nate. But he wanted to know if someone in the company had told Nate that the firm wasn't making a profit yet. He called Deck, who told him he hadn't talked to Nate in weeks, and didn't particularly like the guy. After dinner, he told Stacey that he'd had drinks with Nate a couple of days earlier, and it seemed to him that Nate knew about the company's financial status.

Stacey fielded calls from the portfolio managers on a regular basis and Nate always kept her on the phone longer than the others. She liked the attention, Mark figured. Now when he confronted her, she was evasive.

"Can't you fucking give me a straight answer? Once in your life?"

"Don't talk to me like that. It doesn't take a fucking genius to figure out that we're spending more than we're earning."

With that, she walked out. They'd fought on numerous occasions, but always got over it. This time felt different for him. He was angered by her unwillingness to deny or confirm that she'd talked to Nate about his firm's solvency. He realized that he despised her. Yet, he couldn't even think of breaking up with her. He needed Stacey for companionship and, of course, sex. He had a hunger that was sated only when they were in bed making love. At the same time, he was certain about one thing. He would never marry her.

When she came back to the apartment three hours later, she didn't say a word about where she'd gone or what she'd done. And he didn't ask. She remained aloof and so did he.

At the office the next day, they kept their conversations to a minimum, and only talked about essential business-related matters.

Early in the afternoon, he received a call from Brian, his college roommate, who seemed anxious to talk to him. He was one of the guys Mark considered a close acquaintance. "Dude, it's been a while. I've got something important to talk to you about. What are you doing tonight?"

"Nothing much. The usual stuff."

"Can we catch up at my place or yours?"

"I'll stop at your place about six. The same address, right?"

"Yeah, six sounds good."

Brian lived in Roswell, seventeen and a half miles from his office, according to his GPS. At mid-day, he could make the drive in under thirty minutes. But with Friday rush hour on the 400, he would be lucky to arrive in forty minutes. Stacey left the office at four without even saying she was leaving. She was no doubt waiting for him to apologize, and he'd made no effort to do so.

Stacey had snubbed him, and now he was starting to re-think his unwillingness to call Nate. If he joined the big-money team, it would be a good way to show her who he really was. As soon as the money started flowing, he would fire her ass, kick her out of the apartment, and find a hot new secretary. Stacey would beg him to take her back as soon as she realized he was rich. She would realize what a huge mistake she'd make by turning her back on him.

He left at five and as expected the 400 was a nightmare. But he darted back and forth between lanes slicing through the traffic, and managed to pull into the parking lot outside Brian's luxury condo with five minutes to spare. Brian stepped out on his second-floor porch and waved to him. "C'mon up, Mark. Right on time."

He sensed the excitement in Brian's voice and couldn't help wondering what he had in mind. It better be good, he thought, because he had Nate and Spitzer waiting for him to call. Brian met him at the door and they shook hands. Even though Mark was six feet tall, he always felt short standing next to Brian who was five inches taller. In college, he was gangly and underweight for his size. But in recent years, he'd put on twenty-five or thirty pounds, mostly muscle, it appeared. When Mark commented on his size, Brian said he worked out several mornings a week arriving at the gym at six.

"So what's the big news, big guy? I hope it's good. You know how rush hour is on the 400."

"Oh, it's good. Bro, we go back a long way together. So, I'm going to trust you."

"Always, man. You know me."

"It's sensitive information and potentially quite profitable. But I need to be sure that I won't get into trouble."

"You have my word. Go ahead."

"You know anything about Happ!, the company I work for?"

"Not much, except what you told me, that it's a tech company."

"Yes, it's a niche company and is located in the tech corridor."

"So, what's cooking?"

Brian hesitated for a moment, then continued. "Happ!'s stock is trading roughly at twelve dollars."

"Okay."

"A large IT company is keen on acquiring Happ! and both companies are working at a rapid pace to make it happen. Only high-level leaders are involved."

Mark shrugged. He understood that Brian was giving him a stock tip, but he wasn't convinced that it was a good one. "That could be good for the stock or it could take a dive. You never know on buy-outs."

"No, you don't understand. I didn't finish. Happ! will soon release a game-changing product that can capture market shares very rapidly in a $5 billion dollar segment of the market."

"That's different. What's your reading, if acquisition happens?"

"I think the stock would rise by forty percent immediately on the announcement, and double in two months."

" So, are you buying more Happ! stock?"

"I'm part of the due diligence and it would fall under insider trading, if I buy directly."

Mark smiled. "So does telling me, right?"

Brian returned the smile. "No harm if we both can benefit. Besides, you are a friend and I trust you."

"Thanks, Brian. The acquisition process can get delayed. I'm sure you know that better than me."

"Of course. But in this case I see no hurdles in getting anti-trust approvals and stuff like that. We are small fries. It should be a smooth acquisition."

"Okay, let's stay in touch."

"Sure. But don't wait too long. This is a once-in- a-lifetime opportunity, Mark. Even without the acquisition on the radar, Happ! is a good investment. The stock price surely will accelerate once the news breaks on the new product."

"How much do you recommend I invest?"

"Every penny you can put out there. You have nothing to lose."

"That's cool. Let me think about it and I'll stay in touch."

# # #

When Mark got home, Stacey had left a note saying that she was going to visit her sister and would be back late, or she might stay overnight. Make up your mind, he muttered. He heated up some leftovers and while he ate looked up Happ! on the internet. He saw the company was just turning ten years old, and had been growing steadily for the past seven years. He dived into the company's finances and saw that the stock appreciated by twelve percent in the past year, then spiked another six percent in the last two weeks.

Mark was suspicious about the timing of Brian's call. Ordinarily, he wouldn't consider investing in a company that had already jumped in value so recently. There was no guarantee that trend would continue.

Besides that, Brian's call came just two days after the call from Spitzer and his offer through Nate to park a bundle lot of dirty drug money with him. It was ironic that Brian offered him what he called a killer opportunity, as if he thought Mark had a lot of money to invest.

Was it a coincidence or was there something more going on, he wondered. It seemed that Brian had once told him that his older brother was an FBI agent. Was he being set up by his college roommate? He was getting paranoid, he told himself. There was probably no connection at all between Spitzer and Nate and Brian.

While outwardly he appeared relaxed and carefree, he was under a tremendous amount of stress. His company was failing. At the same time he was being offered a chance to save it and become wealthy. But with a big catch. If he came under investigation, he could lose not only the company, but his freedom.

That evening, home alone, he started drinking, and in the days that followed he stayed mostly drunk, even while he was at the office. In moments of clarity, he would realize that even if the company failed, he could overcome the loss. Considering his work experience and educational qualifications, he could easily find a job with a decent salary. But since childhood—thanks to his father—his life was always about making it big, and now he was being lured into opportunities that offered explosive growth for his company and himself.

However, he still lacked the will power to leap into the void. He didn't call Nate. He didn't call Brian. Instead, he kept drinking, and began fantasizing. He lay on his bed drunk on the third day after his meeting with Brian, and imagined that he had invested ten million dollars in Happ!. The stock doubled in two months after the release of the new product and announcement of the acquisition. He imagined that he cleared ten million dollars in eight weeks.

The party he threw was dazzling. The clients were queuing up to get a chance to talk to him. They all had the same request. We want to put our funds in Maverick Investments and let you work your magic. The firm grew rapidly. He recruited a CEO to run the company and he became the chairman before holidaying in the Bahamas in a yacht full of girls that he'd handpicked from photos, ones he thought were hot and naughty. He gave them expensive gifts and he was looking forward to the orgy.

His fantasy that evening was rudely interrupted by Stacey. "Since when have you become a fucking binge drinker?"

Mark blinked his eyes, trying to focus on her. She was standing over him, hands on hips. That authoritarian stance was all he could take. Somehow, he had allowed her to take charge over him, and he didn't like it. *Mouthy, bossy bitch.* He had enough backtalk coming from every angle. *I'll be damned if some woman is going to call the shots.* His hands curled into fists and a bead of sweat formed on his brow.

"You look like you want to hit me." She leaned forward, as if challenging him.

It took all the restraint he possessed not to pop her in the mouth. "You don't run my life. I'll drink all I want when I want. This is my place, my business, my money and my drink. So shut the fuck up."

"I am your fiancée and you're lucky to have someone like me, who's willing to put up with your shit," she shouted.

He couldn't take any more. "I'm working on a big plan. When it works out, I'll be in the Bahamas in my yacht with beautiful girls, and you will be the ugliest of them all."

Stacey plunged onto Mark and pounded her fists against his chest. He pushed her off, and she landed on the floor and started crying. She climbed to her feet and walked out of the bedroom sobbing. He reached for the bottle of vodka on the bedside table and took a gulp. A minute later, he heard the door to the apartment slam shut.

The next morning, Stacey didn't show up at the office. He was still drunk, but he'd stopped drinking. He was dependent on Stacey for handling all the administrative duties, and didn't hesitate calling her. When she didn't pick up the call, he left a message saying that he was truly sorry for his behavior and that he was done drinking. Before he disconnected, she answered.

"All right, Mark. I'll come back, if you agree to go to counseling with me."

His head pounded; he closed his eyes. Reluctantly, he agreed. But he would do his best to delay it, he thought.

# # #

Two days went by and now as he sat at his desk, he needed a drink. But Stacey had vowed to quit and never come back, if she saw him drunk again at the office. Fortunately for Mark, the family counselor that Stacey wanted to see was on a three-week trip to Europe. Maybe Stacey would just forget about the counseling.

He thought about Nate and Brian and their propositions over and over again, but he remained too wary of the possible consequences of getting involved in criminal activity. His thoughts turned to his mother, who he hadn't visited for three months.

He gave her a call and was disturbed by how confused she sounded. He decided to visit her in the assisted living facility where she'd moved a few months after Mark's father died. When he arrived at her tiny apartment, he was shocked by her physical and mental deterioration. He was particularly spooked that she didn't seem to remember anything about his dad's funeral. She was aware that her husband for thirty years was gone, but she couldn't recall what happened. She kept asking when and how he died.

While she recalled other matters from the past, the memory of her late husband's death and funeral apparently were wiped from her memory. She seemed vulnerable and lost and wondered why she was living in the facility. After half an hour, he told her he would start visiting her more often.

He left her apartment feeling disturbed and went directly to the administrator's office. He was told by the assistant administrator, a petite middle-aged woman with a Caribbean accent that she had tried to contact him several times during the past two weeks. His mother had fallen down in the dining room and been taken to the ER for observation. She was okay, but the ER doctor reported that she was showing signs of Alzheimer's. As a result, she needed more care and could no longer remain in the independent living sector of the facility.

Mark apologized for missing the calls and left feeling even more disturbed. He spent the weekend with her, helping her move to another part of the facility where she would get daily visits by staff members. She had no idea what was happening and Mark's stress level spiked. But on Sunday even when he sat next to her holding her hand, she had windows of clarity and he felt a strange peace.

"I never wanted to be a burden to you, Mark, but if my mental health deteriorates, would you take care of me?"

"Yes, mama, I will. And there are people here who will help you, when I'm not available."

# # #

The next day at the office, Mark saw that Happ!'s stock had climbed up another four percent and the volumes were high. He called Brian and invited him for lunch. This time they met at a restaurant in the tech corridor in Buckhead, not far from Happ!, and just a few minutes from Mark's office. He found Brian tucked away in a back booth, away from the few diners who had arrived for an early lunch. Brian kept his voice low and said he was even more confident about the merger, and said he was ninety percent confident that it was only days before the news would be announced.

"Once the word is out, the stock will soar, probably double from today's price."

"I'm interested, and chances are good that I'll be investing very soon. We'll see how it goes, and work things out between us."

That afternoon, Mark called Nate and said, "I'm in." Nate laughed and Mark's hopes sank. He was sure Nate was going to tell him he was too late. Spitzer had gone elsewhere. But that wasn't the case. "We were just talking about you earlier, Mark, figured you were out. But if you're sure, I'll call Spitzer right away and set something up."

"Do it."

That same evening, Mark drove to meet Spitzer at his office, where he was met by a man in a suit, who he guessed by his size and demeanor, was Spitzer's security guard. He guided Mark past rows of cubicles to a closed door. He tapped on it, stuck his head inside, then motioned for Mark to enter. Spitzer was seated behind a sleek chrome and glass desk in a spacious office. He leaped up from his chair and greeted Mark as if they were old friends. Spitzer was a short, wiry guy, in his mid- to late thirties with thick hair combed straight back. He pointed to a chair next to the desk, then sat back down, put his feet up on his desk. He leaned back in his chair, his hands clasped behind his head. He was wearing a suit minus a tie.

Spitzer engaged Mark in stock market talk for a few minutes, then slid his feet off his desk, sat up and slid in closer to him. In spite of his size and casual behavior, Spitzer now seemed an imposing presence as he turned to the matter at hand. He proceeded to walk Mark through the MO on how funds would arrive through various shell companies, and what Mark needed to do. Now he fully understood the risk he was taking.

"Any questions?" Spitzer finally asked.

"There are a couple of things that we need to agree on."

"Go-ahead."

"One. I'm going to deal only with Nate or you. I'm not going to speak with anyone else."

Spritzer waved a hand. "That's fine."

"I want to operate on a yearly basis. I need a chance to exit after every year with a three-month heads-up."

Spitzer rubbed his chin as he considered the request. Finally, he shrugged. "Fair enough. If you exit after a year, you won't get any fresh money to invest. But you still must deliver the returns on the long-term investments made. Do you understand that?"

"I'm good with it."

"Great. We have a deal."

Spitzer came out of his chair and extended a hand. Mark hastily stood and they shook on it. Spitzer laid a hand on Mark's shoulder and said in a low voice. "You made a good decision. But remember one thing. Discretion and confidentiality are sacrosanct. The actual owners of the money know where their money is, just in case something happens to me. They are reasonable business people. Yes, it's dirty money, but if we remain honest with their money, there will be no trouble."

"I understand." Mark's body was shaking as he left from a combination of excitement and fear.

The money started flowing in through Spitzer's back channels within a couple of days.

He immediately started buying stocks in Happ!. He was thrilled by his double deal. Loads of money from Spitzer and a great stock tip from Brian. He was going to make a killing and would keep most of the profit for himself, while still providing more than decent return on Spitzer's money.

Even though Mark knew that using the inside scoop was illegal, he invited his biggest customers to a high-end bar and talked about the research he had done. "There's a company called Happ! that has a niche space cornered, and the stock is on the rise and will continue going up." When customers asked why he was so certain, Mark talked about a new game changing product that Happ! was working on and would likely launch soon.

"It's going to capture the industry's market shares pretty fast." He was tempted to mention the impending acquisition, but held off saying anything about it, or that he'd received an insider tip.

When a couple of clients indicated that they could make a moderate investment in Happ!'s stock, he ordered a round of shots for the whole bar. He was finally going to make his dad's prophecy about him come true. He would indeed be a spectacular success. His dad's words resonated in his head. "Didn't I tell you Mark that you are special? You are going to make us proud one day!"

3.3 GunO'Pedia

As promised, Robert took Dave to the Big Creek shooting range and Steve came along. It was a four-hundred-acre facility with a six-hundred-yard rifle range with targets at two, four and six hundred yards. It also had a fifty yard pistol range. You could bring your own gun or rent one, choosing from seventy different types, ranging from hand guns to machine guns. Besides using the range, visitors could enroll in classes, purchase firearm accessories, get lunch or snacks at the open-air restaurant, or relax in the club house.

At the check-in counter, they showed their driver's licenses, picked out goggles and sound-blocking earphones. Sometimes, Dave wished he could wear those earphones all day long to block out the random sounds that always distracted him. Steve rented a Walther Creed 9 mm Lugar semi-auto pistol.

He and his dad had brought their own guns that were still in their carrying cases. His dad brought a .22 Marlin 60, another rimfire rifle made by Remington for small game hunting. Last year, Dave had bought a similar semi-automatic rifle, a Ruger 10/22 Takedown, another one his father didn't know about. But today Dave would show off his new Colt 6920.

They picked up their ammunition and headed to the shooting area. Steve went to the fifty-yard pistol range and Dave and his father went to the nearby two hundred-yard rifle range. When Dave took out the weapon from its case, Robert stared at it. "What is that, an AR-15?"

"Yeah, a Colt 6920 semi-auto tactical rifle. It's new. This is my first time shooting it."

"Hm, I figured you had something like that when I heard what you ordered for ammunition."

He couldn't tell how his father felt about his rifle, but then he rarely could discern how people felt about things. "That's the cool thing about it. It takes a 30-round Magpul PMAG magazine. I've got three of them because they'll go fast."

"That's definitely no toy gun."

"That's for sure. It's used by a lot of law enforcement agencies and military operations."

He moved into position, aimed, and pulled the trigger. After several seconds, he paused and peered down the scope at the target. He saw that his shots were scattered across the target. As usual, he needed to work on both accuracy—how close the shots were to the bullseye and precision—how closely the shots were clustered. He aimed and fired off another dozen shots. This time he noticed a tight cluster near the upper left-hand corner of the target, indicating precision, but not accuracy. Only one of the shots hit the bullseye.

There were four rankings of expertise in shooting circles, both military and civilian. They were unqualified, marksman, sharpshooter, and expert. Dave considered himself a marksman, and wished he could become a sharpshooter. But his Asperger's affected his physical as well as mental state, and as a result he did not progress to be sharpshooter.

He emptied the magazine, and reloaded with a new target. This time he fired non-stop just to get the feel of it, and experience of the thrill. He imagined he was on a battlefield and the target was his enemy who was firing at him. He peered down the scope at the target and saw that his shots formed a random pattern with about one out of three striking the inner two circles of the target. So much for accuracy and precision, he thought. He adjusted the stock, then reloaded the last magazine. He took more single shots, and adjusted his aim when he saw a cluster forming several inches to the left of the bulls-eye. But he was soon out of ammunition.

"You're done already?" Robert said.

"Yeah, I'm going to get a snack. Take your time. I'm in no rush." With that he walked off.

He saw Steve aiming his rented pistol and firing at his target on the fifty-yard range. Someday, he might show Steve his Springfield Hellcat 9 mm sub-compact that he kept in the glovebox of his car. But then he remembered overhearing Steve saying something to his father about how it might be dangerous for Dave to spend so much time around guns.

Robert had defended him, which pleased Dave. He knew all the rules and closely abided by them. However, he did have one run-in with authorities when he was stopped for speeding. As soon as the cop approached his car, Dave rolled down his window and said, "I've got a gun. You want to see it?"

He reached for his pistol in his shoulder holster, but before he touched it, the cop pointed a Glock 22 at his forehead. "Raise your hands and don't move." The cop held the gun in place as he called for backup."

"I collect guns. I've got lots of guns, including a Colt Classic 1911 in my glove box. You want to see it?"

"I've got a bullet for your brain, if you don't shut up."

Moments later, a second cruiser pulled up. "Now, slowly open the door and step out."

Dave did so, feeling confused by the way he was being treated. "I own these guns legally. According to Georgia law..."

"Shut up, turn around and put your hands on the hood."

A third cruiser pulled up and Dave was quickly surrounded. He was quickly padded down and the gun removed. "Says he's got another one in the glove box. He was reaching for this one when I approached," the cop told his fellow officers. He's got no ID on him."

A second cop poked Dave in the side. "Where's your driver's license? What's your name?"

Dave was frozen in silence. He remembered the bullies at school and how their attacks led his father to giving him his first gun.

"Are you going to answer me? If not, we're taking you in."

Dave remained silent.

"One more chance. What's your name?"

Dave couldn't hold back any longer. "I have my guns because of people like you. No one can bully me."

"That's it."

Dave was handcuffed and taken to the station. He was charged with obstruction of justice and threatening an officer. Robert found him a good defense attorney and the charges were dropped when the judge was told about his Asperger's. But the judge ordered his open carry and concealed gun licenses revoked and told Dave if he was caught with a gun outside of his home, he would go to jail for at least one year.

Dave went to probate court to challenge the ruling and three witnesses, including his doctor, appeared to testify on his behalf. The judge ruled in his favor, and he was allowed to reapply for concealed carry and open carry licenses. But the entire series of events took five months during which time Dave was not allowed to go to a shooting range. The incident cost Robert $12,000 in fees, half of which came out of Dave's salary from the plumbing company. That was nearly three years ago, and the point when he started using credit cards to purchase more guns.

Dave remained upset about the incident for months and became extremely wary of cops to the extent that he would start hyperventilating if he saw a patrol car on the road behind him. The lawyer had told Dave that he was lucky that he lived in Georgia, which was among the states with the most lenient gun laws.

Dave knew the gun laws by heart. Georgia allowed any person over twenty-one—or eighteen, if in the military—

to openly carry a handgun if the person has a weapons-carry license. Georgia also allowed any person to openly carry a long gun. In fact, if a long gun was carried while loaded, it must be carried openly. The law that fascinated Dave most was an ordinance in Kennesaw City, Georgia, that said all homeowners must own a firearm. He would like to live there, he'd told his father, who said that law was silly and could never be enforced.

He carried his rifle in its case over to the restaurant area that had only outdoor seating. He went to the kitchen window and ordered a sweetened ice tea and a grilled cheese sandwich. "No grilled cheese," he was told. "How about a slice of cheese pizza?"

"Okay, but I like grilled cheese better than cheese pizza because pizza is a clumsy food. It folds down, if you don't hold it with two hands."

The young woman at the window laughed. "I get it. Two hands for beginners."

Dave waited for his food, then walked over to a table and sat down. He knew his father took his time at the range and would take at least half an hour longer. A group of people, four men and two women were eating at a nearby table and several glanced at him as he sat down. He ignored the group and stared at a brochure about guns and ammunition that he'd picked up earlier at the counter. But he couldn't help overhearing their conversation.

"I bought a Taurus 454 Raging Bull over the weekend."

"Isn't that shit a bit expensive? How many rounds?

"Five rounds. Close to a grand. Nice addition to my collection."

"Cool."

The mention of the pistol caught Dave's attention, and he glanced over at the table. The Taurus guy had a shaved head and a muscular build.

"I got it from Hyatt Guns," he said.

"It is so easy to get a gun in Georgia," said another man who spoke with an accent. "I love it, man. It is so much more complex in Paris to own a gun."

"What do you mean?"

"I mean we have a lengthy process and there are strict limits to what one can do and cannot. It is not as easy as it is here in America. I feel jealous of you guys."

"I'm a gun enthusiast, but I think we need better gun laws in America," said a woman with long red hair tied in a single braid. "I don't think broad access to automatic and semi-automatic assault weaponry is a good idea. I mean in Georgia you can have a history of mental illness and if you haven't been confined for the past five years, you can buy a gun."

"It's actually worse than that," responded a man with a goatee and glasses. "If they voluntarily enter treatment when they experience a psychotic breakdown, or whatever, they can still keep their AR-15s or whatever firepower they've got."

"And we wonder why there are so many mass shootings," the redhead said.

A burly man with a beard down to his chest, shook his head. "Guns don't kill.. People do."

"Yeah, people firing semi-autos at a crowd," Red said.

"Cindy, Cindy, if they didn't have a gun, they would find another way to kill people."

"Maybe so. But they can't kill dozens in a minute with a kitchen knife," she responded.

Dave was staring now as well as listening. The French guy looked amused, and spoke up. "Do you guys know that as a country, you have more guns than citizens. There are more gun dealers in the U.S. than grocery stores, McDonald's and coffee shops."

The bearded man looked indignant. "Bad guys will get guns any way and the rest of us will have kitchen knives to protect us."

"We don't need six gun dealers for every Starbucks," Cindy replied.

"Don't throw bullshit statistics at me," he said, raising his voice. "If you want to ban something, make it the damned immigrants who are flooding our southern border."

The bald man, who had talked about his Taurus 454, stood up and raised his hands. "Hey, let's calm down." He held up his phone. "I've found an online quiz that claims to be the hardest Gun Quiz ever. Let's see how we do."

Everyone reluctantly settled down.

"Okay, here we go. We've got fifteen questions folks, and it would be a shame if we don't get at least ten of them right, for the kind of gun-lovers we are."

"Here you go. Desert Eagle, Glock 18, .22 Magnum, and .357 Revolver ..which one is better to use in a gun fight in the streets of a city?"

"I resent that question," Cindy said, sharply. "The only people shooting each other in the streets are drug thugs and other criminals. I'm not even answering it."

"I'll answer it," Bearded Guy interjected. "I think it's the Glock 18. Great design. It's fully automatic and I remember reading that it can fire more than a thousand rounds per minute."

"That is awesome power," the French guy said.

Dave bolted to his feet, facing the table, and laughed. "No, no, not the Glock 18. It's the .22 Magnum. It has little or no recoil. It's not very loud and it's very accurate over medium distances." He avoided making eye contact with any of them. "It's the right answer."

"We'll see about that. Okay, let's go to the second one, Baldy said. "Which of these guns fire a .357: Desert Eagle, Glock 57, Smith & Wesson .500 Revolver, or Derringer Revolver?"

Before anyone at the table had a chance to respond, Dave blurted: "The Desert Eagle fires .357 magnum cartridges."

"He's right," Bearded Guy said.

But Dave wasn't done. "The Glock 57 fires the NATO standard nine by 19 Parabellum round, a.500 revolver

152

can fire a number of different kinds of cartridges, ranging from the old-time Buffalo Bore to the traditional Winchester manufactured fifty calibers. The Derringer Revolver can fire any number of kinds of cartridges, but that also will depend on what type of Derringer you are talking about. I can be more specific if you like, but you probably get my point."

"I think we've heard plenty," Baldy scoffed. "Let's go to the next question. The primary sidearm of U.S. military personnel is the M9. Which manufacturer makes it?"

Dave laughed. "Is this supposed to be a difficult quiz?"

"Beretta," Cindy answered. "I think we've had enough of the quiz."

Bearded Guy shook his head. "No, I want to hear the questions, and see if our new friend actually knows all the answers."

They continued on, with Dave answering all but three of them. He thought those were too easy, and he let someone else answer.

"Holy, shit! We got all fifteen questions. Bullseye!" Baldy chortled.

Bearded Guy laughed and turned to Dave. "You're a fucking nerd, man! How did you know all this shit? What is your name?"

Dave turned to see his father and Steve watching from another table. He picked up the case with his rifle and walked away without answering.

"What a weirdo," Baldy said, loud enough for Dave to hear.

"I saw him shooting just as I finished," Bearded Guy said. "He's not a crack shot, I'll tell you that. But he might be a crackpot."

"He knows more about guns than you guys," Cindy said.

"Don't pay any attention to them," Robert said as Dave approached.

"Hm, I'm ready to go, Dad."

THE SHOOTING

6:41 PM

Watson slipped into the auditorium and immediately ducked down. For just an instant, he'd glimpsed something surreal, like a scene from a horror movie where everyone suddenly dies. Across the auditorium, hundreds of people were huddled low; some under tables. No one spoke or moved. A terrible stillness gripped the air. He lifted his head and spotted the masked killer sitting on the edge of the stage where the band had played, his rifle in hand moving slowly from side to side. A couple of bodies were visible near the stage, a few feet from where Ski Mask was seated.

Watson was hunkered down in the aisle next to a row of chairs on the side of the auditorium where the CEO had talked. There were two doors to the auditorium and the first one he tried wouldn't open. It was either locked or something was blocking it. He'd moved to the other door, the one he and Higgins had entered, what now seemed a lifetime ago. No wonder so few had escaped. They would've had to walk between the rows of chairs and would've been easy targets for the shooter if they'd come this way.

He cautiously peered out again. A sharpshooter with a rifle would have no problem taking out Ski Mask, but firing his pistol from this distance was chancy. If he missed, the shooter would probably start firing randomly, increasing the death toll.

He took out his phone and texted Barrios.

I'm inside the auditorium. Tell cops that the door to the auditorium on the right side is blocked. If they try to open it, he'll start shooting again.

Watson sent the text, and peered out again. The killer hadn't moved, but his head was slowly swiveling from side to side as if he were looking for his next victims. He ducked back down and typed another text to Barrios.

I'm going to call you on Skype and start filming. See if you can link my feed to the cops. I'll keep the video on. If the camera stops moving, it means I'm down and it's time to send in the cavalry.

His former partner now worked in the internet crime division, and Watson knew he would have no trouble carrying out his request. Barrios answered on the first ring. "Be careful, Larry. Make sure the camera's light is off."

"Will do," he whispered.

Watson hit the video record button and held his phone just above the back of the chair next to him. He slowly moved it right to left, then back again. He knew his hand was unsteady, but he kept panning slowly across the far side of the auditorium, stopping from time to time at center stage.

That's where the camera was aimed when he heard a shout. "I told you not to move. Now you pay!" Gunfire, a quick succession of shots, followed by screams and cries.

He'd seen enough. He couldn't wait any longer. He needed to get closer and take his shot.

# # #

After a commercial break, the USN anchor summarized what was going on in Atlanta, then cut to Radcliffe again. He stood silently for several seconds, then raised his gaze to the camera. "This nightmare has to stop soon. Who are these killers, the ones who go into schools and buildings and randomly murder? The average age is 37.8, but don't be fooled by that number. The youngest active shooter was twelve years old, and the oldest was eighty-eight. Imagine that."

Radcliffe shook his head. "Most of shooters are men. Just four percent were women—one out of twenty-five. The majority of shooters have been white—sixty-three percent—but African Americans, Hispanics and Asians have also carried out mass shootings. Being educated doesn't necessarily prevent people from becoming shooters. While some are high school dropouts, others are college educated, including shooters with master's degrees and doctorates. Some shooters are politically motivated and write manifestos; some are angry, and some—like the Las Vegas mass murderer who fired a thousand shots in eleven minutes at a music festival, right into a crowd of thousands of concert-goers, killing 60 people and injuring hundreds of people, seem to have no known motive at all."

Radcliffe paused again, almost as if he expected to hear more gunfire. "There are two commonalities among these shooters. The first is a somewhat surprising one that makes it extremely difficult to pick out these people. The vast majority of the shooters have no prior criminal history. The other commonality is that of course they all own guns."

Radcliffe touched his fingertips to his earpiece, listened. "Okay, now we are going back to the studio to Carole Andrews."

"We're going to a panel discussion that is already under way through one of our affiliates. If there's any breaking news, we'll jump right back to you, Blake." said Carole

Radcliffe kept an eye on police activity outside the event space building. The panel discussion played in his earpiece, and he caught a few of the highlights.

> "Most Americans, by a wide majority, favor stronger gun control laws, including stopping the sale of semi-automatic weapons, like the AR-15."

> "And preventing mentally ill people from buying weapons."

> "Yet, second amendment advocates say that such laws wouldn't prevent these shootings, and that they would open the door to the confiscation of guns from law abiding citizens."

> "Right, the only people with guns would be criminals."

"But you heard Blake, these mass shootings aren't committed by criminals. Most of the shooters don't have a criminal record."

"We blame mental illness for these slaughters, but consider the fact that there's no more mental illness in America than in other countries where mass killings don't occur."

"Sadly, we are getting used to these mass shootings, and there is a collective sense that they have become the new normal, leaving us with a sense of hopelessness and helplessness."

Radcliffe focused on a video playing on his phone that showed a Middle Eastern man shouting at people to get into a room. Blogs start calling him the prime suspect and labeling the assault as a possible terrorist attack.

Chapter 4

Six Months before the Shooting

4.1 Alim's vulnerability

Alim placed his travel bag in the back seat of his Lexus RX, then hugged Rabia and Zamir good-bye, told them he would see them the next day He slid in behind the wheel, eased out of the driveway. He drove slowly out of his neighborhood, then headed for the interstate.

Even though all his air travel expenses would be covered, Alim preferred to drive four hours to Atlanta for a meeting with the management team at Happ!'s corporate headquarters rather than take an hour-and-a-half flight. This way he didn't have to waste time picking up and returning a rental vehicle in Atlanta. What's more, he didn't have to deal with TSA at the airport, a big plus. As someone of Mideast heritage, it was common for him to be pulled aside and subjected to an interview as well as a comprehensive search of his body and possessions. Four hours on I-85 in his own car was much more preferable. Besides, he loved this car and was proud of the fact that he could afford it.

After a ten-minute drive through town, he reached the entrance to the interstate, and picked up speed as he moved into the flow of traffic. Settling into the long drive, he thought about how much Happ! had changed since its early days. While he'd joined the company three-and-a-half years ago when it was well on its way, he was well versed in its history.

The company originated with three seniors at Georgia Tech who wanted to create a software product that would make app development easy and fast, and named their company Happ!. They set up an office in the basement of a house where one of them lived, and established their business.

The university encouraged turning bright ideas into entrepreneurial ventures. In one of the university-industry events, Happ!'s software proposal received funding and that allowed the entrepreneurs to move from the basement to a modest office space measuring 2,000 square feet, enough to accommodate twenty employees. The beta product was ready in seven months and they received their first sales from Fintech. After that, there was no looking back.

By the time Alim was hired , Happ! had diversified into a variety of digital technologies and had grown to a company employing 2,200 in six countries and reporting twenty percent annual growth over the past five years. Happ! Headquarters was located at the end of Atlanta's tech corridor, a two-mile-long stretch.

The company occupied three floors, each one with space for one hundred and fifty employees. A few offices and twenty cubicles were reserved for the visiting employees from the other centers. Four hundred employees filled the remaining offices. The tech corridor was a popular location since it was close to a park-like setting with benches and walking trails that circled an eight-shaped duck pond in the midst of a grove of pines. Food trucks parked nearby, making it a favorite spot during lunch breaks.

Alim's expertise was in security testing software to find if there were any vulnerabilities including attacks by hackers. He kept himself abreast on the latest happenings in his software niche and made recommendations on the latest tools and skills required to certify software products. He also evaluated third-party companies that subcontracted specific assignments. He was happy living in Charlotte and had no desire to move to Atlanta. The city, in fact, attracted upward mobile millennials, who considered Charlotte a popular place to relocate. In the tech industry, the city was known for its pool of talented employees.

For the past month, Alim had been working on security testing of a new product that Happ! was planning to launch within a few weeks. He'd heard that there was a lot riding for Happ! on the new financial technology product, which was considered a game changer and could open a whole new segment of customers.

However, his team had found serious glitches in the new software, and the more he analyzed it, the more convinced he was that there was no easy fix. The developers might have to go to the drawing board again. In Alim's assessment, it might delay the product launch by one quarter. He knew the importance of reporting bad news at the earliest date possible, and promptly informed senior application security consultants about the glitch. Then he'd called his boss.

"Hi Alex."

"What's up Alim?"

"I have the results from the security testing of the new product, and it's not looking good."

"What about it?"

"After our regular tests, we ran some advanced tests running the latest tool set and there are vulnerabilities."

Alex groaned. "How bad?"

"Many critical issues."

"What do you think it takes to fix them?"

"Product design and development can give an accurate response. I think they need to go the drawing board again."

"Are you shitting me?"

Alim could tell that Alex was starting to panic. "Unfortunately, it's not a quick fix."

"The marketing team is working overtime for the launch in a month from now. I thought everything was looking good."

"It was, but this is a new vulnerability."

"Damn, I can't believe that you had four weeks for testing, and you're reporting this out in the last week. Anyway, you need to come here in person. I'll get you in for a 15-minute session with the management team tomorrow. Keep it simple and crisp. Let the product team decide how long it'll take to fix this."

Alim reached the Atlanta office an hour before the meeting began and had time to greet some of his colleagues and go over again what he was going to say. He entered the boardroom and was asked to immediately make his presentation. As he started explaining his findings and the list of things that needed to be fixed, the management team grew restless.

The product leader shook his head and disagreed on the seriousness of the glitch even before Alim had finished. Others offered their opinion on the extent of the problem. After a few minutes, the Happ! CEO, Josh Lane, stood up and that silenced everyone. He was a decade younger than Alim, dressed in jeans, a polo shirt and a sport jacket. He either hadn't bothered to shave for a few days or he was growing a beard. He looked at Alim and said, "Thank you for your diligence in finding these vulnerabilities and presenting them crisply. We'll go deeper into this, but right now we need to move on to other topics."

Alim thanked Lane and the others, and was relieved when he came out of the boardroom. He felt satisfied that he had done his job. Four days later, Alim got a call from Alex, who told him that the CEO himself was looking into the issues and had engaged a top security consultant from LA to help the product team fix the issues.

By the way, Alim, we have a new security consulting project coming up. I'll send you more details."

"What about the current issue? My team needs to test and certify the product after the fixes are done, right?"

"I don't think so, Alim. We have a product launch coming up and we're engaging the best security agency to look into all the issues, fix them and certify the product. You don't need to retest this product."

Alim was surprised and a bit suspicious. The usual protocol was for him to provide the final security certification on any Happ! product. He understood that the new product could take Happ! to the next level, but in his mind that made it even more important to ensure that it was fully functional and watertight from a security perspective.

# # #

Alim called his parents in Baghdad and gave them the good news that he would be traveling to Iraq for the wedding of a cousin. He and Rabia spent hours buying gifts for everyone back home. He purchased the latest Apple watches for his dad and mom. He also had special gifts for his sister and nieces.

At the halal grocery store, they sold a cute plush doll, Aamina. She was a talking doll with a cute, tight purple hijab and a long-sleeved dress over leggings that looked like skinny jeans. If you pressed the flower on her left hand, she would say: *Bismillah ir Rahman ir Raheem,* which translated to: In the name of Allah, the compassionate, the merciful. Her bangs peeked out of

165

her hijab. Press the flower on her right hand, and she recites the first chapter of the *Qur'an, surah al-Qalam.*

"What will the women at our mosque say?" his wife said, feigning being aghast. "Bangs! Cover them! *Astaghfirullah!*"

Alim laughed. "Then it's fortunate that this Aamina is going to Iraq. They will never see it here."

"Everyone will be thrilled to see you," Rabia said. "It's been four years since you visited."

"I know and I wouldn't be able to take this trip if I was still working on that same project. The new product launch."

"That's good."

"Yeah, and good that I got the reservation at such short notice."

"I wish Zamir and I could visit too," Rabia said with a pout.

"We talked about it," Alim said, taking her hand.

They'd had a long discussion, and the key factor for Alim was not the additional cost of airfare, but the travel advisory from U.S. State Department that recommended not to travel to Baghdad. It said that Americans were at high risk of violence and kidnapping. It also made clear that the U.S. government's ability to provide routine and emergency services were very limited. After reading the advisory, Alim took a firm stand that Rabia and Zamir should stay in Charlotte. If he took them to Iraq and something happened to either or both of them, he would be devastated for life, and he would never forgive himself for bringing them into danger.

"I am worried about you, Alim."

"I know you are, and that's even more reason for you to stay back till conditions improve. I don't think I will attract a lot of attention. I'm a local and I'm going to dress like the locals as soon as I land at the airport. Mustafa will be there to pick me." He hugged Rabia. "Nothing to worry about." Yet, he couldn't shake the feeling that something was going to go wrong...probably just his wariness about the airport. Going through security was always intense, even when he zipped right on through. But that wasn't always the case.

# # #

The next day, he boarded a Jet Blue flight from Charlotte to New York City, where he moved through a second security check after he transferred from the domestic terminal to the international terminal. During the security check, his hand baggage was opened and the TSA agent reached a gloved hand into the bag and picked up Aamina. He carefully placed the doll back into the bag, then said, "Follow me."

The agent led Alim to a small windowless room. "Wait here while your name is being compared to the no-fly list." Once again his name had attracted attention. His fear was that another Alim Mubarak would be on the no-fly list some day and he would be confused with that person.

Soon after, another TSA agent arrived, but said nothing about his name. Alim figured it was best not to ask. That might just cause another delay. "Sir, you've been chosen for secondary security screening." The agent acted as if Alim had won a lottery. At the mosque, it was called 'traveling while Muslim' and everyone had stories about invasive searches. Not only did agents finger women's heads through their hijabs, but female agents ran their hands up to their crotches. Men got the same treatment, but were told to remove any headgear they were wearing.

"My flight is departing in thirty minutes," Alim appealed.

"If you miss the flight, your airline will make alternate accommodations."

An angry retort popped into his mind, but he remained quiet. He knew that the shortest distance to the other side of the security check was to cooperate.

The agent, a tall man with a moustache, short curly hair and narrow-set eyes, put on latex gloves, then gestured Alim to stand up. "Spread your legs, sir. I'll be patting you down."

The agent's hands pressed against his back and arms. Alim could feel himself tensing as the agent approached his legs and crotch. No matter how many times he won the lottery for secondary security screening, each time it felt like an encroachment. The agent finished his search, and Alim finally relaxed.

"Wait here, sir, while we screen your carry-on bags again."

168

Alim sighed. This was so humiliating. He wasn't one to walk around with a chip on his shoulder, but the thought of him missing his flight just made him angrier and angrier. And he couldn't express any of his rage, for fear it would mean even more of a wait.

By the time Alim was allowed to pass through the security screening, he had missed his connecting flight. Aamina had been strip searched and his baggage had undergone another thorough examination. Of course, no contraband was found. Annoyed and frustrated, he hurried to the desk of Turkish Airlines. Fortunately, he found a seat on another flight that—if there were no delays—would allow him to barely make his connecting flight in Istanbul.

Two women wearing hijabs sat across the aisle and after they were in the air, Alim overheard one of the women saying that she was right, it was the hijab. She had taken off hers and put it in her purse before going through security. She had gone right through without a problem. Her traveling companion had worn her hijab and had been pulled aside for secondary screening. Alim considered engaging them in conversation about 'traveling while Muslim' but decided to keep to himself. If he had spoken with them, he probably would've told them that his wife not only didn't wear a hijab but donned a UNC Tar Heels sweatshirt before going through the TSA security check.

At the Istanbul airport, he rushed to find his gate for the flight to Baghdad. He arrived as passengers were already boarding and the line stretched out into the concourse. Several people were gathered near a television that hung from the ceiling and he walked over to see what they were watching. He saw a building that had been destroyed and rescue workers digging through the rubble. For a moment, he thought he glimpsed an intact building that looked familiar. But he couldn't be sure.

"What happened?" He asked a man standing nearby.

"Fucking Americans. A missile went off target and killed at least a dozen innocent people."

"Oh, shit. Where?"

"Baghdad."

He heard the last call for boarding his flight. He took one more look at the TV screen, then hurried over to the line of people. Feeling exhausted, he slept most of the way to Baghdad. When he finally arrived, it was a little after 1 PM. His cousin Mustafa, who was ten years younger than him, reminded Alim of his mother, whose twin sister was Mustafa's mother. He was always cheery and happy to see him when he came back.

Mustafa was waiting for Alim when he emerged with his suitcases on a luggage cart. But something was wrong. No smiles, no waves, no shouted greeting from his cousin. Maybe he had been waiting a long time for him. But as he moved closer and closer, he could see tears in Mustafa's eyes.

"Alim, my cousin, you have arrived at a very bad time. I have terrible news. Very bad. I don't want to tell you. But I must."

"What are you saying? What has happened?"

"They are dead. Your family, your father, your mother, your sister. All dead."

"No!" Alim shouted, his voice breaking. "That can't be true. What are you talking about?"

"I'm sorry, Alim, so sorry. A missile strike from the Americans. Off target."

Alim crumpled to the floor, shaking his head. "No, this can't be true. No, no. I will not accept it! Tell me you're lying, Mustafa," Alim pleaded, shouting the words. "Please tell me it's not true."

Mustafa wrapped an arm around his shoulders. "Cousin, let me take you to my house."

Slowly, Alim stood up, tried to take control of himself, but his heart was wrapped in sorrow, his mind was numb. "Where did this happen, Mustafa?

'At your sister's house. Your parents were visiting."

"Are you certain they were in the house? Did you see the bodies? Maybe they were out somewhere."

"I went there, but I couldn't get close. But the neighbors said they were in the house. One of them had left the house five minutes earlier."

"They could be still alive in the rubble."

"No, the explosion killed them all. Please, Alim, come with me. A car is waiting for us.

Alim's head hung, his shoulders shuddered. It was the worst day of his life.

# # #

Instead of marriage, Alim attended the funeral of his family. An American missile, aimed for an ISIS hideout, had gone off-target by nearly half a kilometer, and killed twelve people, including his father and mother, his sister, Kalina, and her husband, and their two daughters. Still in shock, Alim somehow completed the funeral rituals. Finally, everyone left and he was alone in his parent's house, thinking about his parents, who would never again come home. He was lonely and overwhelmed with sadness.

He slumped onto the couch in the living room and memories of his lost family flashed before him. His father had worked for the Baghdad Water Authority as a civil engineer. It was a very important job in a country like Iraq, and he could have gotten twice as much as he received from his humble government salary, if he just took bribes from contracting companies, architects, and the city's elite. But he didn't. Ethics was very important to his father. And he taught Alim that no shortcut was worth losing his moral compass.

His mother had risen from teacher to principal at Baghdad High School for Girls. The city's most elite families sent their girls there for schooling, and his mother encouraged each and every girl, as if she were her own daughter. When Kalina started at the school, mother and daughter bounced out the door as if they were headed for the moon. It was a source of pride for his mother that she would now have her daughter at her school.

He clutched the plush doll, Aamina, that he had carried for his sister's daughters. But they would never see it, never play with it. He had hoped one day he could invite his nieces to attend college in America. He wanted to give back, for all of the sacrifices his parents had made for him. His parents had scraped together every dinar they could, to make sure that Alim could attend Baghdad University. Tears welled up in his eyes as he remembered their sweet faces. He collapsed on the couch and wept.

He wanted more than anything to be with Rabia and Zamir this evening, but he couldn't go back yet. Rabia wanted to fly to Baghdad after she heard the news, but he told her to stay home; that he would be back soon.

Mustafa knocked on the door late the next morning. He stepped inside and looked around as if he expected to see Alim's parents miraculously revived. "May Allah forgive their sins."

"Forgive their sins?" Alim shot back, turning to a phrase his son had picked up from his American Muslim friends. "What the fatwa! They were innocent! Innocent, Mustafa!"

The WTF slang flew over his cousin's head. "I know you are angry, Alim. I want to take you to meet a man I know."

"What man?"

"Brother, I know it is hard. But you must accept the will of Allah. And I know a way that you can find peace of mind. Come to the mosque with me."

Alim felt lethargic and just wanted to go back to bed, but Mustafa was right. He needed to do something to move beyond his grief and his growing anger. They went out and ate kebobs and dolman—stuffed spiced rice wrapped in grape leaves—at a small restaurant that Alim was familiar with, not far from his parent's home. Afterwards, they took a bus to the mosque for the afternoon prayers.

Grief-stricken, Alim moved robotically through the motions of prayer at the mosque. When it was over, a group of men sat huddled around Alim near the middle of the prayer hall. They scolded him. He didn't say his prayers correctly. He held his hands over his stomach when he prayed. The way of the prophet Muhammad was to put his right hand over the left hand on his chest.

"You pray like a *munafiq*," one of the men said.

A *munafiq*? A hypocrite? It was one of the worst insults a Muslim could levy against another Muslim.

"You live in the West. Enjoy the riches of the West. And what do you do for your Muslim brother in the country of your birth? Or your Muslim brothers and sisters suffering in China? Your Rohingya's brothers and sisters? Your Palestinian brothers and sisters? And even you? Is your life not important? America won't tolerate the killing of one American, but when they kill us, do we not bleed? Is their blood lined with gold and ours with soot and ashes?"

Alim was getting dizzy. They talked about the misery inflicted on the Muslim people because of unjust U.S. foreign policies in the Middle East and beyond.

"Who are you?" Alim asked the men.

One of them men stole a glance at Alim's cousin. "It's okay. He's like a brother to me," Mustafa said.

"I am the imam at this mosque," the man said quickly. "We are with the Party of Liberation."

Alim wracked his brain. Party of Liberation? It was not an organization he had known. The imam explained that it was established as a political party with a mission to create an Islamic caliphate, or society. Muslims had been protected for six hundred years by the Ottoman Empire, the Islamic-run superpower that ruled Turkey and large areas of the Mideast, Eastern Europe and North Africa. But with its defeat in 1922, Muslims had a duty to build a new caliphate, the Iman said.

Since its founding, the Party of Liberation had spread to several countries with estimated membership in hundreds of thousands. But the organization was banned in Egypt, Russia, Germany, China, Turkey, Pakistan, Saudi Arabia, Qatar, Jordan, and Indonesia, among others. The imam admitted as much, but then dismissed the governments of those countries. "They are *munafiq*."

The rise of ISIS, or the Islamic State, as they also called themselves, motivated the men of Party of Liberation. It made them imagine that their dream could actually be realized. With so much power in the hands of the Western nations and their lackeys in the Muslim world, the men of Party of Liberation knew they had their work cut out for them.

"We need you, brother," said the imam. "Allah has rewarded you with wealth, opportunity, education. You must give back now. You must help our cause. Don't you care about your family? Murdered by a Western missile strike? Why are these colonial powers still interfering in our lands? The British Raj is dead. The American Raj has risen. And you—you, dear brother—can be the one to stop them. We have a plan of attack. The serpent will strike America."

Alim sighed. He was tired, exhausted.grieving,hurt. And he was angry. He was angry that his family had been buried because of the aggression of his adopted United States of America. The least he could do was support this effort in their name. So they could be rewarded in the afterlife.

The mosque was filling up with congregants arriving for the *maghrib* sunset prayer. Weary from his journey, Alim hadn't moved in the three hours since he had first walked into the mosque. And the imam's appeal had worked. He pulled out his billfold and slipped $500 in U.S. bills to the imam.

"Brother, for my family. For the cause of Allah. May you be rewarded."

"*Alhamdullilah*, brother." Praise be to God.

In turn, the imam slipped Alim a piece of paper. "Here is the phone number for the leader of Party of Liberation in America. Call him. Support him. So your family and you may be blessed."

Alim took the paper and slipped it into his pocket, his wallet a little lighter and his heart a little heavier than it had been a few hours earlier.

# # #

On his journey back to the United States, Alim was tormented by the voices of the radicals he met in Baghdad. Their words still echoed in his mind. They'd touched a nerve deep inside him and his anguish was unrelenting. Outwardly, he appeared calm, but the searing pain of his loss still consumed him and triggered waves of anger that created an urgent need to strike back forcefully.

As he emerged from the arrivals concourse, Rabia stood up from her chair in the waiting area. She approached him, met his gaze, and frowned. She later would tell him that she had immediately sensed that something was amiss. His eyes seemed as if they'd lost all the kindness and love that she'd always seen in them. His gaze was dull; his expression was blank. It was as if he had left a part of his soul in Baghdad, she told him.

She reached out and grasped his hand. His skin was cool and clammy. He didn't take her hand, didn't smile. He moved robotically as they walked away and answered her questions with shrugs or shakes of his head. He said he didn't want to talk about it.

"It's over now, Alim. We have to move on."

Her comment triggered a sharp rebuke. "No, not over!"

At home, he allowed Rabia to lead him to the bedroom. "Alim, Alim", she said softly, pulling him onto the bed, laying his head upon her lap running her fingers through his hair. Images of his mother, father, and sister filled his consciousness. "Rabia, I couldn't save them," he said, burying his head into the soft of her belly and weeping.

"Shhhhhhh," Rabia whispered, doubling over to press her chest against Alim, turning her body into a cocoon for the love of her life.

"It was so horrible. Everything destroyed. Everyone destroyed."

He couldn't keep his secret about the imam that he met. Everything spilled out as if he were a toddler returning home from daycare. Every detail. Every word of the conversation. Every suggestion. Every bit of the plan. Every ounce of his rage, and how the imam had played on it, urging him to act for the good of his family.

"No, Alim. You must not think about revenge. Do you not remember when the prophet Muhammad suffered humiliation in his birthplace of Mecca, fleeing to Medina and waging his war against his ancestral Quraish tribe from there? After much struggle he won, and he set off for Mecca to claim the city for Islam. The elders of the Quraish tribe met him in the desert, and they asked him for patience. They asked him to wait a year and return then? His wife advised him to wait. And he did, returning a year later to victory without a drop of blood spilling."

She caressed Alim's hair and continued, "Victory, my dear, comes in many forms. It is the triumph of the soul. It is the resilience of the spirit. Your mother, your father would like to see you sacrifice for your son as they did for you, not with rage and vengeance, but with *sabr*."

Rabia knew just what to say to ease Alim. *Sabr* was a magical expression in Arabic...somewhere beyond equanimity and noble patience.

"It is written in the Qur'an, Alim: Stand up for justice, even if it is against your kin," Rabia said, reciting the verse to him in Arabic.

Alim breathed deep for the first time in days. And he slept soundly that night, wondering what the next day would bring. Would the anger return? Would he listen to Rabia or turn against her wishes and contact the imam whose phone number remained in his wallet?

# # #

The next morning, he smelled the fresh brewed coffee wafting upstairs from the kitchen. He knew what he had to do. He searched through his desk looking for a business card. Finally, he found it in a drawer and ran his fingers across the gold seal. He picked up the phone and dialed the number for the FBI. He glanced at the card again when a man answered the phone.

"Special Agent Jenkins."

"Uh, this is Alim. I met you when you were investigating the arson attack on our mosque in Charlotte."

"Yeah, hey, Alim. How can I help you?"

"I have some information I want to share."

179

The next morning Jenkins arrived at the house with his partner, Carole Brenner. Both were in their early to mid-forties, slender and fit, dressed in business suits. Alim invited them inside and sat at the kitchen table where he shared every detail that he remembered. The name of the imam in Baghdad. The organization's name. The chapter in the United States. All of it.

As Alim talked, Jenkins and Brenner took notes on FBI iPads. When Alim finished his story, he answered questions for another twenty minutes. Finally, the agents closed their files and turned off their iPad.

"I'm very sorry for what happened to your family in Iraq, Alim," Brenner said. "Thank you for your service to your country."

"You did the right thing," Jenkins added.

It did feel like a service to the country, but had he betrayed his fellow Muslims? Over the next few days, Alim delivered messages to fellow congregants at his mosque from their relatives in Iraq. He also talked with his imam about starting a group to modernize the community further and educate members about how to practice Islam and assimilate in America. He said it would be great to have such plans well established by the time the new mosque was ready for occupancy.

4.2 A Friend Indeed

Dave had tried every chicken franchise within fifteen minutes of home, but none of them compared to Charlie's Chicken Shack, a local place just a mile away. The restaurant was located in a part of the Old Fourth Ward that gentrification hadn't reached. A local guy from the neighborhood, who Dave had worked with briefly in his second job out of college, had taken him to the small restaurant, introduced him to Charlie and the best chicken in Atlanta.

The entrance was set back from the road and required walking through a narrow alleyway. Dave had convinced his parents that it was safe and they had become among the growing number of Atlanta residents who had discovered Charlie and his amazing roasted and barbecue chicken. Then two months ago, *Atlanta Magazine* had reviewed Charlie's Chicken Shack and now reservations were needed.

Nevertheless, Dave came here Wednesdays at 6 p.m. with his parents or without. They knew that the routine was important to him, and that he wouldn't change to an earlier time, that when the restaurant was less crowded. If they couldn't make it on time, Dave would go on his own.

On this evening, Charlie had greeted Dave and his parents and seated them at their favorite table in the corner. The place had eight tables and a bar that would seat six. The wood walls and antique tin ceiling gave the place character like no other chicken place in town.

Their drinks had just arrived when Dave felt his phone vibrate in his hip pocket. He set down his glass of beer after taking one sip, and carefully eased out the phone and laid it on his thigh below the table. His sharp-eyed mother knew what he was doing. "Dave, you know our rules about staring at our cell phones during dinner. We come here with you for the good food and to enjoy your company."

"I know," he said without raising his gaze. It was a text message, and it stunned him.

Coming to Atlanta this weekend. Will call on Sat.

"It's from Laura. She's coming back."

"Really? How nice." His mother smiled. "Invite her over for dinner."

"How's she doing?" His dad asked.

"I don't know, but she wants to see me."

With that, he texted her back.

Looking forward to it.

"I'm glad you've kept in touch," his mother said. "How long has it been, two years?"

"Two years, seven months, eight days. She's my best friend."

He remained quiet throughout dinner, offering only brief answers to his parents' inquiries. His thoughts were lost in the past. He clearly remembered the day he met Laura during his first year at Georgia Tech. He could see the sequence of events clearly in his mind's eye because he had thought about it so many times.

# # #

Dave was relieved when he heard the applause as he finished his presentation of his project. He knew that he was one of the top students in Professor Altman's Civil and Environmental Engineering class. Yet, talking in front of class terrified him. He had memorized everything, but the only way he could give his talk was to avoid eye contact with his fellow students and several guests from the college. So he either looked at the screen where his design plan was projected, or down at his shoes.

At the end of class, Altman called Dave up to his desk and congratulated him on his engineering design—a master plan for renovating two of the college's oldest dormitories, and increasing the number of rooms by twenty-five percent. Dave winced when Altman padded his shoulder. He nodded and thanked him, then quickly left the room. He hurried down the hall and out the door, hoping none of the students would approach. He pulled his hoodie over his head and eyed the sidewalk as he took the least trafficked path in the opposite direction of the student center where the herd liked to gather after class.

Any other first year engineering student would be happy to have been selected to present their final project to the senior faculty and administrators who might actually use his design. But this was the worst thing Dave could imagine. Not only were they planning to formally recognize him, they wanted him to be part of the design meetings. The acclaim and extra credit didn't matter to him, He already had an A in the class. The idea of interacting with a room full of execs petrified him.

"Dave! Dave! Hey, wait up...." He quickened his pace, pretending not to hear the voice. But his pursuer didn't let him get away. A brown-haired girl who often sat one seat behind him in class, ran ahead and then turned to face him, blocking his path.

"Where ya going? I was hoping you'd head over to the student center. I'm Laura... from the class. I wanted to ask you about the design you did. And, well, ask your opinion about mine."

"Going back to my room," he said.

He looked at Laura as if seeing her for the first time. She was plain looking, yet somehow appealing to him. She had large eyes and a friendly smile. She was petite, just over five-feet tall with a slender boyish body. He noticed and liked her earrings, hoops that were big and silver with a smaller hoop inside them.

"Well, we never really got to talk in class, but I wanted to congratulate you. What an honor for a first-year engineering student to get their design actually used for real!"

"I suppose. They are seriously considering it, I was told."

"No shit. Well, if you're not headed to the student center, want to grab a coffee from the food truck? I was wondering if I could have a few minutes of your time to look at my design. I got an extension to turn it in late, but I need an A on it or I'm going to fail the course. I was hoping you might help me."

He shrugged, "Well, er... do you have it now? What is the design?"

She paused and giggled. "You'll probably think it's stupid, but I designed a futuristic amusement park— something I imagined that might be like Disney, or Six Flags." She looked for his response, but Dave didn't show an immediate reaction. "Ah, you're not saying anything. You think it's dumb, don't you? I knew it! Never mind. Sorry, I bothered you."

"No. it's good."

"Ya think?"

"Yeah."

They got coffee and spread-out Laura's plans across the table in the commons area. Dave stuck to the technical talk, but Laura hinted at wanting to attend a weekend event on campus at Tech Square. "They're having carnival rides."

Dave had a rolling ruler and pencil on the graph paper and was measuring the lines on Laura's drawing.

"I was wondering...." she said. "The double ferris wheel.... the linear dimensions. Do you think seeing it at the carnival would give insight to the drawing design?"

He nodded. "That would be good. You should go."

"Dave," she paused and giggled, "You're not getting it. I'm trying to invite you to go with me."

"Oh? Well.... sure. I guess that would be fun. Though carnivals can be kind of chaotic."

"Well, if you don't want to go..."

"No, I do. We'll focus on the Ferris wheel."

She laughed again, shaking her head. "You're different. I don't think I've ever met a guy like you."

"Is that bad?"

"Hell, no. It's refreshing."

The two exchanged numbers and promised to text each other and meet up Friday night. And in the days leading up to the event, Dave ruminated in silent agony, wondering if he should do some research on Ferris wheels, or read a book on first dates. He just hoped nothing weird would happen. He remembered the one and only carnival he'd ever attended when he was nine or ten. A clown had jumped out in front of him, flapping his arms like a bird, and Dave had gone into meltdown, screaming as if he was being tortured.

A red flag went up when Laura texted him suggesting they go to keg party before the carnival. He wrote back that if they went to the party, they might not get to the carnival to research her project.

She texted: *LOL, don't worry, we'll get there. The party is two blocks from the carnival and we can walk.*

Cool, he responded, but felt uneasy.

He wanted to be more social, but he'd heard that alcohol, Asperger's, and women didn't mix. He recalled several disaster stories from older members of the Aspie Club, a social network his mom made him join the summer before he left for college. He was intellectually aware of his disorder, but much of the advice and warnings he'd heard about dating was irrelevant to him back them. Now he wished he could remember more and that he had stayed in touch to ask for advice.

As it turned out, Dave's worries were for naught. They were among the first arrivals at the apartment where the keg party was being held. That was a relief because crowds made him uneasy and would cause him to start looking for a way to escape. The taste of the cold beer was good, and it went down easily. Three or four big red plastic capfuls later, Dave never felt so at-ease in his life. He talked freely with Laura, and she was genuinely interested in his highbrow topics of conversation, even though he tended to linger too long on technical details. He liked that she said what was on her mind. She was able to draw out of him things that he could never seem to express to others.

They walked to the carnival and that gave him time to adjust to the bright flashing lights. Once inside the carnival, he stared just in front of his feet, raising his gaze slightly to avoid people coming toward him.

"Is something wrong? Laura asked. "You seem kind of distracted or something."

"No, I'm okay." He looked up to see the Ferris wheel in front of them. They studied its structure and Dave made some suggestions for altering Laura's futuristic design. He stopped short though when she suggested they take a spin on the Ferris wheel. At first, he didn't know what to say. He didn't want to sound as if he were afraid, or that he might freak out if they got stuck at the top. Then he blurted, "Why don't we go to my place?"

"Oh, that's a good idea."

When they arrived at the dorm, Laura looked around at the orderly room. No clothes on the floor, the Futon bed was in the upright couch position. The desk was clear, except for a laptop and several pens that were neatly lined up. "What, you don't have a roommate. Get out of here! How did you pull that?"

"I just requested it. It costs a bit more, but for me it's worth it."

Laura sat down on the Futon. "This is pretty comfortable." She reached up, clasped onto his forearm and pulled him down next to her.

Suddenly, Dave realized that by inviting a woman into his dorm room in order to get away from the carnival probably had other implications for Laura. Like sex. And now he was at a loss as to how he should proceed. He had read a book about courting and remembered that on the first date you should go easy and maybe just get a kiss at the end. But now he and Laura were on the Futon and he didn't know what she expected of him.

"Hey, relax, Dave. I don't bite."

"Oh, I didn't think so. Neither do I."

They stared at each other a moment, then both burst out laughing. "So let's not bite each other," Laura said.

"I agree, but what should we do?"

"How about this." She wrapped her arms around him, pulled him close, and their lips met. He liked her sweet fresh smell, and the softness of her lips. But he caught his breath when her tongue darted into his mouth. That was in the book, too, but he didn't think it was on the first date. Maybe she didn't know the rules."

He pulled his head back. "You're kind of plain looking and, as far as I can tell, you don't seem to have large breasts. But I like you. And I like kissing you, even with the tongue."

She stared at him, puzzled. "You're full of surprises, Dave."

"Yeah, I've got to tell you something else."

"Let me guess. You're a virgin."

"Well, that too. But the thing is I have Asperger's. Do you know what that is?"

She studied him for a few moments, then smiled. "Well, that makes sense."

"What do you mean?"

"If you got into Georgia Tech with Asperger's, it means that you're super focused and really smart about the stuff that interests you. I have a cousin in high school, Jenna, who's like you."

"Oh, that's good to know."

"Yeah, it also explains why you're a little awkward socially and very blunt. You just say whatever's on your mind, and you probably don't realize how your words affect people."

"Have you talked to my mother, because she says the exact same thing?"

"Let's keep your mother out of it." She leaned in again, embracing, kissing.

Maybe it was the effect of the alcohol, but he trusted Laura, and that was very unusual for him. And he really liked what they were doing. When they came up for air, unlocking their lips, Dave told her that his heart was pounding. "I think that means I really like you."

"I like you too. You're not a player. You're real. And, I guess I feel like I could be good for you."

"How good?"

"Very good," she said with a laugh. "I could guide you through the social mores of our times."

"Yes, I think you're better than the book."

"What book?"

"My book on dating and sex. There's no pictures, though."

"Good to know."

"One of the guys who works for my dad said that doing it is way better than reading about it."

"Smart guy. So let's..."

That was all he needed. As they hugged, he slid his hands under her t-shirt and up her back, pausing at her bra. She laughed when he fumbled with the bra strap, which could have triggered a panic attack and ruined the night. But Laura came to the rescue. Not only did she undo the bra herself, but she pulled it through her sleeve, held it up and showed it to him, and described the design of the clasp in detail, explaining how three curved metal pieces interlocked with corresponding hooks on the bra.

"See? So, that's how that works, pretty ingenious, huh? Do you think you could design a better one?"

"Not right now. Take your shirt off. I want to see your breasts."

She gave him a cockeyed look. "Are you objectifying me?"

Dave felt stupid for a moment, but then she laughed and whipped off the tee. "They're small, but I like them and I don't have any hang ups."

He reached out with both hands to touch and fondle them. She threw her head back with pleasure. "Kiss them, Dave."

"You're so free-spirited. But I hope you're not like this with all the guys." He wanted to be special to her.

"Honestly, I really like smart guys. But I find you very attractive, too. I like your wavy hair, and you have kind eyes. Skinny guys are a turn on for me, and you kind of remind me of this guy I had a crush on in seventh grade. He moved to Seattle and I never saw him again."

Before now, Dave couldn't fathom any real-life scenario in which he would ever make love to a girl, or how anything remotely close to it would happen. He had all the desire and testosterone, like any man, just not the playbook or script to carry it out. But with Laura, he didn't need any of that. She was playful and she made him feel good.

She was also quite adventuresome and dominant. She knew it was his first time, but he didn't think about that. He just followed her lead and let things happen, and it happened fast. And afterwards, they dozed briefly without there being any discussion or analysis. He hoped his performance was okay, but he didn't know the signs to look for as to how she might rate him.

# # #

He heard his mother's voice as if it were coming from a distant place. "Dave, Dave to Earth, where are you?"

He blinked and saw that the waitress had served their meals. "I'm here, of course. I was just thinking."

"And ignoring us," his dad said. "It's okay. Let's enjoy the best chicken dinner in Atlanta."

# # #

When Laura left him to go home that night, he was able to go to sleep satiated, happy, and without the usual looping, self-deprecating, anxious thoughts. He just slept.

In the following days, as the semester drew to its close, Dave helped Laura complete her amusement park project, and spent as much time with her as she would allow. For the most part, she was her usual bubbly self. But she kept putting him off when he asked her to come back to his room. He figured it had to do with school or life pressures and had nothing to do with him. But he wasn't sure about that. He was becoming frustrated and confused, and wondered if she didn't think he was any good in bed. Or, maybe it happened too fast on the first date, and she felt 'objectified', a term he looked up and understood after Laura used it.

He couldn't bring himself to ask what was wrong. Maybe nothing was wrong and he was just overthinking the new relationship. After all, they were texting day and night, working on their projects together in the commons area, even passing notes and funny memes during class when Professor Altman wasn't looking, and laughing about it later.

But when two weeks had passed with no sex, his anxiety was beginning to consume him. He didn't know how to get her alone and make it happen. He couldn't sleep and felt increasingly depressed about the matter.

He texted Laura repeatedly on the long weekend that she went back home to Valdosta. He wished she had invited him to go with her, even though the idea of meeting her parents scared the shit out of him. But he wasn't getting the attention he wanted or thought he deserved. Laura's texts were brief responses to his, or just contained smiley emojis. He didn't want his inner struggles over the relationship to explode into a meltdown, so he tried to occupy his mind with work and playing video games.

When she appeared on campus Monday morning, she told him she had finally turned in the design assignment, but that it would probably not garner a high enough grade to pass the class because of the point deductions taken on lateness, and the fact that she'd failed the most recent quiz. She was thinking hard about her future, she said. On her trip home, she talked with her parents about leaving Georgia Tech and working a year or two before returning to school.

Dave didn't know what to say when she revealed that possible scenario. He couldn't believe she was making such a rash decision that would certainly split them up, based on the sheer distance that would be between them. He'd heard that long-distance relationships didn't work out very well. He felt angry and sad at the same time, and he recoiled. Now his text messages back to her were as short and superficial as hers to him had been while she was away.

He wasn't going to bring it up. His usual modus operandi was not to react to what was going on. Maybe that wasn't what a normal person would do, but Dave only knew how to be Dave, true to himself, no games. Maybe he would ask her to go to the ice cream social after class on Friday and start over on a better note. When she declined because she said was going out with other friends, Dave was beside himself. This time he reacted. He texted her later that afternoon and got a response right away.

Something wrong, Laura?

–Sorta.

What does that mean?

–Ugh. Hard 2 talk about.

Tell me.

–I'm leaving here in a few weeks.

So?

–So? Duh.

What about it?

~I love you to pieces, but figure it out!

????

–You're a great friend and...

Friend??

–Yes, I don't want to get involved because I'm not staying.

Why not?

–It doesn't work.

Says who?

–It's not like we were steady.

What??!

–Oh, Dave. Kisses aren't contracts.

What the hell does that even mean?

She didn't reply. He waited. He checked his phone moments later. Then minutes and hours later. Still nothing. After twenty-four hours, he began calling her and leaving phone messages to call him back, and all the messages went unanswered. She was ghosting him.

Laura didn't show up for the final exam. She never returned to school.

# # #

"Dave, you're just picking at your food. Are you feeling okay?" Robert asked.

"I was just thinking things over. I'm looking forward to seeing Laura again. Do you remember when she came to my graduation?"

"Of course, we do," Mary responded. "That was so nice of her. I'm glad you're going to see her again."

# # #

After Laura left Georgia Tech, to his surprise, she got back in touch with him. She sent a text or emails every couple of months. She never forgot his birthday and reached out to him during the holidays, when she would send a written note or voice mail.

Even though he replied to her with short messages, he still resented how their relationship had ended. He didn't really get over it until Laura showed up for his graduation ceremony.

He remembered being on stage and receiving the diploma from the college president, who moved the gold tassel on Dave's cap to its other side. With that, he graduated *summa laude*—with highest distinction. If only the kids from high school who had bullied him could see him now, he thought, as he walked off stage. Maybe they would retract all the mean things they'd said to him.

Dave left the stage and scanned the hundreds of onlookers, searching for Laura. He couldn't believe it when he spotted her, and it was as if three years hadn't passed. Her hair was much shorter, but she looked the same. They waved to each other, and all the old feelings came rushing back. She had driven all the way to see him—alone! It had to mean something.

She approached him as he exited the arena and met up with his parents. She introduced herself to Robert and Mary. When they realized she'd driven two hundred miles just to see Dave graduate, Mary invited her to join them for dinner. They caravanned and arrived simultaneously at Canoe, a fancy restaurant about fifteen minutes away.

Mary commented on it being a beautiful night, and she asked for a table outside, overlooking the Chattahoochee River. The sounds of the violin and guitar from the band would be best heard there, she told the hostess. Dave didn't notice much of his surroundings. He was more intent on getting a draft beer ordered immediately so he could suck it down to relax. He hoped his father wouldn't say anything stupid in front of Laura. But sure enough, that's exactly what he did within the first five minutes.

"Well, son, you couldn't tie your shoes until you were eight years old. Look at you now! A toast to a new and, let's hope, better future."

"Robby, that's not nice to say in front of Dave's friend," scoffed Mary. She leaned over the table and said to Laura, "He means well, it's just that Dave, well, for as intelligent as he is, it's been a hard life until now."

"You mean my Asperger's, mom? Laura already knows about it, for your information."

Laura giggled. "It's all good. I understand."

Robert's eyes darted at Dave with a familiar and unmistakable look of disapproval, maybe for sharply correcting his mother. Dave looked away. He pulled his smooth onyx worry stone out of his pocket. He rubbed the stone between his thumb and forefinger and, for whatever reason, it provided sensory distraction and calmed him when he felt nervous—like now.

"Where is it, Dave?" asked Robert

"What? What are you talking about?"

"The diploma. I remember the president handing it to you. Is it in the car? I don't remember you holding it when we left the ceremony."

Dave's face flushed. "I... I... I don't know! Are you sure I wasn't holding it?"

Robert stood up and reached into his front pocket and handed him the keys. "Buddy, it better be in the car! Now go look."

Dave got up and bumped into the waiter who was carrying a pitcher of water and some of it spilled. He heard his father make a 'tsk' sound. He felt confused and panicky.

Laura stood up, excused herself, and caught up with Dave. She hooked her arm onto his and together they walked out to the parking lot. Dave was shaking and felt eight years old again. He was mumbling to himself, "Stupid, stupid, stupid," he said.

"Shhhhh stop. I think colleges don't put the real diploma in the book they give you. I think they mail it to you. The cover is usually empty. Can you imagine them having to insert the diplomas and make sure hundreds of students got the correct one?"

"Laura, you're just trying to make me feel better."

"I'm telling you the truth! Seriously! Please calm down. It's all right. Boy, your father really gets to you, I see. I don't like that." She rubbed his back as he opened the back door and bent in to look.

"Oh thank God, it's on the floor!" He held the book close to his chest.

"Geez, Dave, it saddens me to see how upset this made you. Even if you did forget it, this could happen to anyone."

"You don't understand. With me, this happens all the time. My dad gets pissed like this. God!"

"Hey, look inside the binder."

He opened it and saw that contained nothing but a navy silk bookmark. "Told you!" Lacey laughed. "Let's bring it back to the table and show your parents." She rubbed his back again as they walked to the restaurant.

"Your dad didn't need to be so.... well.... what's the word?"

"He didn't need to be such a prick."

"You don't sugarcoat, do you?"

"I can't"

In spite of the annoying interruption, the graduation dinner ended well, and Dave was glad that Laura had met his family, dysfunctional as they seemed though.

He remembered what she once told him, "I feel like I could be good for you in so many ways." She'd proven that today and before driving back to Valdosta, she vowed, "I will always be your friend."

He stayed in touch with her and followed her progress as she completed her bachelor's in business administration and continued with her MBA with specialization in healthcare administration. She joined a healthcare consultant company in Greenville, South Carolina that offered services to large companies in designing health benefit programs that helped employees manage their healthcare needs in a way that saved the money and time for both the employer and the employee.

When she updated her Facebook status to 'In a relationship', Dave understood that Laura would not be his girlfriend again, but he wanted to believe that she would be a true friend, probably the only friend he would ever have.

# # #

They'd finished their dinner and Robert had picked up the check. He paid and left a generous tip, as he always did here, and they were ready to leave. Robert and Mary were standing, but Dave was still in his chair staring at his phone that he held below the table.

"I hope you're not playing a game down there," Robert enquired.

Dave shook his head, but continued looking at his phone, and made no effort to stand up. "What is it, Davey?" Mary asked.

He hated it when she called him by that little kid name. He jerked his head up. "It's Laura. She won't be visiting. She'll be staying. She's moving back to Atlanta."

"Oh, how nice," his mother said.

"Where will she be working?" Robert asked.

"At a company in the Tech Corridor."

4.3 Counseling Mark

Mark couldn't delay it any longer. Stacey was insistent that they needed to go to a counseling session and he didn't want to hear any more whining about it from her. She called it 'pre-marriage' counseling. In spite of continuing spats between them, Stacey apparently was still hopeful about getting the wedding plans back on track. That surprised him, since she seemed so disgusted with him whenever they started bickering.

But she'd noted that he was much more confident about the future of Maverick, and didn't seem worried about the company's high monthly financial outlays. He'd managed to manipulate Spitzer's payments so that she didn't see anything unusual about them. When she'd noted the size of the new deposits, he'd told her about the pitch he'd made to investors about the Happ! stock, implying he had some inside information, and Spitzer had pounced on his tip. That seemed to satisfy her, and she hadn't pushed any further.

Dr. Martha Van Dorn, Stacey's choice from the start, was a big name therapist in Atlanta. Her practice was in the most affluent area of town, just outside the city's largest gated community. She took evening appointments, too, and that was worth the extra expense, Stacey explained. "I've finally got us an appointment for the day after tomorrow, so let's go this time. No more backing out."

It was rainy and cold, and they were still at the office and hadn't had dinner. If she didn't forget about the counseling session, Mark hoped Stacey would cancel it due to heavy rains. They were both overworked and tired, anyway.

"Fifteen-minute warning," she said.

Damn. She didn't forget. "What?"

"We need to go. We'll have to pick up something quick at a drive-through and eat on the way. Remember we're seeing Dr. Martha at 7."

Mark was on the floor, looking for a USB thumb drive he used to save his work.

"You hear me?" she asked.

He reached under his desk where the device had fallen. "God dammit, I'm not deaf, Stacey."

"Don't start."

"We could cancel."

"No way. We've put it off long enough. We need to do this to work things out."

He stood up. "Why can't we work things out on our own?"

"We've tried that and we end up screaming at each other, make up, then do it all over again. I'm tired of it and I'm sure you are, too."

He responded by pulling his keys out of his pocket and walking out the door. Stacey hurried after him, complaining about his stubbornness. He just ignored her. They got in the car and didn't talk much along the way. She pointed at the lighted sign for Rick's Burger Joint at the end of the street, but Mark kept driving.

"No way. I'm not eating that crap. Besides, look at the traffic. We're going to be late."

He heard her mutter, calling him a dick. He turned up the volume of the radio and listened to a recap of the stock market. She could eat after the counseling session. That would keep her from lingering. Maybe they could even skip out early.

The tension between them continued as the rain pounded the car. She didn't say a word when they parked and got out. Her body language said it all. "Relax, Stacey. We're only five minutes late, for chrissakes."

They started walking side by side as they crossed the parking lot. But Stacey purposefully dropped two steps behind him, and the umbrella she held no longer covered Mark. He dashed to the building and stopped under the overhanging awning. He looked back and grinned as he saw her dodging puddles in her high heels.

Dr. Martha greeted them after they entered, then guided Stacey and Mark to her office where she invited them to sit on a leather sofa. She took a seat across from them in an oversized Queen Anne chair. Mark sized her up. *Attractive woman, that is, if you take away the librarian glasses and she let her hair down from that uptight bun. A tad weathered from too much sun or, maybe just aging. Definitely in her forties, no younger.*

Dr. Martha opened up a leather portfolio and reviewed some notes, then peered over her glasses. "Thank you for reaching out to me. I understand you both want to talk about how to give a go to this relationship, or, alternatively, how to part ways."

"Are you shitting me?" Mark turned to face Stacey. He laughed and shook his head. "You told me this was a pre-marital session. Now *you're* the one suggesting we break up? Oh, well isn't that special." He stood up. "I think we're wasting your time, Doc. I don't need a therapist to tell me how to end this relationship."

"Sit down," Stacey pleaded. "We need to get to the bottom of things, please!" She turned her head toward Dr. Martha. "See! This is the kind of alpha male shit I'm dealing with."

Dr. Martha gently nodded and closed her eyes, then opened them. "It's okay, Mark. No therapy. This is an initial consultation. Let's just talk a bit about what's going on at home. Why don't we give you the floor? How do you see things between you and Stacey?"

Mark sat back down and sighed heavily. "Quite frankly, we are on a downward spiral. Look, I'm not easy to live with, I know that. I've got a lot of pressure. A guy like me has millions of dollars of client's money at stake every day. Stacey can't comprehend how intense it is. She gets all twisted up about some shit that doesn't even matter."

"Like what?" the therapist asked.

"Like some silly task list she creates, wanting me to make cash deposits to a ski-lodge for a trip that isn't taking place for months. I've got *real* deadlines every hour. I'll get to the reservations when I get to them. I don't need her yellow sticky notes on my computer screen reminding me what to do and what to pay. She needs to stay in her lane and give me space in mine."

Dr. Martha looked at Stacey, who chimed in, "I can be hard-driving on getting things done that pertain to our personal lives. Mark and I always worked well together—in the office, that is. And he's asked me to oversee a great deal at work to make sure nothing falls through the cracks. I wish he would manage his home life with the same measure of care as he does the business. Sometimes he makes me feel like I don't matter at all." She wiped a tear and Dr. Martha pushed a box of tissues on the coffee table closer to Stacey.

"I hear what you're both saying."

Mark threw his head back against the sofa and rolled his eyes. "Oh, brother. Here we go, again. This is bullshit," he muttered under his breath.

"Why is it bullshit?" asked Dr. Martha.

He didn't answer. Stacey interrupted, "It's so much more than that. Can I say something here?" After the therapist nodded, she spewed off every reason she despised Mark, including a reference to an incident a few weeks ago in which they attended a party and Mark "misbehaved," as she described it.

"He indulged in a line of cocaine and later, got very rough in bed with me. I told him to stop. And do you know what he did?" She squinted her eyes, took a breath and brought the tissue up to face to cry into it. "He.... He..." Her words were garbled as she continued crying.

"Jesus," she's *still* carrying on about some comment I made about there being hotter, sexier girls in the queue, those who appreciate a man who can turn investments of tens of thousands in a day. You know what? That's the *truth!* Stacey doesn't know what she has in me. That's it in a nutshell. I really don't have time for this in my life right now."

Dr. Martha jotted a few notes.

"That's the problem!" Stacey said. "He doesn't care. At.... all!"

The couple bantered as if they were the only two in the room. Dr. Martha allowed the exchange to get heated without interruption.

"You accuse me of interest in other women. Apparently, Stacey, you are writing about other guys in your diary."

"I told you it's not a diary. It's a dream journal. And it's none of your business."

"You left the book lying around. You want to be with your college boyfriend. You said you're trapped in the wrong story."

"It was a dream! You should have never pried into my private journal!" she shouted.

"Yeah, right," he scoffed. "Now that I know what you're really thinking."

"Sneaking around, reading my private stuff.... Then using it against me!" Stacey turned to Dr. Martha. "He's passive-aggressive. He never really wanted to marry me. He's just taken advantage of me. He makes promises, then doesn't follow through. There was no trip to the Caymans. That was just to string me along!"

Mark let the words hang in the air because it was true.

"He's obsessed with flashing money around and being a big shot. It's all about winning, being better than others. I feel like a punching bag when he's feeling down. And when he's winning, he's a cocky son-of-a-bitch."

"Now you're being overly dramatic." Mark wiped his brow.

"Did you say, 'punching bag?'" Dr. Martha made a timeout sign with her hands. "Is Mark physically abusive?"

This was becoming one-sided, he thought. "Now look here, Stacey's the one who sure as shit is coy and sexy when I'm on a good run and gifting her with fine things. Then she's complaining when it's not enough. She doesn't know a damn thing about my work and market cycles. Nobody does."

"Stacey?"

"Yes, he can be abusive." She wiped away a tear.

Mark shook his head, got up, and walked towards the door.

Stacey grabbed her purse. "I'm so sorry. I guess we're leaving."

"Hold on, Mark," Dr. Martha said. "It's okay, please wait in the lobby for a minute." She closed the door.

Mark stopped in the hallway, uncertain what to do. Stacey was wailing and he strained to hear what she was saying about him. He could only make out a few words between all the sniveling, but enough to glean the gist of it. "He's a monster..... lost half of his bank account... brought this on himself... reckless... working some crooked deal now...could end up in jail.... not good father material."

He'd heard enough and left the building. By the time he started the car and pulled up to the front of the building, Stacey was already waiting outside. "I thought you might've stranded me here," she said as she got in.

"We're on thin ice. That old broad can't help us."

"You're right. I'm done with you. I'm moving in with my sister until I find my own place."

"Fine with me. Be a relief."

The tires squealed as the car peeled away.

# # #

After the therapy incident Mark and Stacey didn't speak for a week, longer than any previous silence between the two. She moved out that night and didn't show up at the office the next morning or the rest of the week and the first two days of the following week. They might never have talked again, except Mark turned frantic when he couldn't find the key to the storage locker in the basement of the apartment building. He had packed up some of his mom's legal paperwork, the will, the living trust, stuff he needed right now. He didn't hesitate to call her.

"Sorry to bother you, Stacey. But I can't find the key to the storage locker. Do you know where it is?"

"On the key ring on the hook in the linen closet, where all the extra keys are." Her tone was neutral.

"Let me see.... Oh yep, here they are. Whew! Thanks so much."

"Sure thing. Everything okay? I know your mom's papers are in there."

"She still with us, has good days and bad ones. I just want to be prepared. I'm doing okay. Miss you at the office, of course."

There was an awkward silence.

"Mark?" she asked, sweetly.

"Yeah?"

"Are you sorry?"

He laughed. "About what?"

"You know, about turning into an asshole at Dr. Martha 's."

He couldn't tell if Stacey was kidding or serious. Maybe she was flirting. "Are you sorry you turned into a drama queen at Dr. Martha 's?"

"Yes."

"Then I'm sorry, too!"

They both laughed. That's what was great about Stacey. Mad as a rabid dog one day; then she forgot it all, and was back to her fun-loving self.

"I'm going to the shooting range later today," he said.

"Oooh, you are! Can I go with you?"

"If you don't shoot me."

She laughed. "I promise to keep my aim down-range as long as *you* do the same."

"Yeah, I'll be nice. We both will be nice and very careful with our aim!"

Even a good date with Stacey, Mark knew, had potential for ending on a sour note. She refused to allow the top down on the return trip. "I don't want my hair getting windblown and knotted up, Mark."

He didn't reply and didn't put the top down. It seemed like everything was a power struggle between them. Stacey had become a joy-kill and, quite frankly, nobody—not even Stacey—was going to stomp all over his masculinity anymore. But after a moment he realized it wasn't a battle worth fighting. He used the silence between them as an opportunity to contemplate the power of his gun slinging and shooting skills he was mastering at the range. He was surprised by how much he'd been thinking about shooting. He'd discovered that fantasies were an effective M.O. to deal with negativity around him, and increasingly, those fantasies involved guns.

He followed Stacey's directions and pulled up in front of her sister's house. He turned to her, politely thanked her for joining him at the shooting range. "But you know I should fire you for not showing up for five days of work."

He figured she was ready to come back, but her answer surprised him. "You don't have to fire me, Mark, I quit. I'm out. Now you can get the secretary of your dreams."

"Wow! I wasn't expecting that."

"I've had time to think and part of our problem was that we were seeing too much of each other."

"You mean it's over? We're really done?"

"Let's take a break from each other. It was fun today and reminded me of when we first met. But maybe it was a mistake. As we were driving back, I realized I don't want to fall back into our ways."

"Okay. Bye."

She stared at him a moment, then got out of the car and walked to the house.

He watched her go, then put down the top for the ride home. Fuck her. He was single, he was free, he told himself. He was reminded of happier times driving a fast car with the radio cranked up. He missed that. The s-curves of the tree-lined road were dangerously fun for a hot rod, and he stepped on the gas to recapture that youthful feeling as he sped along the curves and around the bends. He dropped his head back and howled at the top of his lungs.

# # #

For the next couple of weeks, things went well. He realized that it didn't matter that Stacey didn't work for him any longer. Rather than hiring a full-time secretary, he decided to hire a temp to come in when he needed her. He found a mother with two kids who was an experienced bookkeeper. He paid the temp service and put her to work a couple days a week, and he didn't care if she worked at home part of the time, as long as she did what he needed.

The money was coming in at a steady pace and he was no longer drawing down on his reserves. The company was solvent and his personal bank account was growing rapidly. He didn't need to talk to Spitzer and it was best that way. Nate continued on as one of his portfolio managers and passed information to Mark as needed.

Then one day everything changed. He was casually checking the stock market when he saw that Happ!'s stock, which had been making small gains over the past couple of months, dropped by twenty-two percent in a single day. And right on the expiry date, the day when the stock options were settled. He snatched his phone, called Brian, and shouted at his old college buddy.

"What the fuck is going on, dude?"

After a startled pause, Brian said, "Hi, Mark. Nice to hear from you."

"Well?"

"I was going to call you today. There's some glitches in the software of the new product and Happ! is pushing back its plans for the launch by a couple of quarters. No big deal. The stock will recover."

"What about the acquisition you were trumpeting?"

"Yeah, that's being delayed, too. And frankly, it might not happen. No guarantee."

"But you gave me a guarantee."

"No I didn't. I told you that it looked good, and at the time it did."

"Shit, Brian. This is all bullshit. You're cutting me off at the knees. I'm losing big. It's going to have devastating consequences for me." He'd invested heavily in Happ! options, but investors thought he'd only signed them up for shares in the cash segment mode. He was looking at losses of hundreds of thousands of dollars. Before he had a chance to explain what he'd done, Brian said he had to go and disconnected.

"Shit! Fuck! Going to kill that bastard," Mark muttered.

Now he would have to scramble and assure his investors that the stock would go back up once the issues were fixed with the software, and that the company was working on it. He was completely shattered and clueless. Spitzer's clients were taking big losses, and he had to keep that fact from them as long as he could.

That night he had a terrifying dream of how they were going to torture and kill him. His dad was looking on from a corner of the room with a smirk on his face. Mark woke up with beads of sweat on his forehead. It was after 3 AM before he fell back to sleep.

# # #

The rays of the early morning sun beamed through the white venetian blinds. The bright light awakened him from a short night of slumber. Sleep was becoming a forgotten luxury in the two weeks since the Happ! stock had tumbled. Mark added up the hours he estimated that he'd slept after eliminating the unrestful tormenting and lingering time spent obsessing about the accounts he'd lost, or the latest news about mom's worsening condition. Today it was three hours of superficial sleep, which was worse than the day before and the one before that.

He dragged himself to the bathroom. He lifted the faucet and let the water run warm to wash his face. The mirror on the wall revealed the toll the past weeks had had on him. He ran the bar of soap over his jaw, which was now hidden by whiskers that had grown unkempt. He noted the thinness of his face and the heaviness of his eyes from sleeplessness.

He walked past the kitchen. His stomach felt acidic. Coffee, which he loved so much, had zero appeal. He stared at the computer screen displaying icon links to the company log-in site, his work files directory, and the internet. Everything seemed so pointless.

While Mark and Stacey continued to live separately, he'd managed to get her to work at the office on a part-time basis after his temp had walked out on him. He'd shouted at the temp when she'd made a mistake in the payout to a client. He told her she was stupid and useless. That was the last he'd seen of her.

He needed Stacey at the office, especially during this critical time with the collapse of the Happ! stock. So they'd put their differences aside. Besides, Stacey said she needed a paycheck to pay rent to her sister and buy groceries. You wouldn't know that by her Facebook page, Mark thought, where it appeared she was living the high life. Photos showed her with some guy clinking champagne glasses at a classy restaurant. It pissed him off, but he didn't want to drive her off like the temp. So he stayed quiet about it.

Today he found more new guy photos, including a beach scene with the two of them posing next to jet skis. He cross-referenced the man's name in the photo with his online profile and jotted down his name, location, and workplace, just in case he ever needed to find the bastard. He fantasized about how he would bring him down to his knees, begging for his life.

Mark picked up the phone and called Stacey. "Where the fuck are you? You back from the islands? Thought you were coming in today. I need the accounting sheets."

"Whatever happened to saying, hello, like a normal person? About the accounting sheets, you're in the red on the checking account. The overdraft protection kicked in."

"That's no big deal." He knew he sounded defensive.

"I was wondering when you would ask me the status on the account. Another thing, why did you tell me that you paid up on all the accounts? You haven't. Why are you lying to me? You know I run the reports. Something's not right."

"Hey, look. Everyone in business cheats, some more than others. It's just the way things are." He could hear the purr of a car's engine and he heard a man coughing in the background.

"Are you in a car? Who the fuck are you with? Don't talk about Maverick in front of anyone."

"Nobody," she said. "I with nobody."

"That's a lie. Get your ass over here and let's go over the reports. Confidentially," he added.

"Don't talk to me like I'm a child! Sheesh, I hardly know you anymore the way you lash out. Yes, I'll stop by. I need my paycheck and I want to talk with you, anyway."

He hung up.

# # #

Later that day, Stacey came in and they looked at the accounts. She stood over him at his desk, and highlighted the pages where withdrawals were shown with no reference or associated client number. "Something is very wrong, here. What about that?"

Mark punched a few numbers in his calculator and didn't answer her.

"And here on line 15, it shows a check made out to you for $47,743 on the fifth, but the category is blank."

He punched in a few more numbers into the calculator.

"And here..." She slid the tip of her pen across the spreadsheet to show him a column. "Look at this one. It's a withdrawal and..."

"Dammit, Stacey. Just leave the report here for me to read. I wanted the report; not your analysis. You don't understand the transactions like I do."

"That's for sure." She threw the pen down on the paper in frustration.

Mark ignored her as he expanded a window on his computer screen showing stock pages. He scrolled the pages like a mad man, searching for information.

She pulled up a chair next to him. "Mark? Please look at me."

"Stop with all the fucking questions!" He continued scrolling the data.

She put her hand over the computer screen to distract him. He finally turned and looked at her. She moved her hand over his fingers on the keyboard. "Putting everything aside, everything between us, the wedding, the on-again, off-again relationship, the business.... Just the two of us. I'm closer to you than anyone. I know you! You're falling on the job. You're losing it. Things are going awry. I'm worried you're going to do something reckless."

"What are you talking about?"

"You look disheveled. Hung over. Have you had any sleep recently?"

He hated what she had to say, but at the same time this was the Stacey that he remembered, the sensitive one who could call him out on his own shit, who used to comfort him, who withheld judgment, before everything got crazy. He *was* tired. "The pressure...."

"I know. Shhh. Turn off the computer and let this go until tomorrow. Please come with me for counseling tonight at 7. I see Dr. Martha every week and she totally understands. Even if she can't help *us*, she has helped me immeasurably. And she can help you, too. Maybe she can prescribe a relaxant. Please come."

It was a moment of desperate weakness, perhaps. A tranquilizer sounded good right now. Heart palpitations, night sweats. He hadn't eaten a decent meal in weeks and was losing weight. His thoughts meandered. The coke dealer wasn't responding to text messages. He needed a quick snort. He was feeling withdrawal symptoms. Withdrawal from coke, withdrawal from booze. Vodka no longer carried him through the rough patches, and the taste of it was beginning to make him puke.

He agreed to see the therapist if it meant some medicinal relief. Legal, too.

Stacey left the report on his desk. She called him later at 6:30, and he was still at his desk.

"Did you eat something?" she asked.

"Stop always asking me about what I ate. I had a protein bar."

"Well, I'm outside. Come on out, and let's go together."

# # #

What the fuck am I doing here? Mark felt manipulated and duped. Dr. Tight Ass Bun Head looked like she'd eaten a canary, so proud of herself she'd gotten him back in her office. Aside from feeling hateful about everyone and everything in his life, Mark was also loathing the man he was becoming, shamefully submitting to a woman who led him on this desperate move to the therapist's office, all for the hope of getting a drug.

His head was in a fog between reality and unreality—alert to the therapist's talk that pertained to him, then in a fog when it was about Stacey's issues. She and Dr. Tight Ass talked long about Stacey's progress in therapy – blah, blah, blah—and Stacey said that she wanted very much to "iron things out with Mark on a new playing field." Maybe even start over again and find what they once had in the beginning. Mark's thoughts were singular... Just give me damned pills.

"It's perfectly appropriate to consider individual therapy in addition to couple's therapy," Dr. Martha suggested. "What do you think, Mark?"

He nodded, realizing the stupidity of his response and the nonsense of this whole charade. He saw Dr. Martha 's overture as nothing more than a ploy for increased therapy fees to line her pockets, not intention to help him. *Just write me a script, and let's get out of here.*

"Yes, Mark will definitely benefit from individual therapy," Stacey said. "It's difficult to watch his decline in the ways I have. No sleep. Losing track of the money on the books. Did you notice the weight loss since the time you met him?"

He felt like a goddamn circus freak show animal being observed by zookeepers. But he bit his tongue. *Write the damn prescription.* Stacey continued on about her assessment of how the surrounding circumstances of his mother's sickness was just too much for him, that Mark's business was failing..."

Mark cleared his throat, "Failing? I'm going to ask you to not talk about company business. That's confidential. Nothing we can't fix in due time. Not a topic for here."

Dr. Martha smiled, "Everything is confidential here."

"I'm going to ask one more time if we can avoid any reference to the business," he said. His piercing stare was intended to threaten Stacey, who was entirely too chatty. It didn't seem to faze her, and Mark's agitation began to escalate. His head was pounding.

He noticed Stacey rolling her eyes as if to communicate to Dr. Martha that they were dealing with an idiot. What a pair these two women were! Two against one. If that wasn't bad enough, Stacey cupped her hand up to one side of her mouth to gesture to Dr. Martha a little secret, "The company is a loser and as you can imagine, we have a lot of unraveling to do at the office, which keeps both me and Mark pretty busy." The gesture and comment lit Mark up and an intense wave of rage washed over his body.

Loser? This was *my* company she was talking about. She was so cavalier to say that." Zip it up, Stacey. You're only a part-time secretary, not a partner. You don't know what's going on behind the scenes."

"Nothing legal in my estimate," she shot back.

'Watch your mouth, you..." He lunged toward her across the sofa and she cowered and put her arms over her head in natural defense.

For a few seconds, Dr. Martha seemed to lose any sort of decorum in the room. She stood up. "No sir, that is not how we behave in my office. Before I call the cops, I'm going to have to ask you to leave." She pointed to the door. "Stacey, stay here. We'll get you a cab. It's not safe for you to leave with him."

There was a long awkward pause, then Mark walked out. His thoughts were all over the place. A woman is supposed to stand by her man, not throw him under the bus. *Two* women busting my balls in that room? He wouldn't put up with that. He wished he never mixed personal and business relationships. Stacey had twisted him in knots, spun a web of deception around him. What other cliches fit, he wondered. Oh yeah, *Don't shit where you eat*, and now he knew why. Stacey knew way too much. She judged, she criticized, she demeaned. It was bad enough he had clients kicking his ass. He needed and wanted a comrade, a friend, a woman, an oasis. She turned out to be none of those things.

THE SHOOTING

6:45 PM

Larry Watson crawled between two rows of chairs toward the party area where the shooter remained seated on the side stage. He held his Glock in one hand, his cell phone still recording on Skype video in the other. He wasn't concerned that the video was only recording his movements. That was the signal that he was alive and active and moving toward the kill.

When he reached the end of the row of chairs, he would be about seventy-five feet from his target, if the shooter remained where he was.

Twenty more feet, fifteen, ten. Somewhere out in the party area a child cried softy. He dropped to his belly, then edged forward, pulling himself along on his forearms. Finally, he saw the stage, then glimpsed the killer. Instantly, Watson knew he had a problem.

Ski Mask was holding a hostage, a girl of seven or eight who was whimpering. He must be expecting police to charge in at any time, Watson thought. The madman would use the girl as a shield and shoot as many people as possible. He held up his phone to record the scene, to show the shooter and the girl to the police.

But after several seconds, the reflection from the phone caught the shooter's attention and he swung his weapon around, aiming at Watson over the girl's shoulder.

"Oh, shit."

# # #

If USN's Blake Radcliffe had any hopes of learning new information from Fulton County Sheriff Trevor Atkins, he quickly realized that wouldn't be the case. Atkins, who was in his late fifties, tall and lanky with salt and pepper Afro hair, convened a press conference near the duck pond, and told reporters that his comments would be brief. "Everyone should stay away from the tech corridor and allow law enforcement to carry out their duties," began the sheriff.

"This is an on-going law enforcement action, and we don't have much to tell you. There are many rumors being spread on the internet, and they are just that, rumors. The facts will come out, but right now we need to put our efforts fully into ending this terrible event."

"Chief Atkins," a local TV reporter asked. "There is a video showing a man with a Middle Eastern accent who is shouting at people, telling them to lie down. Do you know if he is the shooter, or one of them?"

"We're looking at that video. It was taken shortly after gunfire was first heard. We don't see any weapons in his possession."

"But don't you think he should've been telling people to escape, instead of laying down?" she persisted.

"Not necessarily, ma'am. There were reports of an active shooter in the lobby. So attempting to escape could've been very dangerous. One more question."

"Do you have videos of the shooter or shooters from cameras inside the building?" another reporter asked.

"We have videos of a man wearing a ski mask throwing towels over the cameras. There are reports of more than one gunman, but we don't know if they are true. Thank you all and stay safe."

As Atkins started to walk away, Radcliffe called out to him. "Chief, do you have anyone inside?"

Atkins paused and looked over at the USN reporter. "No comment."

If ever *a no comment* meant yes, that one did, Radcliffe thought.

Less than a minute later, two pops were heard. As if in response, Klieg lights blossomed, illuminating the Red Oak building. Anyone emerging from the building would only see bright lights, while police on the outside would have an enhanced view of anyone coming out.

Radcliffe moved as close as the police lines allowed, his cameraman filming the scene. He waited expectantly, but didn't have to wait long. A tactical squad of five or six officers charged the building and entered the lobby.

"Something must've happened," Radcliffe muttered.

# # #

In the moment after Ski Mask spotted him, Watson had a shot at his head. He could've taken it, but the girl was too close to the line of fire. Suddenly two people leaped from their hiding places. They ran to the door that was locked and pounded on it. Few more ran to the door. Ski Mask turned and fired on those trapped by the door.

Someone broke open the door at the other end of the auditorium. Dozens of others raced for their lives, crossing the auditorium, and clambered through rows of seats, some leaping over the chairs, scrambling for the door. Just as they crowded the doorway, police in tactical gear struggled to get inside. Blocked by the mounting number of escapees, they pulled people through the doorway as more gunfire erupted inside.

Watson lay on his belly next to the bodies and waited to take a shot. But everyone who was still alive was in motion, blocking his way, running, shouting and crying for friends or family members. He held his phone out in his left hand filming the chaos, and providing real time video of the onslaught, which he knew was being monitored. No doubt a tactical squad was ready to charge in and kill the shooters. Would they shoot him too, if they saw his gun? Probably.

The best way to prevent that from happening was to take down the shooter before the tactical teams charged into the auditorium, before the madman added to his death toll.

# # #

Radcliffe touched his ear and listened to an update from the studio. Hackers had broken into a Skype feed sent to authorities from someone inside the auditorium, and it was streaming for anyone to see. A commercial ended and the studio anchor said, "We are going to connect with a live video feed from inside the auditorium. You may not want to watch what's coming up now. This is unedited footage. We don't know what we are going to see. I believe it was intended for the police, but it's on the internet, so we are going to patch into it."

Radcliffe shook his head and looked over at his cameraman. "Unbelievable. The more blood, the higher the ratings."

Like millions of people around the world, Radcliffe watched events as they unfolded inside the auditorium. A maniac, a bloodbath, a shaky camera blurring some of the worst of it. People screaming, fleeing for their lives, some covered in blood. It went on for several minutes.

The shooter was firing like a robot in a video game. Nothing mattered to him. Their age, their gender, their frightened screams, their pleas to spare them. Bodies littered the floor of the auditorium. Radcliffe watched in horror as the shooter hunted a couple who were desperately trying to crawl under a table.

The shooter, meanwhile, had cornered a group of people, and they were the ones he was focused on. Radcliffe guessed they were his hostages. Everyone else was dead or dying or escaping.

Chapter 5

Three Months before the Shooting

5.1 Secret Garden

Checking Stacey's Facebook updates was a repeated exercise in masochism for Mark. She had a new boyfriend, and of course, he was tall and stacked with muscles and had a man bun and gleaming teeth that looked like they'd been whitened. Here they were sunbathing side-by-side in the Bahamas in one photo; Frenching on the Jumbotron at Braves game on opening day; dancing at Coachella, covered in dirt, and hugging Beyoncé.

Mark desperately needed a distraction to break his depressive thoughts and loneliness. He had no interest or energy to look for a new relationship. But if Stacey can enjoy herself without him, he can have a good time too. He drove to a bar and had a couple of drinks to clear his head.

As soon as he reached home, he opened his laptop again. He created a proxy email ID and used his credit card to buy credits worth $50 and went to an adult chat site. He noticed that there were rooms that charged from $1.98 per minute to $4.98 per minute. It was similar to economy, business and first class on a flight. He picked a room that charged $4.98 credits per minute, named Secret Garden and found that the host was a woman in her early thirties who seemed eager to get rid of whatever little dress was covering her body. Her nickname was Spicy Pink.

He chose to enter with his video disabled so that he could see her, but she could only hear him.

He was immediately showered with digital kisses and virtual hugs.

"Hi! Thank you for coming to my room."

He loved her seductive voice. "My pleasure."

"How are you doing today?"

"Good and you?"

"Horny and hot." She spoke with such feeling and voice that Mark believed her and made him feel warm.

"Okay."

"I can do role plays, play with toys, pretty much whatever you want me to."

"I want to first drown in your big eyes, brush your absolutely kissable lips with my lips and run my tongue on your perfect front teeth."

"Wow how poetic!"

Poetry in a porn room.

"You seem like a very sensitive and sweet person." She acted the part well, he thought, and that was exactly what he needed right now. An acknowledgment, a praise, a connection however brief it is. They played around for some more time.

The dialogue quickly turned dark and dirty. As Mark's credits ran out he became restless and angry as credits points started reducing. It reminded him of the bitterness he felt about the crash of the Happ! stock on the expiry day. He started walking about restlessly as his mind returned to the depressive thoughts he'd been experiencing ever since that financial mishap.

# # #

Word had leaked that Maverick Investments was in deep trouble and clients started pushing him. One nasty call in particular had spooked him. The caller threatened his life promising a slow torturous death. He was at his rock bottom. He reached out to his friends and was snubbed. All of his backhanded compliments came back at him with a vengeance. Nobody had time for a loser.

He called his mom from the office. The advanced stage of the disease was clouding her thinking, and that just stressed him even more. Much of what she said on the phone was incoherent, babbling about imaginary people who were after her. "Mom, those people aren't real. You're just imagining that stuff." The ones that were after him, on the other hand, were very real. He was frightened, and also angry with himself. He was mad with the world, mad that he was spiraling downward, mad that he wasn't going to join the financial elite.

The phone didn't stop ringing, and he felt sick when he listened to the messages being left. Besides threats of physical assault, there was talk of his possible arrest. The damn thing was he still couldn't figure out why he'd believed Brian about the Happ! stock. He wondered about it as he drove home. His throat was dry; he felt thirsty. All these bastards had conspired against him, he thought. That night, he twisted and turned and barely slept.

With each passing day, he worried more and more about the physical harm that some of Spitzer's clients were capable of inflicting. He went to the shooting range to relieve his stress and forget about his precarious life. Until now he'd never thought about buying a firearm for protection at home and in his car. Purchasing a gun was not a problem in Georgia. Pretty easy and straightforward stuff. But which one to buy? That evening he started researching handguns with a simple question. "What is the best gun for self-defense?"

The sheer number of responses bewildered him. There were hundreds of sites about pistols, rifles, and shotguns. Focusing on handguns, he found dozens of options to choose from with detailed analysis of each gun with comparison based on portability, ease of use, weight, affordability, stopping power, and so on. One website said shotguns were good home defense weapons as they were relatively cheap, easy to use and had plenty of knockdown power. He kept surfing late into the night and came upon statistics that surprised him.

In 2018, Small Arms Survey reported that there were more than a billion small arms distributed globally, and 857 million (about 85 percent) were in civilian hands. The Small Arms Survey stated that U.S. civilians alone accounted for 393 million (about 46 percent) of the worldwide total of civilian held firearms. He found that in the U.S. more people used a gun in self-defense each year than the number of people who died in car wrecks. Almost all national surveys indicated that defensive gun uses by victims were at least as common as offensive uses by criminals. One report Mark read said that the Department of Justice confirmed a total of 338,700 defensive gun uses in both violent attacks and property crimes over a five-year period, or 67,740 defensive gun uses every year. Now he knew he needed a gun.

Not surprisingly, a window popped up on his screen about a gun show in Atlanta. Over the past few years, he'd become used to his online searches attracting advertisers with related products or services. The gun show promoters claimed it was a great way to spend the weekend for any gun collector, hunting enthusiast, or those interested in buying their first gun. There would be a variety of vendors displaying a wide range of guns, hunting supplies and outdoor gear.

Mark paid $15 for the special ticket for no line, no wait. The parking lot was full when he arrived at the Howard's Gun Show in a convention hall north of Atlanta. Mark was stunned by the scale of the show, even though he'd read that it was 27,000 square feet, the size of half a football field. The exhibition hall was awash in a sea of Confederate flags. Table after table was covered with display of handguns and rifles. He stared at a poster promoting a private militia group, called Oath Keepers, next to posters of Confederate flags with the words, Never Give Up...and Deal With It.

There were so many different types of weapons, so many brands that he was at a loss. He stared at a display behind glass, of a pistol that looked like it was made of gold. The sign with it said: Colt Second Amendment Founding Fathers Tribute Pistol. Nearby, a banner read: *AR-15s $499.99 & Up.* He took a look at the row of rifles, then moved on.

Most of the shoppers were white males between forty and seventy, he figured. He saw a few women, including one who was a vendor. The only black person he noticed at first was a guy who stood out not only by his race, but because he was a head taller than most of the crowd.

Mark strolled by three middle-aged men in camouflage and boots and stopped by a table covered with a wide variety of handguns. The proprietor of the display, a balding man with a thick moustache, was engaged in a conversation with a young man who looked familiar. After few moments, he realized it was the same young man he'd seen at the shooting range. That day the tall, slender man was silent and unwilling to respond when Mark greeted him.

Waiting for the vendor to become available, Mark stood at the table, scrutinizing the guns. The young man was talking incessantly about the guns which he thought were the best ever made. The dealer was trying to wind up the conversation and make a sale, but the young man was simply not getting it, or didn't seem to care. It took ten more minutes before the vendor closed the conversation and turned his attention to Mark.

"I'm really sorry that I had to keep you waiting." He spoke in a deep voice with a smooth Southern drawl.

Mark shrugged. "That's okay. I understand. You need to take care of the customers—or potential customers—in order."

"That young fellow is a regular and a collector, so I had to oblige, though he wasn't buying today."

"Oh, a collector, huh."

"Yes, Yes. He's very knowledgeable about firearms. So, what are you looking for today? By the way are you a first timer?"

"Yeah, but how did you know?"

"Experience, I guess. I could tell by the way you were looking at the display."

For the next several minutes, Mark looked at various handguns, as the dealer described them. When Mark explained that he was looking for protection with something that would be inconspicuous, but powerful, the dealer nodded. "Well, that narrows it down to the pocket pistols or sub-compacts, as they're called."

With the dealer's help, Mark settled on a Glock G42 with a Lirisy ankle holster. The gun weighed just one pound with a loaded magazine of .380 caliber cartridges. The dealer gave him a thumbs up. "Good choice. As long as you're wearing long pants that aren't too tight around the ankles, no one will notice that you're carrying."

He then demonstrated the most effective way of unholstering the pistol. Standing in the aisle next to Mark, he dropped to his left knee, pulled up the cuff of his pants on the right leg and withdrew an imaginary weapon. He aimed it down the aisle, and said, "Bang."

He placed his invisible pistol back in its non-existent ankle holster and pulled down the pant leg. He stood up, rubbed his lower back with a hand, then smiled. "I would've demonstrated with a real gun, but I probably would've been thrown out of here. Either that or shot," he said with a laugh. "Look, since I'm not a private seller, you need to fill out a form and I'll run a background check. Okay?"

"Fine with me." Mark took the form, which was issued by the Federal Bureau of Alcohol, Tobacco, Firearms and Explosives. After filling in details about himself, he started answering the questions which were straightforward:

Have you ever been convicted of a felony? Have you ever been convicted of a misdemeanor crime of domestic violence? Are you a fugitive from justice? Have you ever been committed to a mental institution?

Mark quickly checked 'NO' to those questions, but paused when he came to a question accompanied with a warning. Are you an unlawful user of, or addicted to, marijuana or any other depressant, stimulant, narcotic drug, or any other controlled substance?

Warning: The use or possession of marijuana remains unlawful under Federal law, regardless of whether it has been legalized or decriminalized for medicinal or recreational purposes in the state where you reside.

He looked up and saw the dealer looking at him. "Just curious. What about a medical marijuana card holder?"

"Are you one, sir?"

Mark shook his head. "No, but I've considered it."

"Well, for a marijuana user even if he is a medical user, technically it's illegal to have a gun. There is no way they can buy a gun without committing perjury."

Mark quickly ticked another NO and moved on to the other questions.

"What next?" he asked, handing over the filled form.

"I just need to make a background check. It'll take a few minutes."

Mark had done his homework. The dealer would use the system created by FBI that was supposed to instantaneously let a firearms dealer know whether a buyer is legally allowed to purchase the gun. The system used a database called the National Instant Criminal Background Check System (NICS) to comb through their customer's records as it scans three federal databases—the National Crime Information Center, the Interstate Identification Index, and the NICS Index, for a match.

The dealer came back in a few minutes again with a thumbs up sign. "Everything is cool."

Mark used his credit card to make the payment. As he strolled about examining table after table of weapons, he saw a man walking with a backpack. A sheet of paper taped on the back of the backpack listed handguns and rifles along with the price details. Mark noticed that the Glock 19 listed on the backpack was priced $75 dollars less than what he had just paid. He figured the guy must be a private seller, and he knew that private gun sales in Georgia didn't require a background check, and that was known as the "gun show loophole." After that, he saw several vendors with signs that read: *Private Collection, Cash Only, No Questions.*

He meandered around a few minutes longer, then headed for the exit. As he crossed the parking lot towards his car, he saw the same lanky guy with sharp facial features that he'd seen talking to the dealer. Now he was standing behind his Toyota with the trunk open just two cars away from Marks' BMW. He was wearing a Georgia Tech tee and shorts that were too loose and riding below the waist, his checked boxer shorts peeking above them. Five younger males, surely no older than fourteen or fifteen, were crowded around, peering into the trunk. Mark stopped next to his car and watched the curious scene.

The man showed the kids a pistol, then stuffed it into a cloth bag, and pick up another one. Mark wasn't sure if he was witnessing a benign show-and-tell session or something much more sinister, the sale of firearms to minors. He was curious and wanted to know what the man was saying. When one of the kids looked over at him, he pretended to be scrolling his cell phone. He kept his head down as he listened. One of the kids called the man Dave, and Dave seemed to know the teenagers by name. By his brazen behavior, Dave either lacked fear of cops or was just stupid, thought Mark.

"That's not real, is it?" one of the boys teased. The other kids laughed. "Yeah, Dave, you're full of shit, I think," one of the others said.

Mark saw Dave shake his head in frustration, "The Casull cartridge for this little gem has been used to hunt animals as large as Cape Buffalo. You kids don't even know what that is."

"I know what a gun cartridge is. I also know what a buffalo is," one of the kids said. "But what the fuck is a Cape Buffalo? A bull dressed as Superman?"

The kids laughed.

"Biggest sub species, bovine. An ungulate inhabiting only limited areas of Africa."

The kids elbowed each other, snickered at the terminology, but Dave was oblivious as he continued to describe African buffalos, with equal emphasis to the specifications of the Taurus 454 Raging Bull, how it got its name and so forth.

"I don't believe it's all that great," the tallest of the boys said. "Man, this is all crap-talk unless you let us try out that baby. Let's go shoot!"

"Nobody touches my stuff," said Dave. "You can look, and that's it."

Mark peeked over his cell phone and observed the boys as they trivialized what seemed to be a massive amount of gun supply. "Bah! We've seen enough," the tall kid said, and motioned the others to leave.

Dave looked troubled as he neatly unzipped a pouch to put away ammunition. He certainly didn't look like a criminal type. Maybe he was just a geek. Maybe he had guns for sale as a private seller.

"Excuse me..." Mark called over to him.

Dave looked up and cupped his hand to his ear.

"I said, 'scuse me.." Mark said loudly.

"What?"

Mark motioned him over to his car.

Dave shut the trunk of his car and walked a few steps to the driver's side of Mark's car.

"Are you talking to me?" Dave asked.

"Yeah. This may seem strange to ask you, I mean you don't know me from Adam, but we bounced into each other a few times. I saw you at the shooting range earlier and today in the show, and now here in the parking lot."

"Who is Adam?"

"Adam?" Mark looked puzzled and then laughed, "That's just an expression."

"My name is David Pruitt. I go by Dave."

"Okay, well, I knew that."

"How do you know my name?"

"I overheard the kids calling you Dave. You should be careful when you talk about guns with teenagers."

"They are from my neighborhood and all of them have taken shooting lessons at ranges with their parents."

"Oh. Are you a private seller of guns?"

Dave shook his head. "I have some guns in my collection but I'm not really looking to sell them."

"I saw you at the range. You go there frequently?"

"Not really."

"Maybe we could meet up sometime, you know, and talk about guns. I'd really like to know more, and I think you're someone who could help me. I just made my first purchase today. I'd love to see your collection. Maybe I'll start my own collection down the road."

Dave looked toward the highway. "Down the road?"

"You're a character, Dave. I mean sometime later, you know, down the road."

"Yeah, down the road," Dave repeated, trying out the unfamiliar phrase.

They exchanged numbers, and Mark drove away. He immediately started feeling lonely. His mother's mental health was deteriorating fast, and she was no longer able to have meaningful conversations. He had no friends. All he could think about was his impending financial ruin and the prospect of drug gang thugs coming after him. He had no one he could talk to about his predicament. It was getting to be too much to handle.

5.2 Mindless Massacre

Construction on the new mosque had begun several weeks ago. Meanwhile, over the past year his mosque was merged with the next nearest Charlotte mosque, that was led by a conservative imam. It was an interim measure, but everyone from his community was anxious for the new mosque to be completed and open.

As they talked, he told his imam about the meeting he'd attended in Baghdad, and the radical group's plans for an attack. He confessed that he had informed the FBI about the meeting and gave them the slip of paper he had received from the imam in Baghdad.

"Brother, you did the right thing," the imam told him, gripping him by the shoulder.

But within days, rumors about his actions began to spread. Zamir told him that kids from the mosque were calling his dad a snitch. Soon the Muslim community began shunning not only Alim, but Rabia and Zamir. The invitations to the pot luck dinners stopped coming. The calls asking Alim for advice about their children stopped. Alim felt isolated, betrayed, and alone.

Still, every Friday, he arrived early at work so he could leave for an early lunch to drive to their interim mosque for the weekly Friday prayer that was like Sunday service for Christians. As he shaved one Friday, he was listening to National Public Radio on his phone when he heard something shocking.

The show's host read the breaking news. "A lone gunman has shot worshippers at two mosques in Christchurch, New Zealand. The shooter had videotaped his rampage on a Go Pro camera that he live-streamed to Facebook."

Alim put his razor down on the sink. His shoulders tensed, his heart racing. He took three steps backward into the bedroom.

"*Inna lillahi wa inna ilayhi raji'un,*" he whispered to himself, sinking onto the edge of the bed. His mother had taught him to say these words upon news of anyone's death. "We belong to Allah and to Allah we shall return."

It was from chapter two of the Qur'an, Al-Baqarah, verse 156. He flopped backwards onto the bed as images of his homeland flashed on his mind's eye. Al Qaeda's attacks on Shia mosques. Blood spilled on plush prayer carpets. Muslims killing Muslims. Alim knew many studies indicated that globally maximum people killed by the Muslim terrorist attacks are the Muslims themselves.

Now, what was happening, thousands of miles away in New Zealand?

Whites were now killing Muslims in mosques? Wasn't it enough that we were killing our own? Did they need to kill us too? Alim gripped his chest. He felt as if he'd been gunned down himself.

Didn't we have enough hate in our own Muslim community? Hate against other Muslim groups? Hate against the Jews? The Christians? Gays? Atheists? Now, the hate had come back at us, like a boomerang.

Many Muslims had spent so much energy, so many years, so many TV interviews, so many press releases, so many talking points, denying our extremism. Denying the Islam in Islamic state. Denying the jihad in violent jihadi terrorism. Covering up Wahhabism. Deobandism. Salafism. Call it by any name. It was perceived as an ideology of hate, extremism, and destruction.

It wasn't the Islam his mother had taught him. It wasn't the Islam he taught his son. But it was the Islam that embedded itself in the psyche of so many who feared Muslims and hated Islam.

There were equal number or for that matter far greater number of Muslims are continuously advocating peace and harmony. Advocating compassion for all. Expressing gratitude to non-Muslims for their contributions. Their voices don't get so much attention and coverage while every statement from extremists make headlines.

The townhall incident came back to him. Some participants calling out that every Muslim is a terrorist. Some trying to stop reconstruction of the mosque probably set on fire by people who believed that all Muslims are bad people. He was earnest and eager to explain that most Muslims believe in peace and harmony but not all locals supported him. Finally overall majority supported and reconstruction of the mosque has started. "No!" Alim shouted to the heavens. "No!" There had to be a better way, a way to pierce the distrust and the hate on both the sides.

# # #

5.3 Guns, Guns, Guns

In the first couple of weeks after Dave met Mark outside the gun show, they talked on the phone and exchanged emails. Mark was a new friend, who was keen on leveraging Dave's encyclopedic knowledge of his guns. For his part, Dave liked the fact that Mark wasn't judgmental about his Asperger's or about his passion for guns. After some hesitation, he finally scheduled a time to show Mark his guns and to loan him several issues of *Guns & Ammo* and *Firearms News*, which referenced some of the guns Mark was interested in acquiring.

"So tell me where you live and I'll pop over to take a gander at the stuff," Mark said over the phone.

"No," Dave said.

"What the fuck? What do you mean? You just said I could come see everything and you even had magazines to loan me."

"Let me finish. I said, no, because I don't keep my collection at home. I have everything locked and stored safely offsite. The reason for that is that I'm renting my apartment on the third floor, which is directly above dad's business. So, I don't want guns here for several reasons. I found a storage unit the size of my bedroom, and that's where I have everything locked up and stored."

"You mean like one of those storage facilities that have rows of tiny spaces with padlocks on metal doors?"

Dave shook his head. "Way better. I found this old guy who lives on several acres. He's got a portable building. It must be an acre out behind his house."

"Sweet. But where is it?"

"Southwest of the city, about thirty miles away."

"Are you hiding your guns from your parents?"

"They know I collect guns and magazines about guns. They just don't know the volume I have of either of them. I just can't seem to throw away the magazines and books I collect, so I've catalogued everything and set up shop at the shed. I don't want dad to know how many more guns I've bought in the last couple of years."

"Well, I want to see them."

"It's great there... it's like a man cave. Well, to me, it is. I could almost live there, if I had running water."

"Are you going to blather on all day? Can we just go?"

Dave picked up Mark an hour later and they made their way to I-20. It was about a 45-minute drive, much of which they spent talking about guns. For Mark, it was time well spent; he had Dave's undivided attention and he could ask virtually any question. Dave enjoyed talking about guns, but also quizzed Mark about his knowledge.

Before they reached the interstate, Mark asked: "So, Dave, how many assault rifles do you own?"

That term hurt Dave's ears. "I don't have any assault rifles."

"I thought you told me you had an AR-15."

"I do, but it's a semi-automatic carbine. An assault rifle is a battlefield weapon that's fully automatic like a machine gun, or a select-fire rifle."

"What's that?"

"A select fire rifle can fire either in a burst mode, automatic, or semi-auto depending on how the switch is set."

"But I thought the AR stood for assault rifle," Mark countered.

"Wrong. It stands ArmaLite Rifle, the name of the manufacturer who created the semi-automatic in the 1950s." Dave turned onto the entrance to I-20 and moved into the flow of traffic. "If you're going to get into collecting and going to the gun shows and shooting ranges, you need to know the proper terms."

"I'm not completely ignorant about guns. I know the difference between a handgun and a pistol."

"Oh, what is it?"

"All pistols are handguns, but not all handguns are pistols. There's also revolvers that have the circular cylinder for the bullets. Pistols are semi-autos."

When Dave didn't respond right away, Mark asked: "Well?"

"That's what a lot of people say nowadays, but if you study the history of guns you'll realize that's wrong. The term pistols was used long before semi-automatics were invented. By the late sixteenth century, pistols referred to all handguns. So handguns and pistols are interchangeable terms. Also, the NRA Firearms Sourcebook says, and I quote, that a pistol is a generic term for a hand-held firearm, often used more specifically to refer to a single-shot, revolver or semi-automatic handgun.'"

"Damn, you memorized that?"

"I find that memorizing things that I want to know is a good way of accumulating knowledge. But I don't memorize anything I don't understand. That would be like a parrot that memorizes the sounds and repeats them. But parrots are pretty smart, so who knows how much they understand. Regardless, I am not like a parrot."

"Yeah, I get that, Dave."

"Do you know the difference between a pocket pistol and a sub-compact?"

Mark shrugged. "Sound like the same thing to me."

"No. A sub-compact is a small, concealed-carry-friendly version of a full-size pistol. For example, the Springfield XD 9mm Subcompact has a 3-inch barrel compared to the 5-inch barrel of the full-size 9mm XD. A pocket pistol is a standalone model that's unrelated to any larger pistol."

"But pocket pistols and sub-compacts are the same size, right?"

Dave shook his head. "There are no standard dimensions. They vary among manufacturers. But sub-compact barrels are typically around 3.25 inches. The overall length is usually about 6.2w5 inches. Some with stubby barrels are a bit shorter."

"What other terms should I know if I'm buying a gun?"

"Do you know the difference between a bullet and a cartridge?"

"Tell me."

"A bullet is the projectile that exits the barrel. It's a piece of lead, copper or other material, including rubber. The cartridge includes the case, primer, propellant and projectile. When you go to the gun store, you ask for cartridges of a particular caliber that fits your gun, not for bullets. The caliber is the diameter of the bullet. A magazine is a device that holds ammo and has spring action that feeds cartridges into the gun's chamber."

"Got it. So what's the difference between a magazine and clip?"

"Glad you asked. A clip feeds cartridges into a magazine."

"How did you develop such passion for guns?"

"It started in high school, when I was a junior. Something happened at school that messed me up."

"And so you went out and bought a gun on the street from someone?"

Dave laughed. "No, that's not it."

When Dave didn't offer anything further, Mark pushed him. "C'mon, Dave, tell me. I'm your friend. I won't be judgmental."

It took a few moments for Dave to find a way to begin his story. "You see, I never understood the high school hierarchies and non-verbal rules of the group."

"You mean you didn't have any friends?"

"I wasn't part of any clique and didn't recognize that these two guys, Andy and Jeffrey, were bullies and leaders of a pack."

"Ah, the big bad wolves. So, you messed with them?"

"There was this incident where those two guys sat down at the nerd table at lunch. They never sat there and I didn't know what that meant. The other guys were sitting very still and not talking. I tapped Andy on the shoulder and told him that he was in my seat. He turned around and said it didn't have my name on it."

"What did you say to that?"

"I said that they need to move it. They got up from the table, laughing. Jeffery put a hand on my shoulder, which I didn't like, even though I thought he was trying to be friends. Then Andy punched me in the gut and they walked away."

"Did you report them?"

"No, the others guys said it was best just to ignore them. But after that they began bullying me in the hall, calling me names, hitting and pushing me when I walked by. I was puzzled and didn't understand why they were so hostile towards me. Sometimes, I would freeze or crouch down under a stairwell."

"Did you finally report them?"

"I could never explain it to the teachers. I was living in fear. I still feel a sense of dread just thinking about them."

"That's too bad. But how did all this lead you to guns? Did you want to shoot them?"

Dave shook his head. "No, nothing like that. One day they forced me into playing dodgeball. Andy put his hands on his hips and stood about ten feet away, and asked me to throw the ball at his face. I didn't realize that he was just showing off in front of others and to establish his authority over me. He yelled at me to hit him on his face with everything I got. I took him literally. While he was grinning and continued to say come on retard, I turned my body away from Andy, to get my throwing arm behind me, took a step forward and used my arm to convert all that force into propulsion for the ball."

"Yeah, yeah, but what happened?" Mark asked.

"Andy didn't realize what I was doing. His hands were still on his hips. The ball broke his nose. It took him two weeks to recover."

Mark laughed. "That is hilarious. Well done. The son of a bitch got his due. Did he leave you alone after that?"

"Unfortunately not. When he came back, four of them locked me in a toilet stall and punched the hell out of me. I had cuts and bruises all over my body. I wished I was dead. I limped back home somehow and refused to go back to high school. I was very adamant. When my math teacher called, I cried. I loved math and really enjoyed the math classes."

"What did your parents do? Did they lodge a complaint?"

"They did, but I wouldn't go back to school. My dad told me he was very disappointed. He tried his best, but I wouldn't budge. He was desperate to get me back into school. As a last-ditch effort, he drove me to a local shooting range. He said that no one would ever bully me physically if I could protect myself."

"Wow, that was radical."

"My mother didn't like it. But I fell in love with shooting the very first day and it has grown since then."

"Did you get a hunting license at that age?"

"My dad had a hunting license and I went hunting under his direct supervision. First, I got my education certificate and later the license. I've studied everything about guns since then."

"I believe it."

Dave was impressed that Mark was listening and following him so intently. Besides his mother, the only other person he could open up himself up to was Laura. But he never discussed guns with either of them. Laura probably wasn't even aware of his fascination with guns. He started to like Mark more, because he seemed to respect him and appreciated his knowledge of firearms.

"Dave, I know how you feel about bullies. I've had some people bullying me lately and I hate it."

"I'm sure you would feel safer if you have a gun to defend yourself."

"That's true."

Dave was surprised by how quickly they reached the dirt road leading to the house where his storage shed was located. When he stopped at the gate, Dave let out a low whistle. "You were right, Dave. This is very private and countrified. I like it. I can't wait to see what you've got out here. Maybe you can loan me a gun or two?"

Chapter 6

6.1 Fingers Crossed

Every time Mark found an e-mail from one of his former clients, he worried that it would be another threat—a law suit or a threat of violence. But this morning, a former client who had lost thousands, sent him an attachment, an article about Happ! in the business section of the Atlanta Journal. An anonymous employee at the tech company had told a reporter that Happ! had exaggerated the revenue potential of its new product to increase its valuation during acquisition talks. If they hadn't fudged these numbers, the acquisition talks would never have started.

Mark called Brian, who confirmed that Happ! top brass had fudged the accounts and artificially increased the valuation of the company. Mark felt even more victimized and more convinced that the odds were stacked against him, that the social norms had collapsed, that everyone in business was out to cheat and steal. The scales needed to be made right.

He reached out to Stacey, hoping to meet her for lunch. If anyone, she would understand how he felt. "No way," she told him, before hanging up on him.

He wanted to tell her how crooks had wronged him at Happ!, but she wasn't interested. He sent her text messages, mentioned all the money he'd spent on her, and asked her to talk to him, even if she wouldn't meet him. She threatened to report him for harassment and blocked his number.

# # #

He visited his mother, who turned eighty-four today. She lay in bed in her nightgown, holding a small stuffed bear. A birthday balloon floated near the ceiling, and a baseball cap that said WILD WOMAN, lay on a chair, her eyes looking straight ahead, expressionless. "Happy birthday, Mom."

Her lips moved, but no words came out. It seemed that she could no longer engage in conversation. Even the short answers had stopped. She was blank, expressionless.

A nurse who came to the room to check on her said, "Your mom had a big day today on her birthday. We had a pineapple cake. You can talk to her, but she won't understand."

"I know. It's very sad."

"You need to move her to twenty-four hour care. She's getting to the point where she can't bathe or dress herself without help."

"Thank you. I know she needs more help than she's getting."

Sleepless and surfing the TV, he stayed with his mother and watched the news about a shooting earlier in the day at a restaurant in which six people were shot, three of them killed, in the outdoor seating area. The shooter had walked by the diners and randomly fired shots, then run off. Authorities were searching for a cook, who had been fired by the restaurant two days earlier.

Random shootings were commonplace now, and with only three dead the incident would quickly fade into the past, Mark thought. Even shootings that received widespread attention, like the Las Vegas mass shooting at an outdoor concert, soon disappeared from the headlines. Mark vaguely recalled hearing quite a while ago that the FBI had closed the investigation on the Las Vegas mass shooting.

He hadn't pursued the story any farther, but now he was curious about the shooter's motive. He went to Google and within seconds the FBI's report from January 2019 was on his screen. The investigators concluded that there wasn't a single or definite motivating factor. He started watching every YouTube video he could find on the Las Vegas shooting, then spent the rest of the night watching other mass shooting videos.

Late into the night, his mother dozing soundly beside him, Mark found videos that Ryan Jasper, a student from Michigan, had recorded before he murdered ten people and wounded twenty two others in 2008 at Michigan Institute of Arts & Science in Detroit. The words captivated him more than any other he had read, and he started to read again and again the parts of the message.

You trashed my dreams, wrecked my hopes and ravaged my path. You turned blind when I'm in front of you and turned deaf when I spoke. You smiled when I'm in pain and scoffed when I tried to smile.

Do you know what it feels like when you crawl for a mile and arrive at a mirage? Do you know what it feels like to kneel in prayer for a lifetime and never receive a single answer?

You had everything but that was not enough. You had expensive cars and boats. You had dollars and diamonds. What you had was never enough for you. All your debaucheries wouldn't satisfy your hedonistic cravings. It was not enough that you were in heaven. You had to peep into hell for that extra pleasure.

You thought you can cripple my conscience, murder my mind, steal my soul and watch the fun. I refuse to be a shadow, a phantom being, a freak show. I will no longer hide, no longer flee. I am striking back. I die as a hero, an inspiration for generations of the downtrodden to come.

Your expensive wines will now forever taste like blood. Your dreams will only be nightmares. Your memories will always be painful. That is how it should be as I am just a bullet that you triggered. The fingerprints on the gun are yours's. Not mine. You will rot in hell for this evil act. Not me

"Genius message. Isn't it mom?" he asked. His mother had woken up, but she didn't reply.

"Remember the silver medal I won?"

"Hmmmmm?"

256

"Come on mom... you remember. The competition at the lake? Please tell me you remember?"

"Okay."

"I was supposed to get the gold medal, you know. I was thinking about that last night. The quizmaster was friends with Kevin's dad and asked him easy questions. I told you. Don't you remember?"

She nodded.

"Mom, that gold medal was supposed to be mine! Do you hear me? It was mine. Are you hearing me? It always happens to me, mom. Why does what is mine get snatched away from me? I'm not a loser, mom. I'm not." He was growing aggravated.

She patted him.

"I just finished work on a big plan, mom. I wanted you to be the first to know, because it's top-secret work that I'm about to carry out. You're going to see it on the news. On TV."

His mom was a bit more responsive now. "Is it a big surprise for *me?*" she asked.

"It is... and if dad were here, it would be his surprise, too."

"Oooooh!" She squeezed the stuffed bear. "Will there be balloons?"

He laughed. "Do you like fireworks?"

"Oh, yes! I love fireworks. At the beach? Will I get candies and cookies?" she asked.

"Mom, no, not at the beach, not like that. I don't know yet where it will be, but it won't be the beach. You're thinking of the Fourth of July celebrations. Mom! Listen, this is different than that! Bigger! Get the idea out of your head that it's a copycat of Fourth of July. Jesus Christ, mom, this is important and *bigger*. Listen, listen to me, because you're going to see it on TV."

"This is bigger?" she said, stretching her hands.

"Mom."

"Yes?"

"Look at you. You always helped your brothers and sisters and their kids. I called them, mom, and they don't have time to come and see you. They say they are sorry, but don't mean it, mom. They don't care. "

She was irritated now and didn't answer.

"Are you listening, mom? I want you to listen."

"Okay."

"I tried, mom. I don't want to punish them, but I have no other option. My act will immerse them in a sea of grief, but that is what their actions did to me. They will curse me; they will be sick of me, but that is what they deserve, mom. They have created a cruel society, and I'm a victim. I'm not a loser, mom. I am going to get even, and end up the winner I always wanted to be."

She didn't say anything.

"You approve my actions. Don't you mom?"

She was still silent. Mark reached out to her and gently helped her get out of the bed and sit in a chair. "Where are the aides this morning? They should be here helping you."

He went down on one knee and hugged her. "You want me to stop, mom? Remember you said medal or no medal, you will always love me. Do you still love me mom?" he asked, almost in a whisper. "Hug me back, mom."

His hug provoked a violent reaction in his mom, and she started screaming.

An aide hurried in and helped her back into bed.

"It would be good if she rests now."

Mark stood up, gave his mom a long look and left. He walked out, as if he was in a trance.

# # #

Just like yesterday, he didn't go to the office. He went to the shooting range again. He was testing Dave's guns. Yesterday, he worked with two semi-auto pistols. Today, it will be the AR-15. Dave was pressuring him to return the guns, and he couldn't hold him off much longer. He needed to buy his own guns.

He loved the feel of the AR-15 in his hands when he took it out of its case at the lane he'd been assigned. Since he wasn't renting the gun from the range, all he needed was the ammunition and the targets, ear plugs and goggles. He fired off three magazines as rapidly as he could until each one was spent. He didn't care how accurate he was with individual shots. When you fired this many shots in rapid succession, something was going to hit.

When he left, he felt charged and ready. Something was coming up. He just needed to figure out what it was, where it was.

# # #

Later that day at the apartment, he opened his laptop and started typing.

"I am crossing over to the dark side. I know it all right. I tried staying on your side. As I stand on the edge of darkness and look at you, I realize that I am just an ugly manifestation of the world we live in. You have created a fucked-up society where so many of us feel alone, left out and irrelevant. At times I do know that I am turning into a monster not able to deal with my painful loneliness and irrelevance that is extenuated by indifferent bastards around me.

"I am not a fucking solitary wolf; I am human, and I need to connect. I need something to cling onto. I have my eyes on you guys. In work places, in homes, in schools, in public places I am observing how you bastards create hostility to cover your ass by ganging up and mocking and punishing weak people.

"Do you ever care about anyone but yourself? I think it is okay to cross over to the dark side in such a selfish world. But I haven't given up yet. I will try and try hard to stay connected and find something to hang onto. I don't know when my patience will run out, though. Fingers crossed."

6.2 They never call it Christian Terrorism

Even for Rabia who was always strong and ferociously righteous the slaying of 51 Muslims in the New Zealand mosques was too much to cope. The gutting of local mosque was still fresh in her mind though she sided with Alim that without solid proof it cannot be tagged as a hate crime. She went into a mild depression and was fearful of things that can happen to Zamir as he grows up in a world full of hate. She was fearful of going to the mosque and said. "Let us pray in the home for now."

Alim was devasted to see her so vulnerable. Grief and anger consumed him. No matter how badly some fringe groups of Muslims had responded to the problems with extremism, there was no justification for the slaying of innocents. It could have been him, his wife, his son, his friends. And, now as he stepped into the mosque's main hall, he wondered: could it be them next?

He slipped into a row in the back and moved through two *rakats*, or prostrations of prayer, before settling onto the carpet to hear the Friday sermon. "We are called to condemn extremism in Islam. And we do: we condemn Muslim extremists," the imam said, as if reading Alim's mind. "What about Christian extremists? Why don't we use that name? Do Christians disavow the hate in the name of their faith?"

Alim jolted to attention. Sure, Christians must condemn the violence in their communities. But the imam was talking apples and oranges. We still had a disturbing ideology of Islam, being preached from our pulpits, teaching hate. Christians had been called to task for violence they had sanctioned, such as calling their wars holy and the terrible excesses of the Spanish Inquisition. And now they recognized, for the most part, that the terrible violence they'd promoted was wrong. They acknowledged 'with great shame' and apologized for Church's use of violence in the past. They apologized to Jews, women, Muslims killed by crusaders and for over 100 wrong doings. That is the public position they have taken on violence committed in name of Christianity. That's where Muslims had to get to."

Whatever the name, though, the hate was real. Would his path of self-righteousness work in such a mad world? Alim too felt very vulnerable.

Outside in the parking lot, he opened the Telegram app on his phone and called the imam he'd met in Iraq. He had told the FBI about him, but he'd kept his phone number, and now he wanted to hear the imam's reaction to the mass killing of Muslims. May be he now recognized the futility of revenge. An eye for eye leaving the whole world blind.

"We will get vengeance for the blood our brothers and sisters spilled! We will strike back!" the imam said.

Alim's heart sank as the imam continued: "The prophecy is written. The days of *qiyaamat* are coming."

He was talking about Islamic 'end times'. The Muslim apocalypse. Christians had their Book of Revelations. Muslims had their *hadith*, which spelled out the signs that would portend the end times. They included: men on black horses from Khorasan, a region in the modern day northern Afghanistan and Iran; a *dajjal*, or Muslim version of an anti-Christ; the *Mahdi*, or Muslim messiah.

"Haven't you seen the signs? Tsunamis. Earthquakes. Men marrying men. Women marrying women. Children born outside wedlock. *Yahudis* everywhere, controlling everything?"

The Jews. It always ended with the Jews.

Alim focused again on the conversation. The imam was actually trying to sell him on the idea that seventy-two virgins awaiting for any man, including Alim, who sacrificed his life for the greater good of Islam. Alim struggled not to laugh out loud. He'd read a translation by a Bangladeshi-American playwright that said it was actually 72 *grapes* that martyrs received. Not virgins. Grapes.

He thought about the imam's proposition for another moment. He would pass. He wasn't that fond of grapes, anyway.

# # #

That night Rabia turned to Alim and said softly, "I will also come to the mosque from tomorrow. For the inter faith vigil."

She pursed her lips, defiantly. She didn't have to speak a word. He knew that look. She was determined to stand up to the fear that gripped her heart. Local community members had asked the imam if they could host an interfaith vigil for the lives lost in New Zealand.

263

After he and the host imam at their temporary mosque agreed to the vigil, word quickly spread.

"We must go," she whispered.

When they arrived at the mosque, the parking lot was filled. Cars also filled the curbside slots on the neighboring streets. A steady stream of congregants and visitors walked past them as they rounded a corner and finally found a parking spot.

Alim took his wife's hand and led his son inside the main hall. Rows of folding chairs now covered the space where the congregation had prayed earlier in the day. A rabbi stood in front of at least three hundred guests.

"We are with you," the rabbi said.

Alim knew how much hate still existed within the community against Jews. The rabbi probably knew also. But, still, there he stood, in solidarity with their community. Alim recognized a woman in the front row. It was the blonde woman from the city planning meeting, the one who had yelled in fear about sharia courts coming to Charlotte. She caught his eye and rushed over.

"I'm so sorry," she said.

Alim looked around him. A rabbi says he was with us, the Muslims. A woman who feared Muslims was now sympathetic. But when the shock of the tragedy in New Zealand receded, where would their sympathies lie? Which path was the truly righteous one, which path would he choose?

6.3 Dave's Nightmare

It was an unseasonably chilly afternoon when Dave made a second trip of the day to the duck pond. He parked in the lot next to the larger event space building and walked over to the pond. He also came here this afternoon because it was near the site of a volunteer project he was working on.

He stopped as he spotted Laura sitting alone on a park bench overlooking the pond.

He smiled and moved ahead, noticing that Laura was wearing a red sweater and her face was buried in a paperback. Three months had passed since she'd moved back to Atlanta. She'd come over for dinner and afterwards, she and Dave had taken a walk to an ice cream shop. It was good to see her again, but it was still difficult to know that she would be living in the same city and yet they would never be as close as they once were.

He stopped in front of her, but didn't say anything. Her big eyes looked up at him and her mouth opened into a broad, toothy grin, "Fancy meeting you here, Mr. Pruitt!"

"Oh, you can just call me Dave still."

She laughed. "Sometimes I don't know when you're serious and when you're joking."

"Well, I don't joke very well. And, when I'm serious, people sometimes find me funny. But when I'm being funny, people don't laugh."

"Seriously? I'll laugh at your jokes, Dave."

"Good, and thanks for calling me Dave."

She stood up and wrapped her arms around his neck, a hot dog in one hand, the book in the other. "Don't be so silly. You know we will always be good friends." Normally, Dave hated any public display of affection, any touch at all, really. But he never minded being close to Laura, and now it brought back the old feelings of longing in his heart.

But he pushed it away. "That hot dog smells good."

"I'm having a late lunch. You, too?" She stepped back and took a bite.

He nodded. "I am kind of hungry."

"Then go get one; come back and plant your butt here next to me!"

"Plant my butt?"

She laughed and patted the bench. "Sit with me."

"Yeah, I will." He turned away and headed to the food truck. He was still occasionally getting fooled by slang phrases. He used to collect them and their meanings in a notebook, but after college he threw it away, thinking he knew all the idioms—those phrases that said one thing and meant another, or even the opposite. He was wrong about that.

When he returned to the bench, he sat down and muttered, "Planting my butt."

"Hot dog!" Laura answered.

He frowned. "Yes, it is. Just like yours. Oh, wait, was that another idiom?"

266

"I guess. Actually, it was kind of a joke, too. It's another way of saying that I'm happy you're here—hot dog! And you had a hot dog in your hand. Get it?"

"I think I understand that. Hot dog, me too. Glad to see you here." He took a bite, then said, "I learned so much slang when we were together in college, you know."

"Yeah, that was a long time ago. How are things going with your job? Still with your father's company, right?"

"Going okay, it's just plumbing. But I like to work on the plumbing design for new buildings, and the re-design of old ones."

"Cool."

"I've also got a special project I'm working on now with an architect, and it's not plumbing, either. I'm designing a small skatepark on the other side of the pond near the smaller building on the right."

"Really? A skatepark. How did you get that project?"

"It came to me through a Georgia Tech alumni group I joined. Many of the companies in the tech corridor recruit from Georgia Tech so this is a way for the school to contribute to the corridor."

"Nice. But what kind of design is involved with a skatepark? Isn't just like a big empty swimming pool without the steep sides?"

"That design doesn't work very well because everyone is skating in the same area. Too many chances for creating crash-up derbies."

"What?"

"You know, collisions. So I'm creating skating pods for different skill levels and keeping skaters in separate areas."

"I can't wait to see it."

"How's your job, Laura?"

"So far so good. Greenville was beautiful, but quiet. I like the buzz of the city. Happy to be back in Atlanta."

"I'm happy that you moved back."

"How are your parents?"

"Good. You should come over for dinner again."

"Yeah, I will one of these days, with Bill."

She tapped on her phone and showed him pictures of her and Bill from a recent trip to Miami. "He had a business thing there, and I went along. We spent a couple of extra days there."

Dave stared at the photos, including one where she and Bill were cheek to cheek, smiling. When he didn't offer any comment, Laura said, "I think you'll like Bill when you meet him."

"I'm sure you're really happy that he was able to follow you to Atlanta."

"Oh, he wanted to go right away, but decided it was better if he kept his job in Greenville until he found something here."

After an awkward moment of silence, Laura asked, "By the way, I saw you here from a distance the other day. I had to get back to work, so I couldn't come over and talk."

"Was I feeding the ducks?"

"No, you were talking to a guy. Do you remember, who was that?"

"Oh, that was my new friend, Mark. We have something in common that we're very passionate about."

"Oh, really, tell me."

"We are both all about guns. I'm a big collector."

"Guns? You collect guns? You never told me that."

"Do you own a gun?"

"No."

"See. Not much to say. Unless you and Bill would like to become gun owners. I could show you everything you need to know."

"Thanks, Dave. But Bill thinks there are too many guns in the hands of Americans. I guess I agree."

"I understand. Some people don't abide by the rules of gun ownership."

"Or the laws."

"Yes, too much of that. But I don't want to talk about politics, Laura. It's not my favorite part of the gun world."

"Well, I'm glad you have someone, a new friend, to talk to, about guns."

"Me, too. But I'm getting a little concerned about Mark's interest in my guns."

"Really, why?

"He's obsessed with guns. Well, so am I. He wants to buy half a dozen guns from my collection - maybe more."

"You want to sell them?"

"It would help me pay off my credit card debt, but I would hate to lose my collection."

"What are you going to do?"

"I lent him the guns. So he could try them out, to find out which ones he wants to buy from a gun shop, if not from me."

Laura looked concerned. "Dave, is this guy someone who might go down a bad path? These are weapons! It's not like you're talking about you loaning out a book or something. I don't like what I'm hearing."

"Mark wants me to get him a really large supply of the ammunition, too. I'm just wondering why he wants so much. I mean a collector just collects the gun - not cartridges."

"Dave, just tell him 'no'. Don't buy him any ammunition, and get your guns back, if he's got them."

He finished his hot dog and looked straight ahead.

"Now you're being quiet."

He shrugged. "I'm just thinking."

"You're a good guy. I know you'll do the right things. I've got to get back to work. Ciao." She collected her bag and walked off.

Dave remained seated, staring into the pond.

# # #

The talk with Laura was both helpful, but also distressing. It brought to light what had been weighing heavily on Dave's mind and gave some direction. But that night he had trouble falling asleep and couldn't stop thinking about the situation with Mark. He felt paralyzed because he didn't like confrontations, especially with a friend. It took a few days, but Dave finally decided to send Mark a text message.

You done with the six guns I lent you? Do you want to return them to me?

A few minutes later, Mark replied.

I'd like to hold on. You'll sell them all to me, right?

Dave's breathing intensified and his hands shook as he typed his reply.

Not selling them. I want my collection complete. They are registered to me. You need to make your gun purchases legal and with the proper documentation.

Mark: *Dave, man, I thought you were going to help me! This is a bummer.*

Dave: *Sorry. I can give you the contact information and you can buy your own from the same dealers I dealt with, if that helps.*

When Mark didn't immediately respond, Dave worried that his friend was mad and that wouldn't return his guns. He thought about what Laura had said; how worried she'd seemed. More determined than ever, he wrote again.

Can I stop by to pick them up?

Mark responded in pieces.

I'm out to dinner....

If I can't buy yours, will you help me buy them from dealers?

Can we get together tomorrow to do that?

Dave answered right away.

Yes, after you return my guns.

Although he felt the communications went well, Dave was still feeling insecure as he waited for Mark that evening in a parking lot a mile from his apartment. Mark lugged a large gym bag from his trunk to Dave's. Dave immediately opened the bag, found four guns and without comment placed them into a cabinet and locked it.

He slowly turned to Mark. "What about the other two guns, the semi-autos?"

"I haven't tried them yet. I'll get them back to you once I do. I'm a little disappointed, Dave, that you won't sell me any of them. But I know how you get. You know... the autism thing, Asperger's, whatever you call it. I don't want you to flip out on me, that's why I brought them back so quickly."

Dave's shoulders tensed. "I don't flip out."

"I'm not saying you do. I'm being sensitive, but I need a favor. I want to get these guns immediately. I mean, can you start working on it tonight and make some call tomorrow for me? The licensing, everything? I want you to come with me when I pick them up, and I want to go to the same dealers where you made your purchases. I want you to set everything up."

"Why can't you do it?"

"I'm asking you because you're the expert, and I trust you. You know I've got a shit-ton going on at the office, so I will pay you for your time, pay you well. "

"I can make some calls."

"Look, Dave, the quicker you do this for me, the faster you'll have all your guns back."

"How do I know you'll give them back?"

"Because I'll be buying my own."

These situations were difficult for Dave. He wanted very badly to trust his friend, but he also wondered if Mark was taking advantage of him. It had been a long time since he had a male friend, and the two of them had shared a lot of laughs. He hoped the friendship was real, an unbreakable bond.

"Do you really need my help?"

"Duhhhhhhh. Yes, I need you my friend. Please."

"I'll do it."

Chapter 7

Day of the Shooting

7.1 The Headquarters

Alim left home after an early lunch and set out on a four-hour-plus drive to the Happ! headquarters in the Atlanta Tech Corridor. This evening would be the company's big party celebrating ten years in business. A young company with many young employees. At forty-five, he was one of the older members of the Happ! team. He was looking forward to the event with food, music and drinks, and a chance to renew acquaintances. More than a dozen people he had known at the Charlotte Happ! office had migrated to headquarters over the past couple of years as the company expanded.

His boss had offered Alim a promotion with a raise, but it would've required moving to Atlanta. He'd turned it down, which probably meant that he wouldn't advance any further with the company. But it was hardly a sacrifice. He was paid well and enjoyed his job for the most part. He'd lived and worked in Charlotte ever since he'd gotten his PhD at UNC and was hired by a tech company. He and Rabia were established in the community. Rabia enjoyed her job as a college counselor, and Zamir didn't want to leave his hometown, school, and life-long friends.

As he motored along at seventy-five miles an hour on I-85, he tried to relax and think about this day as one to enjoy, joining fellow workers in a festive event to celebrate the company's success. But that wasn't so easy for him. A niggling thought kept creeping into his mind.

He'd taken an action three months ago that he'd felt was necessary, but one that could've endangered his career. He'd become a whistle blower, exposing the glitches in the software in an anonymous leak to the media. He'd acted after he realized that management was pushing ahead with the release of the software in spite of unresolved glitches. A contact from the Los Angeles company that had taken over the security duties on the project from Alim's team had asked him for information. From what Alim had gathered in the conversation, the company's fix on the glitch had resulted in new issues, and regardless, the Happ! management was moving ahead.

After the leak, there was another news that accounts were fudged to increase the valuation. Happ! stock took a beating, but the company management reacted quickly. They sent out a press release saying that from the moment they were aware of the glitch, they immediately informed all relevant stakeholders and made a concerted effort to fix the issue. They followed that with an update that they'd found a solution to the glitch. When questioned by reporters about acquisition, they responded that they didn't comment on market speculation. The stock recovered and the company tied in that news with the announcement of the tenth anniversary celebration.

Alim was relieved that Happ! had taken the proper action to repair the glitch and that everything was on schedule for a release of the software. However, he'd also heard rumors that management was attempting to identify the source of the leak, and that worried him. No one had questioned him about it, and he hadn't seen Josh Lane, the CEO, since he'd leaked the information. He was concerned though that if he bumped into the CEO while at headquarters, that Lane would look at him, see something in his expression, and know that he was the one. Or worse, that Lane would call him into his office and ask him directly. No doubt Alim would admit that he was the one.

But the more he thought about it, the more he realized that worrying about it was useless. There was nothing he could do about it. He'd done what was right. If he paid a price for it, so be it.

Those thoughts reminded him of how the local Muslim community had reacted to him and his family after he'd gone to the FBI and exposed the imam and his plans for a violent attack. In his estimation, the eye-for-an-eye attitude of some Muslims would only make the whole world blind. He'd taken action and he stood behind it, no matter what the consequences. He felt the same way about his work ethics. In both matters, he was at peace with what he'd done.

Yet, he wasn't happy with the foreign policies of the west in the Mideast. He was sure it was all about controlling the oil. The long-term solution, he believed, was for the countries to bring in social and religious reforms based on values of peace, welfare and pluralism. He knew it is easier said than done.

He'd become so wrapped in his thoughts that he was surprised by how quickly the time had past. It seemed he'd only left an hour or two ago when he pulled into the parking lot adjacent to the Happ! headquarters. He stepped out of his car, took a deep breath, ready for whatever awaited him. Holding his head high, a smile on his face, he headed for the front door.

7.2 The Sign

Mark was sitting at his kitchen table feeling groggy from lack of sleep and being hung over. He pushed aside an empty bottle of vodka, a reminder of last night's private binge, and stared at a text message on his phone. He blinked, focusing, and saw it was from Brian, the finance manager at Happ! He read it slowly, let it sink in, read it again. The stock was back up to 90 percent of its value before the plunge. Yeah, if he'd only invested in Happ! stock, the loss wouldn't have been catastrophic. But he'd gambled in the derivatives market, and lost nearly everything.

Brian had attached links to media coverage about the tenth anniversary of Happ! at an event space at the Atlanta Tech Corridor. Just as he hit one of the links, he heard a pounding on his door. He set his phone down and stood up. He wasn't expecting anyone. *What the hell? Who could this be? How did they get into the building?*

The pounding continued as he walked toward the door. He had a bad feeling. They were coming for him. He stepped aside in case they started shooting through the door. He had nowhere to go, nowhere to hide. His only hope was that they would go away, but at the moment that didn't seem very likely.

"Mark McCarthy, open up! We need to talk." The voice was calm, but firm.

When he didn't answer, a gruff voice growled. Open up, McCarthy! Now!"

Was this really happening? Maybe it was a bad dream.

No, it's happening, a voice said. *Bad people, bad people. At your door. Here they come.*

He backed away, then heard a laugh, a sarcastic laugh. *They're coming for you, Mark. They're coming for you. They won't stop.* The derisive laugh again. He covered his ears with his palms, but it didn't help. The pounding continued, the voice in his head laughed louder.

Then abruptly it all stopped. No voice, no pounding. Did they go away? Maybe they were never there. Maybe he'd imagined it, all of it. Lack of sleep. That had to be it. Nobody was coming for him. He was safe.

Prove it. The voice again.

"Okay, I will," he muttered. He walked to the door, paused, listened. Another minute passed. He unlocked the deadbolt, opened the door a few inches, stretching the chain, and peered out. "Hello, who's there?" No response. He smiled, relieved. "See, no one." He closed the door, unlatched the chain, then opened it wider. *Bad move! Bad move!*

Suddenly, a hand reached around the door frame and clamped onto his throat. Two hulking beasts rushed him, pushing him into the apartment. One of the men closed the door, then joined his partner, who was lifting up Mark by the throat and pushing him into the kitchen. "Where's the money, McCarthy? You are out of time."

Mark tried to say something, but the only thing that came out of his mouth was a gurgling sound. The thug lowered him, released his throat and grabbed his shirt collar. "The money, McCarthy. You got it?"

"It's gone, lost in the stock market."

"Not the right answer." He slapped Mark hard across the jaw and his head jerked back. The other thug planted a fist into his gut. "Any better answers?"

"I've lost it all."

Fists and feet pounded him from all sides. He covered his head with his arms and crumbled to the floor. The intruders kicked and stomped on his back, his ribs, his legs. He curled into a foetus position and one thought broke through, one desire, one hope. He reached down, pulled up his pant leg, and yanked the Glock out of its holster. He twisted around rolling onto his back and fired, one shot at each of the startled men. They stumbled back and he fired again. They collapsed and he slowly sat up. One of the men was still moving and he fired a shot into his forehead.

Mark dropped the gun, gasping for breath. He struggled not to pass out, but collapsed into unconsciousness. When he awakened, he winced at the pain, but managed to sit up. Two bodies lay on the kitchen floor in pools of blood. What was he going to do? Slowly, he reached for the kitchen table and pulled himself up into a chair.

He ran his hands over his torso feeling the bruises. He might have a couple of cracked ribs, but it would've been a lot worse if he hadn't stopped them. The voice again: *Good job, Mark. And now you're really fucked.*

"No I'm not," he responded. He would call the cops and tell them that these two men had broken into his apartment, began beating him up, and he'd killed them in self-defense. Sure, they'd believe him. Strangers, his own home, self-defense. That was a sure winner. He was about to call 911, but hesitated. If the authorities began investigating who the men were, they would ask more questions. Why did they come after him,:why was he armed inside his house, why did he open the door? Eventually, if they persisted, his corrupt dealings with the drug boss would be exposed.

Even if he managed to avoid getting pinpointed as a player in a drug money laundering scheme, the boss would come after him again, and this time no doubt the end result would be torture and death. He was fucked.

He started feeling more and more desperate as blood from the bodies crept towards him. He was trapped and there was no way out. The only thing he could do was strike out against the injustice of it all.

He looked down at his phone, tapped it, and saw the link that Brian has sent him.

It was an online news story about the tenth anniversary of Happ! at the event space in the Atlanta Tech corridor.

They are celebrating your annihilation, you fucking loser! They are all in it together mocking you.

He stepped around the bodies, nearly slipping on the blood. He didn't know what to do with the bodies. He had no plan, no future. As far as he was concerned, all was lost. He hobbled to the bathroom and slowly peeled off his t-shirt, jeans and underwear, wincing several times in the process. He turned on the shower and stepped right under the cold water that hit his head ran down his face and over his body, numbing the bruises.

He stood under the shower until his brain calmed down. Finally, he turned off the water, grabbed a towel, and stared at himself in the mirror. He hadn't shaved for days. He told his portfolio managers that he was down with a bad flu. Over the last few days, he'd slept for less than three hours. Last night, he hadn't sleep at all. He started drying his hair.

He closed his eyes, and another voice spoke, his father's voice. *You are special Mark. You will make us proud one day.* There was no question about it. It was him. He felt a pat on his back and spun around. Nobody there. He stared at the bathroom door as a thought came to mind. He ran into the hall, picked up his phone, and stared at Brian's message again. He looked at the date for the event. It was this evening! It was perfect. It was the answer. What better way to strike back! All was not lost. Big Bang time, he thought and laughed.

"It's a sign, Dad. Oh, my god!"

It was the solution he needed so badly. Now he knew when and where to send out his message. It was crystal clear now.

A massive jolt of energy passed through Mark, shaking his entire body violently. Once the shaking stopped, he felt as if he suddenly possessed the strength of a thousand elephants. He went back into the bathroom, opened the medicine cabinet and rummaged through it until he found the pill bottle he was looking for. Four pills left, pills that would take away the pain for eight hours or more. He tossed them into the back of his throat, leaned over the sink, and sucked a mouthful of water, swallowing the pills.

He stared in the mirror, smiled. His mission was clear now. "Poetic justice." He started shaving.

He put on one of his 1000 dollar suits got into his car and drove toward to the tech corridor. His haziness in thinking was gone. Everything was clear now. He would scope out the event space, find the entries and exits. He had Dave's guns with him, and he would look for a place where he could hide one or more on the property.

There were two event space buildings at the end of the tech corridor. He noticed a truck and men unloading equipment in front of one of the buildings, and he figured that was where the Happ! celebration would be held that evening. He parked in a lot at the side of the building, and watched what was happening. He didn't see any suits entering or leaving the building, only the workers moving equipment.

He tightened his tie, got out, and walked to the building confidently, as if he belonged there. He carried the case with the AR-15 as if it was a businessman's briefcase. He nodded to the workers and he asked one how it was going. "Right on schedule, sir. Everything will be set up by five."

"Great."

He entered the building, walked through the lobby where tables were being set up. He stepped into the auditorium where more equipment was being wheeled onto a stage. He backed out of the auditorium after scanning it again, then crossed the lobby and moved down a hallway wondering where he could hide the weapon. He came to double glass doors that led out to a courtyard where he saw bushes. A perfect hiding place. But he realized that he would be locked out and there was no way for him to unlock the door.

He pressed the bar across the door, opened it, and stepped out. He searched for something to brace the door. He saw a stick near the bushes about twenty feet away. He wedged the gun case between the two doors, then walked over and picked it up. He tried breaking it to get a smaller piece, but didn't have any luck. Finally, he spotted a six-inch stick that looked like it might work.

He turned toward the door and caught his breath as he saw a man standing in the doorway holding his gun case staring at him. He was a burly middle-aged man with a hard edge about him, a no-nonsense type of guy.

"The man nodded to him. "What's going on?"

"Oh, I was just coming out for a smoke, and was looking for something to keep the door open."

"Sure." He handed Mark the case. "My name is Higgins. I'm the security chief on the corridor. Who are you?"

"Ah, Trent Wallace, I'm with Happ! and...and we're having our tenth anniversary celebration this evening."

"Yeah, I know." He leaned down, picked something up to one side of the door and held up a rubber door stopper in the shape of a wedge. "This will work."

"Oh, thanks a lot. I appreciate it."

"No problem." He pointed at the case. "If you don't mind my asking, what is that?"

"It's audio equipment."

Higgins pointed to the BMW parked at a distance and said "I saw you driving in. Enjoy your day."

"Thanks."

After a few minutes, he went back inside and made sure that Higgins wasn't anywhere nearby. Then he backtracked, and quickly hid the case under the bushes. He left the stopper in the door and took the back way to his car. He took deep breathes as he slid behind the wheel. He was in a kind of trance.

# # #

7.3 Dave's Destiny

It was mid-morning and Dave was at his desk in the office staring at a new project, the rehab of an older house in the neighborhood that would include adding an additional bathroom and re-modeling two others in the historic two-storey Tudor.

His phone jangled, and he saw that Laura was texting him.

Hey, Dave, the Mexican food truck is out by the pond today. How about grabbing a bite together?

They decided to meet in an hour, and Dave started feeling better. He'd already shown his completed design for the skatepark to the patrol cops this morning when he went to feed the ducks, and now he would proudly show it to Laura. He arrived at the food truck with his design scheme rolled up in a tube under his arm. Laura was just picking up her order and said she would claim the last available picnic table.

When he sat down with his chicken tacos a few minutes later, he realized it was a perfect spot. From the table, they had a view of the area where the skatepark would be located between the duck pond and the smaller event space building. Before he had a chance to say anything about it, Laura pointed to the building and said she was going there this evening for a company event.

"We've invited some of our local clients to come by for drinks for the unveiling of the company's latest products and newest features."

"Sounds like fun," Dave said as he started to pull his design sheet out of the tube.

"Not really, it's a sales event and everyone is required to attend, unless you've got a really good excuse. So what you got there?"

"My skatepark design."

"Oh, show it to me."

"It has four pods, plus the central speedway. So skateboarders of different skills and ages can participate at the same time, and there will be a minimum of collusions."

"When does the construction begin?"

Dave felt a zinging sensation at the back of his neck and down his spine, as if he'd just gotten a mild electrical shock. He turned and stared at the larger event space building. A truck was parked outside it and workmen were carrying folded tables into the building.

Laura followed his gaze. "Looks like they've got something going on there this evening, too." She glanced up at the sky. "Hope it doesn't rain."

Laura talked about how Bill was already moving up in his company and their plans for a week's vacation in Bermuda in a few weeks. Dave asked if she really wanted to go there, and she said, "Of course. It's going to be fun."

"I've never been out of the country. I don't like to travel. I've only been to Florida, to Disney World, and I don't think I liked it very much. Too many people and too many things going on. I was young, though. Maybe

I would like it better now. But I have no plans to go there."

Laura nodded. "Yeah, travel can be challenging, but there's always new things to see and learn about."

Dave was quiet for a few moments. "I suppose. I'll be interested in hearing about your trip. Take some pictures ...of Bermuda, not of you and Bill."

She smiled. "I will, and I promise I won't show you any silly selfies. Okay, gotta get back to work." She stood up and he did the same. "I'm looking forward to seeing your skatepark, Dave. But I'll just watch the skateboarders. I'm not going to try it."

"I cannot skateboard on a flat sidewalk, much less down a concrete ramp. I won't try it, either."

She gave him a hug and walked off. Dave watched her, feeling the usual mix of emotions, and reminding himself that she would never be his girlfriend. He walked over toward the larger building where there was even more activity. Laura was right. Something was going on there, or would be, later on.

He headed to the nearby parking lot and stopped when he saw a silver BMW. It looked just like Mark's car. He walked around to the rear of it. He liked to memorize license plates, and he knew instantly that he'd stumbled upon Mark's Beemer. He looked around, but didn't see him.

He considered texting him, but he'd already tried several times over the past few days. He'd arranged for Mark to buy guns from his favorite dealer, but when they went together to the gun store, Mark only wanted ammunition for the two semi-autos that he still hadn't returned. He'd said he wanted to go shoot them at the range and would give them back and then decide what to buy. But that was a week ago and Mark wasn't responding to his texts.

Finally, he made up his mind and wrote a brief text.

I'm standing next to your car. Where are you?

He waited a couple of minutes, then walked over to his car and sat in it for another five minutes. He slowly drove out of the parking lot, scanned the sidewalk. No sign of Mark. No response. He didn't like it, not one bit.

# # #

Dave had just finished eating dinner with his parents, had gone to his room and settled in front of his computer. He was anxious to see what members of the alumni club had thought of his design for the skatepark. He'd uploaded it yesterday to the full club list after his architect partner had suggested he do it.

Just as he was about to go into his email account, a text arrived from Laura. She was probably just thanking him for meeting her for lunch and showing her the design plan. He was about to ignore the text until after he'd read any emails on the park plan. But he felt an inner nudge, a hunch that he should read it right away. After all, it was from Laura. His eyes widened and his jaw went slack as he read her message.

There's a shooter, Dave. We heard shots and a blast. People are running from the other event space building.

He responded as quickly as he could.

Did you get away? Are you okay?

A minute later, her response arrived, and he didn't like it.

I got knocked down when everyone went out to see what we going on. I hurt my knee, but I'm okay. I'm back in the building, hiding with a few others.

Dave: *I'm coming.*

Laura: *No, stay away. I told Bill the same. Send me anything you find out.*

Dave knew what she meant. He went to Instagram and immediately *#atl.techcorridor,* popped up. He saw a string of brief fear-laden posts from people trapped in the larger event space building. *Shooter...maybe two or more...shots...explosion...people down...he's here.*

Dave leaned closer, focused on a pic of an automatic pistol that had been discarded by the shooter. He zoomed in and was able to read part of the serial number. "No! Shit, shit, no!" It was his .357 Sig. Mark must be in there with his guns. He bolted out of his chair, raced across the apartment, and down the stairs as fast as he could. He had to stop him.

THE SHOOTING

7:05 PM

Just when Larry Watson thought he would finally get a shot at the killer, a young man ran towards the Ski mask shouting, "Stop it Mark".

Ski Mask froze for a moment listening his name being called out and jerked his head towards the young man running towards him with a gun in his hand. The young man fired two shots at the ceiling.

"I thought you were my friend, Mark," the kid shouted at Ski Mask. "That's my AR-15 and you're killing people with it."

The shooter laughed. "Dave, Dave, that's what it's for. You know that. Watch me now!"

The AR-15 sputtered off a dozen quick shots, exploding into the bodies of people huddled under tables and on the floor. The gunfire reverberated throughout the auditorium and was followed by screams and shouts. Several people staggered and fell.

"No! No!" Dave shouted.

Mark turned on Dave, aimed at his head. "Drop your gun!"

"What are you going to shoot me, Mark?"

"I will if you don't drop it."

Dave laid the gun on the floor and raised his arms as he stood up. But he did not stop talking to Ski Mask.

"Mark, Mark, put it down. You can end this right now."

Ski Mask scoffed, ""What do you know, Dave? You're fucking autistic. You don't have any feelings. I have"

Dave continued trying to reason with him. "I'm not shooting people, Mark." He pointed to the hostages, thirty or forty people clustered together near the locked door. Bodies lay nearby. He struggled to articulate the emotions he is going through. "Let them go. Look, there are children. They have families. They have lives to lead. Please, c'mon, Mark."

Watson could see Mark's head over Dave's shoulder, but he would probably take off Dave's ear if he hit the shooter. If he hit missed or hit Dave, the killer would empty his weapon on the hostages. Who was Mark, anyhow? An angry ex-employee fired unjustly? A terrorist with origins in the Mideast? A white supremest, angry because the company's leadership was multi-racial? Abruptly, the shooter pulled off his ski mask, finally revealing himself. He looked about thirty, unshaven, bloodshot eyes, unruly hair and crazed look on his face. The worst part was that he seemed to be admiring his handiwork as he gazed at the bodies and pools of blood around him.

Then he turned to Dave again. "But I'm not done yet, Dave."

Neither am I, thought Watson.

He couldn't wait, not for another minute. Maybe he was about to die, but at least he would go down attempting to stop this abomination. He cautiously crawled out from under the table. He aimed his Glock from near the floor, and finally Dave stepped aside, and he had a clear shot. Mark was protected by a bulletproof vest. So Watson needed a head shot, which was much harder than shooting into a torso, and it was a difficult angle.

# # #

Alim was huddled with the hostages,. Most of them seemed in shock, unable to move. He couldn't stand by any longer. He had to do something. He held up his hand and stepped forward toward the shooter, who immediately charged toward him.

"Don't kill these people," he called out to Mark. "Some are children."

"I'll shoot you then."

Mark pulled the trigger, but nothing happened. He was out of bullets, the magazine was empty.

Alim lunged forward, but Mark responded by striking him in the stomach with the barrel of the semi-automatic. Alim groaned, bent over clasping his belly. Mark jabbed the rifle at him, pushing him back toward the other hostages.

"Stay the fuck there, or I'll blow your head off."

# # #

Watson moved closer while Mark reached into his backpack for a fresh magazine and casually reloaded. Easy shot, he thought and aimed.

"Finish it," Mark said aloud to himself. "Winners finish strong."

I'll finish it, Watson shot and pulled the trigger. Nothing happened.

"Winners don't go around shooting people," a voice shouted.

Mark's head snapped around. "Who said that?"

"I did." A man in a green sports coat stepped away from the hostages and toward Mark. Watson recognized the CEO. So did Mark.

"Look who's still alive. Boss man," Mark said. "How many other lives have you destroyed with your reckless criminal actions?"

"Let's talk about it. Put down your gun. Please."

"Let's not." Mark fired several shots and the CEO hit in the shoulder collapsed. Then he fired a couple more.

A sickening feeling overwhelmed Watson, not only at the sight of the slaughter, but he had realized his mistake. When he'd left home, he'd grabbed his Glock and the shoulder holster, a snap decision to impress Higgins, to show him that he was ready to take the job. But the Glock wasn't loaded.

He'd removed the cartridges in the aftermath of losing his wife. After she'd left, he'd considered killing himself more than once during the following weeks, and he'd finally emptied the gun. Now he wished again that he'd picked up Higgins' pistol.

He was still on his hands and knees next to the table, but he was as vulnerable as the hostages. If Mark turned this way, he was a dead man. But Mark was now focused on Dave. He pulled a pistol from a holster on his hip and pointed towards Mark. "I'm tired of your whining. Why did you follow me? What are you doing here?"

"I didn't follow you. I came here to protect for my friend, Laura."

Mark's features twisted into an expression of hatred. "Oh, you have a friend, do you, and she's here? Then she's one of them. She's with these bullies, and now they are getting their due."

"What bullies? You don't know them. They never bullied you. You are killing strangers Mark"

"They're all bullies, Dave. You don't understand, you fucking autist. They are all the same. They need to learn."

"Learn what? What are you teaching them? Your name will be added to the list of lunatics, Mark. That's all you will achieve."

Mark moved closer, his pistol pointing upward, as if he were unconsciously following the procedure he'd learned about not recklessly endangering any lives.

Watson slowly stood up, his clothing soaked with blood of the dead. He crouched low, edging closer.

Mark stepped away and looked at the people still huddled near the door. "This fucking bullshit company cheated me. My mom can't even recognize me. I tried, I tried. This is what they deserve, what you deserve. Now I'm going to finish off the rest of you."

Alim turned to Mark and pleaded, "No one deserves this. So that you know, my entire family died in a missile attack. I can never overcome the pain and the grief but I am not going to go around shooting people. Please stop this now."

He is a nobody Mark. You are special. The voice said.

"Shut the fuck up you moron. You are a fucking nobody and you can die like a nobody. Not me. I'm special. I must achieve. I have no choice." Marks shoulders dropped for a moment before he turned his weapon to the hostages who huddled in a corner for maximum kill.

Alim ran towards Mark, patting the air with his hands.

Watson lunged from behind, wrapped his arms around Mark's chest, tackling him. They crashed to the floor, rolled over. But Mark managed to free his gun hand and aimed the pistol at Watson. Dave jumped in and grabbed Mark's arm just as Mark fired off three shots. Alim rushed forward and kicked the gun from his hand. At that moment, the tactical squad charged, weapons aimed. Alim raised his hands, certain he was about to be shot. He dropped to his knees and laid down. Dave did the same.

Watson lay on top of Mark. He lifted his head, and looked at the squad members surrounding them. "We got him. It's over."

AFTERMATH

Dozens of bouquets of flowers were strewn along a plywood barrier outside the Red Oak Event Space building where twenty-nine people had lost their lives. It was Sunday morning, three days after the horrific event, and a memorial service was under way with a minister, a rabbi and an imam all participating. Victims had belonged to many faiths. USN's Blake Radcliffe stood off to one side of the crowd that he estimated at eight or nine hundred, and more were still arriving.

But his thoughts were on the victims. Just a few moments before gunfire erupted, they were laughing, cheering and celebrating. Then death sprang upon them like a lurking lion on an unsuspecting lamb. Their everyday concerns, their dreams and desires, their heart-felt plans for the future wiped away in cruel blasts of hot lead. He shook his head to clear his mind and turned his focus to the memorial service.

The Christian minister wearing a black Geneva gown walked to the podium. A large cross with an American flag-like design imprinted on it dangled from his neck. "We make many mistakes. We commit sins. Jesus made the ultimate sacrifice and died for everyone's sins. Amidst the grief and sorrow caused by this horrendous violence, we recall the victims with love and affection. Their souls receive eternal blessing."

A few minutes later, the Imam dressed in white cotton garb and a white *Taqiya*—a round skullcap—spoke next, "As we read in the Qur'an, one life lost is like all mankind, and one life saved is like all mankind. To God, all life is sacred and precious. Kindness is not just a matter of the heart. The Prophet Muhammad, peace be upon him, said that kindness is a mark of faith, and whoever is not kind, has no faith."

When the imam stepped away from the podium, the rabbi took his place. He wore a prayer shawl over a long black coat and a *kippah* over his head. "When we bid farewell to the beloved departed, we say: "Go in peace. Go in peace and may your memories contribute to a world blessed with peace."

Radcliffe approached a woman, standing near the wall, who had lost her husband in the mass shooting. He'd interviewed her before the memorial service began. She turned to him and motioned toward the stage. "If all of them are saying the same thing, why is there so much hate in the name of religion? The sky, the water, the air, the nature, they are same everywhere. If an Almighty created the universe and all of us, does it really matter what we call him?"

"You would think not," Radcliffe said in a soft voice. "You would think not." He looked over at his cameraman who was filming messages scrawled with markers or painted on the wall. They ranged from expressions of love and peace to the frustrations of mourners. One simply said: WHY??? Another nearby seemed to answer with an opinion: GUNS, GUNS, GUNS. THAT'S WHY! Someone else had painted flowers in the shape of a peace symbol, while yet another declared, INSANITY REIGNS AGAIN!

The message that Radcliffe found the most interesting was one that asked an important question: WHO KNEW? Dozens of reporters were trying to find out who knew Mark McCarthy, and did they have any inkling of what he would do? Revelations about Mark McCarthy and his failing investment business had already come out, and two bodies found in his apartment had been linked to organized crime.

With the memorial over, people started to drift away from the stage area. Some were tearful and hugging friends. Others looked upset or disconsolate. It seemed as if everyone knew someone who had died, or had been inside the building and escaped. And some of the survivors were here.

Alim attended the memorial with Rabia. He was devastated that his act as a whistleblower to expose the glitches in the Happ! software had resulted in the company's stock crashing and that had pushed McCarthy over the edge. Rabia consoled him. "You did the right thing, Alim. You couldn't have known how that man would react."

"I am afraid for the future, Rabia. Not our own, but about Zamir and future generations in a world full of such hate and mutual suspicion." His head hung in regret and he wept.

Rabia hugged him. "I know, Alim. I know."

"I lost my parents," he said through his tears. My heart is filled with grief, but not hate. It's the same feeling I have when I think about twenty-nine lives lost in a mindless shooting."

"You're not a hateful man, Alim."

After a few moments of silence, he locked his gaze on Rabia. "When I was returning to America after the funeral, my heart and mind were filled with rage. I lost my entire family and I wanted vengeance. But your love and guidance stopped me in my tracks. Without your love, I don't know which way I could've have gone."

Rabia shook her head in disbelief. "Remember how welcome we felt when we first came here, Alim? Sure, 9/11 changed things, but we still see so many acts of love and kindness. Many people are supporting us in rebuilding the mosque, and many stood in solidarity against the killings in the New Zealand mosques."

"I know. Good and bad are ubiquitous."

"We must be kind and gentle to people around us."

"I agree. You never know what pushes someone to go over the edge. Our actions and words have the power to be the last straw or they can give that little peace, that little hope, that little comfort" He took her hand. "Let's go home."

Dave and Laura remained near the front of the stage long after it was over. Dave refused to leave. "C'mon, Dave. We should go now. Let's go get some lunch."

"I can't, Laura. Not yet. I should never have loaned my guns to Mark. How could I have done that?"

"You didn't know, Dave. Not until it was too late. The police cleared you. They know you weren't responsible.

McCarthy would've gotten weapons from someone else, if not you. You were just a convenience. He knew he could manipulate you."

She was right and that made Dave angry. "Maybe I will take all of my guns and bury them where no one will ever find them, and I will never make another stupid mistake like that."

Laura hugged him. "Dave, you are not a criminal. You would never hurt anyone with your guns. You just were not able to understand that his intentions were bad."

"People say I don't understand how other people think, how they feel, or how they will react to what I say. I've gotten angry, really angry many times. I've felt lonely and depressed. But my mom, dad and you were there for me. You supported me. Maybe that is what love is. I think it's the only thing that can save us. Love."

Lightning Source UK Ltd.
Milton Keynes UK
UKHW020918301121
394854UK00010B/1057